CAMINO
GHOSTS

John Grisham

CAMINO
GHOSTS

HODDER &
STOUGHTON

First published in Great Britain in 2024 by Hodder & Stoughton Limited
An Hachette UK company

1

Copyright © Belfry Holdings, Inc. 2024

A CIP catalogue record for this title is available from the British Library

Hardback ISBN 978 1 529 34250 5
Trade Paperback ISBN 978 1 529 34251 2
ebook ISBN 978 1 529 34252 9

Printed and bound in Great Britain by Clays Ltd, Elcograf S.p.A.

Hodder & Stoughton policy is to use papers that are natural, renewable
and recyclable products and made from wood grown in sustainable
forests. The logging and manufacturing processes are expected to
conform to the environmental regulations of the country of origin.

Hodder & Stoughton Limited
Carmelite House
50 Victoria Embankment
London EC4Y 0DZ

www.hodder.co.uk

CAMINO GHOSTS

CHAPTER ONE

THE PASSAGE

1.

None of the fifty or so guests wore shoes. The invitation specifically ruled them out. It was, after all, a beach wedding, and Mercer Mann, the bride, wanted sand between the toes. The suggested attire was *beach chic,* which may have had one meaning in Palm Beach and another in Malibu, and probably something else in the Hamptons. But on Camino Island it meant *anything goes.* But no shoes.

The bride herself wore a low-cut white linen gown with an entirely bare back, and since she had been on the island for the past two weeks she was superbly tanned and toned. Stunning. Thomas, her groom, was just as lean and bronzed. He wore a brand-new powder blue seersucker suit, a starched white dress shirt, no tie. And of course no shoes.

Thomas was just happy to be included. He and Mercer had been together for three years, sharing an apartment for the past two, and when Mercer finally got tired of waiting for a proposal she had asked him, three months earlier, "What are you doing on Saturday, June sixth, at seven p.m.?"

"Well, I don't know. I'll have to check."

"Say nothing."

"What?"

"Say you're doing nothing."

"Okay, I'm doing nothing. Why?"

"Because we're getting married at the beach."

Since he was not exactly a detail person, he had little input into the planning of the wedding. However, had he been detail-oriented it would not have mattered. Life with Mercer was wonderful in so many ways, not the least of which was the absence of responsibility for making decisions. The pressure was off.

A guitarist strummed love songs as the guests sipped champagne. She was a creative writing student of Mercer's at Ole Miss and had volunteered for the wedding. A server in a straw hat topped off their glasses. He, too, was studying under Mercer, though she had yet to break the news that his fiction was too weird. If she were a blunt person she would point out that he was likely to earn more money tending bar at small weddings than trying to write novels, but she had yet to gain tenure or the ability to discourage students with little promise.

Mercer taught because she needed a salary. She had published a collection of short stories and two novels. She was searching for a third. Her last one, *Tessa,* had been a bestseller, and its success had prompted Viking Press to give her a two-book contract. Her editor at Viking was still waiting for the next story idea. So was Mercer. She had some money in the bank but not enough to retire, not enough to buy the freedom to write full-time with no worries.

A few of her guests had that freedom. Myra and Leigh, the grandes dames of the island's literary mafia, had been together for decades and were living off royalties. Back in their glory days they had cranked out a hundred steamy romance novels under a dozen pseudonyms. Bob Cobb was an ex-felon who'd served time in a federal pen for bank fraud. He wrote hard-boiled crime stories, with a penchant for prison violence. When drinking, which was practically all the time, he claimed he had not pursued honest labor in twenty years. He was a writer! Perhaps the wealthiest of the group was Amy Slater, a young mother of three who'd hit pay dirt with a vampire series.

Amy and her husband, Dan, had taken a chunk of their money and built a splendid house on the beach, about half a mile from Mercer's cottage. When they heard about the wedding, they insisted on hosting it along with the reception.

Like every bride, Mercer envisioned a lovely walk down the aisle with her father. He, though, got cut from the ceremony, as did the aisle. Mr. Mann was a complicated soul who had never spent time with his wife or daughters. When he complained that the wedding might conflict with his busy schedule, Mercer said never mind. They would have more fun without him.

Her sister, Connie, was there and could always be counted on for family drama. Her two rotten teenage girls were already sitting in the back row and staring at their phones. Her husband was gulping champagne. On the more pleasant side, her literary agent, Etta Shuttleworth, was there with her husband, as was her Viking editor, who no doubt wanted to grab a moment and inquire about the next novel, now a year overdue. Mercer was determined not to talk business. It was her wedding, and if the editor got the least bit pushy then Etta was expected to step in. Three sorority sisters from Sewanee were there, two with husbands. The third was fresh off an acrimonious divorce that Mercer had heard far too much about. All three had the hots for Thomas, and Mercer was keeping an eye on them. The fact that he was five years younger than his bride made him even sexier. Two colleagues from the Ole Miss faculty had survived the final cut of the invitation list and were spending a week on the island. Mercer got on with them well enough, but was cautious. She had invited them only to be polite. She was on her third campus in the past six years and had learned a lot about faculty politics. She was the only professor in the history of the Ole Miss English department to crack the bestseller lists with a novel, and at times she could feel the jealousy. An old pal from Chapel Hill had been invited but declined. Two friends from high school and one from kindergarten were there.

Thomas had a more stable family. His parents and siblings and their young children filled an entire row. Behind them was a rowdy bunch of college chums from his days at Grinnell.

The fake minister was Bruce Cable, owner of Bay Books and onetime lover of the bride, who began asking everyone to take a seat and squeeze closer to the front where a white wicker arch had been erected. It was laden with red and white roses and carnations and flanked by trellises on both sides. Beyond it was a hundred feet of white sand, then nothing but the Atlantic at high tide, a gorgeous view that stretched for miles until the planet curved. North Africa was four thousand miles away, a straight shot.

The guitarist kept strumming until Mercer and Thomas appeared on the boardwalk. They came down the steps, holding hands and smiling all the way to the arch where they were met by the fake minister.

It was not Bruce Cable's first wedding. For some vague reason, Florida allowed almost anyone to buy a cheap permit from a clerk's office, become an "officiant," and conduct a civil wedding ceremony. Bruce had not known this, and had no interest in it whatsoever, until an old girlfriend wanted to get married on Camino Island and insisted on Bruce doing the honors.

That was the first. Mercer's was the second. He wondered how many officiants had slept with all of their brides. Yes, on one occasion not too many years earlier he had slept with Mercer when she was spying on him, but that was ancient history. Noelle, his wife, knew about it. Thomas had been informed. Everyone was cool. It was all so civilized.

Well aware of Bruce's tendency to go off-script, Mercer had carefully written their vows. Thomas, surprisingly, had been consulted and even added some language of his own. A former student from UNC rose and read a poem, an impenetrable hodgepodge in free verse that was supposed to heighten the romantic mood but instead caused the crowd to gaze at the waves breaking gently along the shore. Bruce managed to refocus things by giving brief bios of the bride and groom and got a few laughs. The guitar player could also sing and she delighted the crowd with an impressive version of "This Will Be (An Everlasting Love)." Connie read a scene from *Tessa* that was based loosely on their grandmother. In the story, Tessa walked the same stretch of beach every morning looking for turtle eggs laid the night before. She guarded the surf and dunes as if she owned them, and several in the crowd remembered her well. It was a poignant piece about a person who had greatly influenced the bride.

Bruce then got them through the vows, which, in his learned opinion, were a bit on the wordy side, a recurring problem with Mercer's prose and one he was determined to correct. He loved his writers and nurtured them all, but he was also a tough critic. Oh well, it wasn't his wedding.

They swapped rings, had a kiss, and bowed to the crowd as husband and wife. The crowd stood and applauded.

The entire service lasted twenty-two minutes.

The photography took longer, then everyone climbed onto

the boardwalk and followed Mercer and Thomas over the dunes to the pool where more champagne was waiting. They had their first dance to "My Girl." The DJ followed it with more Motown and the dancing caught on. Almost ten minutes passed before the first drunk, Connie's husband, fell in the pool.

The most popular caterer on the island was Chef Claude, a real Cajun from South Louisiana. He and his team were busy on the patio while Noelle supervised the table arrangements and flowers. She was mostly French, and in matters of fine dining with all the trimmings she had no peer. Amy asked her to take charge of flowers, china, place settings, crystal, and flatware, along with the wine, which Noelle and Bruce were happy to select and order from their broker. Two long tables were set on the terrace under a canopy.

As the sun was setting, Chef Claude whispered to Amy that dinner was ready, and the guests were directed to their assigned seats. It was a rowdy bunch, with lots of laughter and admiration for the newlyweds. When the first bottle of Chablis made the rounds, Bruce, as always, called for quiet so he could wax on about the wine. Then platters of raw oysters arrived and covered the table. During the second course, shrimp remoulade, the toasts began and things began to go off-track. Thomas's brother did a nice job but wasn't much of a speaker. One of Mercer's sorority sisters played the obligatory role of the crying bridesmaid and went on far too long. Bruce managed to cut her off with a splendid toast of his own. He then introduced the next wine, a fine Sancerre. Trouble started when Mercer's brother-in-law, still wet from his splash in the pool and still drunk since midafternoon, stood and wobbled and tried to tell a funny story about one of Mercer's old boyfriends. His timing was bad. His remarks were mercifully cut off when Connie snapped loudly, "That's enough, Carl!"

Carl roared with laughter as he fell into his chair, and it took a few seconds before he realized no one else thought it funny. To break the tension, a frat brother from Grinnell jumped to his feet and read a raunchy poem about Thomas. As he read, the main course of grilled flounder was served. Verse after verse, the poem grew dirtier and funnier, and when it was over everyone was in stitches.

Amy had worried about the noise. The homes were built close together along the beach and noise carried. So, she had invited the neighbors on each side and introduced them to Mercer a week earlier. They were laughing and drinking harder than anyone.

Myra took the floor and told the story of the first time she and Leigh met Mercer, five years earlier when she returned to the island for the summer. "Her beauty was obvious, her charm was contagious, her manners were impeccable. But we wondered: Can she write? We secretly hoped that she couldn't. With her latest novel, a masterpiece in my opinion, she proved to the world that she can indeed tell a beautiful story. Why do some people have all the luck?"

"Now Myra," Leigh said softly.

Until then, most of the toasts and remarks seemed to have some measure of forethought. After that, though, everything was off the cuff and fueled by wine.

The dinner was long and delicious, and when it was over the older guests began leaving. The younger ones returned to the dance floor where the DJ took requests and turned the volume down.

Around midnight, Bruce found Mercer and Thomas at the edge of the pool with their feet in the water. He joined and told them again what a lovely wedding they had put together.

"When do you leave for Scotland?" he asked.

"Tomorrow at two," Mercer replied. "We fly from Jackson-ville to Washington, then nonstop to London." The honeymoon was two weeks in the Highlands.

"Could you run by the store in the morning? I'll have the cof-fee ready. We'll need some."

Thomas nodded and Mercer said, "Sure. What's up?"

Bruce was suddenly serious. With a smug grin he looked at her and said, "I have the story, Mercer. Maybe the best I've ever heard."

2.

Bay Books opened at 9:00 a.m. every Sunday morning when Bruce unlocked the front door, from the inside, and welcomed the usual crowd. Though the demographics were unclear, he had always surmised that about half the permanent residents of Camino Island were retirees from colder climates. The other half were locals from North Florida and southern Georgia. The tourists came from all over, but primarily the South and East.

At any rate, there were plenty of people from "up north" who missed their favorite newspapers. Years earlier he began han-dling the Sunday editions of the *Times, Post, Enquirer, Tribune, Baltimore Sun, Pittsburgh Post-Gazette,* and *Boston Globe.* Along with the newspapers, he sold legendary hot buttered biscuits from a restaurant around the corner, on Sundays only, and by 9:30 the café upstairs and the reading area downstairs were packed with Yankees reading news from home. It had become a ritual of sorts and many of the regulars never missed a Sunday morning at the bookstore. Though women were certainly welcome—Bruce had long since learned that most books were bought by women—the Sunday morning crowd was all male, and the politics and sports talk often became rowdy. Smoking was allowed on the outdoor terrace and a layer of rich cigar smoke usually hung over Main Street.

Mercer and Thomas arrived late in the morning, now legally married, remarkably clear-eyed and dressed for their trip. Bruce invited them into his downstairs office, his First Editions Room, where he displayed some of his finest rare books. He poured coffee and they chatted about the night before. The newlyweds were ready to go, though, with a long adventure ahead of them.

Mercer smiled and said, "You mentioned the greatest story of all time."

"Yes I did. I'll be brief. It's a true story but can also be fictionalized. You've heard of Dark Isle, just north of here."

"Maybe. I'm not sure."

"It's deserted, right?" Thomas asked.

"Probably, yes, but there is some doubt. It's one of two smaller barrier islands between Florida and Georgia and it has never been developed. It's about three miles long and a mile wide, with pristine beaches."

Mercer was nodding and said, "Oh yeah, now I remember. Tessa talked about it years ago. Isn't it supposed to be haunted or something?"

"Or something. Centuries ago, sometime around 1750, it became a haven for runaway slaves from Georgia, which, then ruled by the British, allowed slavery. Florida was under the Spanish flag and though slavery was not against the law, runaways were granted sanctuary. There was a long-running feud between the two countries about what to do with the slaves who escaped to Florida. Georgia wanted them back. The Spanish wanted to protect them just to irritate the British and their American colonies. Around 1760, a slave ship returning from West Africa was preparing to land in Savannah when a fierce storm from the north, what we call a nor'easter today, spun it around, shoved it south, and badly disabled it. It was a ship from Virginia called *Venus,* and it had around four hundred slaves on board, packed like sardines. Well, it left Africa with four hundred, but not all made it. Many died at sea. The conditions on board were unimaginable, to say the least. Anyway, the *Venus* finally went down about a mile out to sea near Cumberland Island. Since the slaves were chained and shackled, almost all of them drowned. A few clung to the wreckage and washed ashore in the storm on Dark Island, as it became known. Or Dark Isle. It was unnamed in 1760. They were taken in by the runaways from Georgia, and together they built a little community. Two hundred years went by, everybody died or moved away, and now it's deserted."

Bruce took a sip of coffee and waited for a response.

Mercer said, "Nice, but I don't write history."

Thomas asked, "Where's the hook? Any sign of a plot?"

Bruce smiled and picked up a plain, thin book the size of a trade paperback. He showed them the title: *The Dark History of Dark Isle.* By Lovely Jackson.

Neither reached to take the book, which didn't bother Bruce. He said, "This is a self-published book that sold maybe thirty copies. It was written by the last living heir to Dark Isle, or that's her claim anyway. Lovely Jackson lives here on Camino, down near the old canneries in a neighborhood called The Docks."

"I know where it is," Mercer said.

"She claims she was born on Dark Isle in 1940 and left there with her mother when she was fifteen years old."

"How do you know her?" Mercer asked.

"She first came in a few years back with a bag full of these books and wanted to do a big signing. As you've heard me complain, the self-published crowd can drive a bookseller crazy. Very pushy, very demanding. I try to avoid them but I really liked

Lovely and her story is fascinating. I was quite taken with her. We had a signing. I leaned on our friends, most of whom will do almost anything for a free glass of wine, and we had a nice party. Lovely was forever grateful."

"I'm still waiting for a plot," Thomas said, rather dryly.

"Here's the plot. Florida being Florida, the real estate swingers have scoured every square inch of the state looking for an undeveloped beach. They found Dark Isle years ago, but there was a big problem. The island is too small to justify the cost of a bridge. The developers could never configure enough condos, hotels, water parks and T-shirt shops, et cetera, to convince the state to build a bridge. So Dark Isle was off-limits. But Hurricane Leo changed all that. Its eye went directly over the island, split off the north end, and shoved tons of sand into a massive reef that links the southern tip to a spot near Dick's Harbor on the mainland. The engineers now say that a bridge would be much cheaper to build. Like vultures, the developers are all over it and they're leaning on their pals in Tallahassee."

Thomas said, "So, Lovely Jackson is the plot."

"You got it. She claims to be the sole owner."

Mercer said, "If she doesn't live there, why not just sell to the developers?"

Bruce tossed the book into a pile and drank his coffee. He smiled and said, "Because it's hallowed ground. Her people are buried there. One of her great-grandmothers, a woman named Nalla, was on the *Venus*. Lovely is not selling. Period."

Thomas asked, "What's the position of the developers?"

"They have lawyers and they're a tough bunch. They say there's no record Lovely was even born on the island. Keep in mind, she's the only living witness. All other relatives have been dead for decades."

"And the bad guys have big plans?" Mercer asked.

"Are you kidding? Wall-to-wall condos, resorts, golf courses. There's even a rumor that they've cut a deal with the Seminoles for a casino. The nearest fancy one is two hours away. The entire island will be paved in three years' time."

"And Lovely can't afford lawyers?"

"Of course not. She's in her eighties and gets a small Social Security check each month."

"In her eighties?" Mercer repeated. "Do you know for sure?"

"No. There's no birth certificate, no record anywhere. If you read her book, and I suggest you do so immediately, you'll realize how isolated these people were for centuries."

Mercer said, "I've already packed books for the trip."

"Okay, your business, not mine. But allow me to offer a teaser. One reason they were so isolated was because Nalla was an African witch doctor, some sort of voodoo priestess. In a scene you'll remember for a long time, she put a curse on the island to protect it from outsiders."

Thomas shook his head and said, "*Now* I smell a plot."

"You like it?"

"I do."

Mercer said, "I'll start reading on the plane."

Bruce said, "Send me a note from Scotland when you finish."

3.

As soon as the plane leveled off, somewhere over South Carolina, Mercer pulled the book from her tote bag and studied the cover. The artwork wasn't bad and depicted a narrow dirt road lined with huge oaks and drifts of Spanish moss hanging almost to the ground. The trees grew darker and faded into the title:

The Dark History of Dark Isle. Across the bottom was the author's name: Lovely Jackson. Inside there was a half-title page, then the credits. The publisher was a small vanity house in Orlando. No dedication, no author photo, no blurbs splashed across the back cover. And no editing at all.

Mercer was expecting a simple writing style. Easy words of no more than three syllables. Short, direct sentences, only a few commas. Certainly no literary flourishes. However, the writing was easy to read, and the story so compelling that Mercer quickly set aside her rather snotty editorial and professorial thoughts and got lost in it. When she finished the first chapter without a break, she realized that the writing was far more effective and engrossing than most of the stuff she was forced to read from her students. Indeed, the writing and storytelling were more interesting than most of the hyped debut novels she'd read in the past year.

She realized Thomas was watching her. "Yes?"

"You're really zipping right along," he said. "How is it?"

"Quite good."

"When can I read it?"

"How about when I get finished?"

"How about we tag-team and alternate chapters? Back and forth?"

"I've never read a book like that and I'm not inclined to start now."

"It'll be easy since I read twice as fast as you."

"Are you trying to provoke me?" she asked.

"Always. We've been married for about twenty hours. It's time for our first spat."

"I'm not taking the bait, dear. Now stick your nose in your own book and leave me alone."

"Okay, but hurry up."

She looked at him, smiled, shook her head, and said, "We forgot to consummate our marriage last night."

Thomas looked around to see if other passengers might hear them. "We've been consummating for three years."

"No, Romeo, a marriage can't be official, at least in the biblical sense, until the vows are said, we're pronounced wife and husband, and we do the deed."

"So you're still a virgin, in the biblical sense?"

"I'm not going that far."

"I was tired and a bit wasted. Sorry. We'll catch up in Scotland."

"If I can wait that long."

"Hold that thought."

4.

Nalla was nineteen when her short happy life changed forever. She and her husband, Mosi, had one child, a three-year-old boy. They were of the Luba tribe and lived in a village in the southern part of the Kingdom of Kongo.

The village was asleep. The night was quiet when loud, panicked voices cut through the darkness. A hut was on fire and people were yelling. Nalla awoke first, then shook Mosi. Their son was asleep on a rug between them. Along with everyone else, they ran to the fire to help, but it was far worse than a fire. It was a raid. The fire was deliberately set by a murderous gang from another tribe that had previously tended to their own business. Now they were known as slave hunters. They attacked from the jungle with clubs and whips and began pummeling the villagers. As seasoned marauders, they knew their victims would be too stunned and disorganized to fight back. They beat them, sub-

dued them, and chained them, but they were careful to kill as
few as possible. They were too valuable to kill. The elderly were
left behind to care for the children, who, in a matter of minutes,
became orphans. The women screamed and wailed for their children, who were nowhere to be found. They had been led away to
the jungle where they would be released the following day. Small
children were worth little to the slave traders.

Nalla screamed for Mosi but he did not answer. In the darkness, the men were separated from the women. She screamed for
her little boy and when she could not stop screaming, an attacker
struck her with a club. She fell down and felt blood on her jaw. In
the light of the fire she could see men armed with long machetes
and knives shoving and herding the villagers, her friends and
neighbors. They shouted harsh commands and threatened to
kill anyone who disobeyed. The fire grew in size and got louder.
Nalla was knocked to the ground again, then ordered to get up
and walk toward the jungle. There were about a dozen women
chained together, almost all of them young mothers who cried
and yelled for their children. They were ordered to shut up, and
when they kept crying a man with a whip lashed them.

When they were away from the village and deep in the jungle,
they stopped in an opening where an oxcart was waiting. It was
filled with chains, cuffs, and shackles. The women wore only
their usual loincloth around their waists. These were stripped
off, leaving them naked. The assailants hooked iron cuffs
around their necks and clamped them tight. One neck cuff was
chained to the other a few feet away, and when they began walking again single file the women were linked together so that if
one tried to run away, the entire line would stumble and fall.

But the women were too terrified to run. The jungle was
dense and pitch-black. They knew it well and knew its dangers,
especially at night. The oxcart led the way with a teenage bandit

guiding it, a torch in one hand, the reins in the other. Two other armed raiders escorted the women, one in the lead, the other in the rear, both with whips. When the women tired of crying they plodded on; the only sounds at times were the rattles of the chains.

They were aware of other movements in the jungle. Perhaps others from their village being led away. Perhaps their husbands, fathers, and brothers. When they heard the men's voices, all of the women immediately began calling the names of their loved ones. Their captors cursed them and cracked the whips. The voices of the men faded away.

The oxcart stopped at a creek, one the women knew well because they used it for bathing and washing clothes. The captors said they would stop for the night and ordered the women to gather by the oxcart. They were still chained together, and after an hour the neck cuffs were rubbing sores on their skin. A heavier chain was tied to a wheel of the oxcart and looped around the necks of two of the women. The captives were secured for the night.

The teenage boy built a small fire and cooked a pot of red rice. He mixed in cassava leaves and okra, and when it was ready he and the other two men had dinner, eating from the same wooden spoon. The women were too tired and frightened to be hungry, but they watched the men eat because there was nothing else to watch. They huddled together, their chains rattling with every small movement. They whispered among themselves and grieved for their children and husbands.

Would they ever go home again?

There had been rumors of slave hunters in the northern part of the country, but they were still too far away to worry about. The ruler of their village had met with other tribes and heard the warnings. He had ordered the men to keep their weapons close at night and take precautions when hunting and fishing.

As the fire went out, the night grew even darker. Their whispers could be heard by the men so they kept their thoughts to themselves. The teenage boy fell asleep by the fire. The two men disappeared. One of the women whispered they should try and escape, but it seemed impossible. Even breathing rattled the chains that bound them together.

Suddenly the two men were back. They grabbed the youngest captive, Sanu, a girl of fourteen whose mother had been left behind. They unlatched her neck cuff and freed her from the chains. She jerked and protested and they hit and cursed her. They disappeared with her but for a long, terrible period of time the women could hear the assault as the men took turns. When the girl returned she was sobbing and shaking as if in a seizure. The men chained her again and threatened the women with the same treatment if they spoke or tried to escape. They huddled even closer in terror. Nalla stayed close to the girl and whispered soothing words, but nothing stopped her trembling.

The men were spent and exhausted and soon fell asleep. For the captives, though, sleep was impossible. Physically, they were too uncomfortable. Emotionally, they were devastated and wanted to go home to their children and husbands.

At daylight they began walking farther away from their village. The jungle thinned and the sun rose high and hot. By midmorning they were in a valley most had never seen before. The oxcart stopped and the women were led to a tree and told to sit. The teenager built a fire and cooked another pot of red rice and okra. The men ate first, from one wooden spoon. The leftovers were offered to the women, who let Sanu eat first. She said no, she had no appetite. The sparse amount of food was carefully

rationed by the others and everyone took a few bites. They were
starving and needed water.

In sad single file they moved onward; the only sounds were
the axle of the oxcart and the constant rattling of the chains
that stretched from neck to neck. The men took turns riding in
the back of the oxcart where they napped. They also watched the
women constantly, as if sizing them up for the night. At a creek
they stopped to drink and rest for an hour or so in the shade of
a cotton tree. Lunch was a small apple and a piece of hard bread.
After eating and getting enough water to drink, the women were
allowed to wade in the creek and bathe themselves.

After dark on the second night, a woman named Shara was
selected. As the men removed her neck cuff, she tried to free herself and fought with them. They beat her with a walking stick,
then tied her to a tree and bullwhipped her until she was unconscious. They cursed the other women and threatened the same
punishment for those who resisted. The women were terrified
and crying and clutching each other.

One of the men walked over and pointed to Nalla. She knew
better than to resist. Shara had fought back and was now practically dead. They took Nalla into the trees and raped her.

Though exhausted, starving, dehydrated, frightened, and in
pain, the women found sleep almost impossible for the second
night. Poor Shara didn't help matters. Still tied to the tree, she
groaned pitifully through the night. At some point during the
night, the groaning stopped.

5.

At dawn the men began arguing. Shara had died during the
night and they blamed each other. They forced the women to
walk close to the tree as they left. They cried as they said goodbye

to their friend. The neck cuffs made it impossible to turn their heads, but Nalla managed one look back. Shara still hugged the tree, her hands bound to it with rope, her naked body covered with dried blood.

For days they walked the hot dirt paths and grew weaker and weaker. They knew they were headed west and the ocean was getting closer, though they had never seen it. It was part of the lore, the legend of their Africa. Their village was so far away now, they knew they were not going home. For over two centuries the Congolese and other West Africans had been attacked, chained, taken away, and sold into slavery to the colonists in the New World. The women knew what awaited them. Nalla's only remaining hope was that she would see Mosi again.

The days blurred into each other and time meant nothing. Survival was their only thought, when they could contain their emotions. The fierce and unrelenting sun made everything worse. The hunger and dehydration wore them down, hour by hour. At night, when the winds blew from the north, the women piled even closer together to stay warm while their guards slept by a small fire.

When they were out of food, the men began to argue. They ordered the teenager to turn the oxcart onto a trail heading south. At dusk they smelled the smoke of cooking fires and came to a small village at the edge of the woods. Fencing of boards and wire encircled a farmyard that was filled with captives like themselves. Dozens of them, with the men separated from the women and children. Slave pens. Several of the guards had rifles and they watched as the women approached. A gate came open and they went inside where their shackles and chains were removed. A gray-haired African lady in a sack dress soothed their blisters and sores with animal grease from a bowl. She gave them beans and tasty bread and they ate until they were full.

She and her husband owned the farm and charged a small fee to the slave traders who passed through. They would probably be sold to another gang who would take them away. She was sorry for their plight but could do little about it.

There were several children. Nalla and the other mothers from her village watched with longing and pity. They ached for their own lost children, but weren't they better off being left behind? Surely the older villagers would take care of them. The poor children in the pen were weak and hungry. Many had sores and insect stings. They did not play and smile and skip around like normal children.

The pen was divided by a tall wire fence. The men and the women met there to examine one another, to look for a familiar face. Mosi was not there, though Nalla did recognize and speak to another man from their village. He said they had been divided into three groups after the first day. Mosi was led away with some others. No, Nalla had not seen his wife or his two daughters.

It rained hard that night, with fierce lightning and heavy winds. There was no shelter in the slave pens. They packed together between the stilts of a small hut and slept in the mud. In the morning the gray-haired lady brought bread and red rice, and as she distributed the food she noticed a rash on a child. She feared it was the measles and took the child inside a hut. She said that three children had died of smallpox a month earlier.

After a week in the slave pen, the women were divided again and told they were leaving. A different group of guards rounded up twenty women and three children and brought out the chains and shackles. Nalla and her friends had just been sold for the first time.

There was a new device, a new form of torture. It was called a coggle board and was nothing but a crude plank of wood six feet long with metal loops at each end, one for each prisoner. The loops went around the necks, so that the two women were not only joined firmly together but would have to support a heavy piece of wood with each step. A chain went around their waists and was looped through a shackle around the neck of a child, who walked between the women and under the board. To make bad matters worse, the guards placed water and supplies on the coggle boards to further burden their prisoners.

After a few minutes on the trail, Nalla almost missed the iron shackle around her neck. It really didn't matter. One form of torture was as bad as the other.

Days passed and the sun grew hotter. The women became weaker and began fainting from heat exhaustion. Attached by a coggle board, one fainting caused both women to go down. The guards reacted by offering water, and if that didn't revive the woman, they pulled out their whips.

Justice arrived in a small dose when a guard, the most sadistic of the three, stepped on a large green mamba and went down screaming. The snake got away as the prisoners scattered in a panic. They were corralled and shoved under a tree, where they rested in the shade and watched in both satisfaction and horror as the guard convulsed, wretched, vomited, and groaned until he died. Good riddance.

One day they topped a hill and saw the ocean in the distance. The blue water was somewhat comforting because it meant the end of an arduous journey. It was also devastating because they knew the ocean would take them away forever.

Two hours later, they approached a village and saw small boats anchored in the bay. The oxcart squeaked along and came to a stop at an encampment called a "fort." The women were led to a shade tree and told to wait. Through the perimeter fencing they could see others inside the fort, women and children close by and men in another large pen. They searched in vain for familiar faces.

The boss finally appeared, an African, but he wore Western clothes and army boots. He barked at the women and told them to stand up. Then he immediately began examining each one. He fondled their breasts, probed their pubic areas, pinched their backsides, and in doing so tried to seem bored with it all. He took his time, and when he was finished he told the two guards that they had brought him a nice selection. Twenty women, all young and somewhat healthy and likely to be good breeders, and three hungry children who weren't worth much. The boss and the guards began talking money and the conversation grew animated; a lot of headshaking, some arguing back and forth. It was obvious the men knew each other and had bargained before. When they finally came to terms, the boss pulled out a small bag of coins and paid for the captives.

Nalla and the others were sold for the second time.

They were led through a gate and into a dirt yard where the coggle boards, chains, and cuffs were removed, and they were allowed to move around. They met other women of their tribe and swapped stories, all of them dreadful. Some of the women had open sores across their backs where they had been whipped. Almost all were young mothers who cried for their lost children.

On the other side of the fort was a larger pen where several dozen men were loitering and trying to see the women. Nalla and the others walked as close as possible but saw no familiar faces.

Bread and water were served and the women retreated to the shade behind one of the huts. A ship had left three days earlier with almost two hundred on board, but the fort was fill-ing up again. The slave trade was booming. No one was certain when the next slave ship would arrive to take them away. The only certainty was that they were not going home. Everyone had lost either a husband or a child or both. Nalla admitted she had been raped and some of the others did too, reluctantly. All of the women were gaunt, underfed, and naked.

The terror began each evening after dark when the soldiers came around. For a few cents, the boss allowed them into the fort to assault the women, all of whom were fair game.

Conditions in the fort were deplorable. Most of the captives had no shelter and slept on the ground. The few huts were given to those suffering from dysentery and scurvy. A brief rainstorm turned the red dirt to mud. Food was sporadic and consisted of hardened loaves of old bread and whatever fruit the boss could find. The only effort at sanitation was a large hole filled with raw sewage in one corner. Using it was treacherous. Its walls were slick with waste and at least once a day someone fell in. The entire fort was a breeding ground for rats and mosquitoes, some as large as hornets. At night, no one protected the women. The guards were as likely to assault them as the soldiers who were always lurking.

And so they waited, day after day. The fort slowly filled up, with more people meaning less food for everyone. In desperation, the women began looking at the harbor and wishing a slave ship would appear to take them away.

6.

One morning, two weeks or so after they arrived, though they had no idea what day of the week it was, Nalla awoke in the dirt and got up. Two women were pointing to the harbor. There, finally, was a ship. Hours passed and nothing happened, then a strange sight appeared. It was the first white man they had ever seen. He and the boss met on the porch of a hut and negotiated.

After the white man left, the atmosphere throughout the fort changed considerably. The guards opened a hut and removed piles of chains and iron cuffs for necks and ankles. They ordered the women to stand in a line and began shackling them again. When one resisted she was whipped as the others were forced to watch. Nalla was in the first group of about thirty who were led from the fort as everyone, men and women, watched. Their turn would come soon enough.

They were led down a path toward the bay. The villagers stopped what they were doing and watched with pity as the captives were taken away. At the dock, Nalla and the others were marched down a narrow pier to a boat where some harsh white men growled at them in a foreign tongue.

It was English and they were Americans.

The women were shoved onto the deck, then down a flimsy ladder to a sweltering hold with closed portholes. The boat, a cargo canoe, could carry fifty slaves at a time, and it took two hours to load it with the cargo. Meanwhile, Nalla and the women waited in the dark below, in the stifling, disgusting air. At times they could hardly breathe. They gasped and struggled and cried out in fear. A guard opened a porthole and allowed in some air. Finally, they shoved off and the cargo canoe rocked slightly. The air flowed through the hold. With no experience on the ocean, the rocking of the boat made them nauseous.

Half an hour later, they were ordered out of the hold and off the boat. They stepped onto a gangplank and climbed up the steep walkway to the deck of the *Venus*.

What they saw shocked them. For humans hardened by cruelty and abuse, the sight was even more alarming. Dozens of African men squatted or sat in tight groups waiting to be told what to do. They watched the women come aboard. Around the edge of the deck were white men with guns, glaring at their captives. Tied to a mast in the middle of the deck was an African man in the process of being bullwhipped. His blood dripped onto the wooden boards. Next to him, on another mast, was a white man, also naked and bloodied. The brute with the whip was laughing and talking loudly in English. One lash for the African. The next for the sailor. He was in no hurry.

7.

Mercer had passed through Dulles International before. It was a major airport, an important crossroads that welcomed people from all corners of the world. In the main terminal, the arrivals and departures boards listed hundreds of flights to and from everywhere. Every airline of any significance had a presence. Mercer enjoyed gazing at the boards and dreaming of all the places she wanted to see. The world was at her fingertips, and carriers such as Icelandair, All Nippon Airways, Royal Air Maroc, and Lufthansa could take her away.

They were killing three hours as they waited for their flight to London. Thomas was off stretching his legs and hunting coffee. Mercer put down the Dark Isle book. She was halfway through and needed a break. Somewhere back there in the distant memories of her education, she was certain she had been forced by a well-meaning teacher to read about enslaved people in America. She knew some of the basics, but history had never held her interest. She'd read *Uncle Tom's Cabin* and *Huckleberry Finn*, and had a general idea of how horrible things had been, but she had never taken the time to dwell on it. Her reading tastes had always leaned toward contemporary English and French literature.

A crowd of Africans approached. The women were adorned in brightly colored robes and head scarves. The men wore fashionable dark suits with white shirts and loud ties. They were in a lively mood and talked at full volume in richly accented English. Other passengers stared as they walked by and gave them a wide berth. They rolled their luggage to the Nigerian Air desk and got in line.

Mercer flashed back to the haunting story of Nalla and the inhumanity of her first and only trip across the Atlantic from West Africa. She smiled at the Nigerians and asked herself how her ancestors could have tolerated such cruelty to their ancestors. The very idea was overwhelming.

Thomas was back and handed her coffee in a paper cup. He said, "You've hardly spoken to me since we left."

"So?"

"So, we're newlyweds and we're supposed to be thoroughly smitten with each other."

"Are you smitten?"

"Of course, and I'm thinking of nothing but more consummating."

"Sorry I brought it up. I'm smitten too. Now you feel better?"

"I suppose. Not really. How's the book?"

"It's pretty amazing. The people who settled on Dark Isle were slaves from West Africa. Ever been to West Africa?"

"No. I've been to Cape Town and Nairobi."

"Me neither. It's a fascinating story."

"You found a plot yet?"

"Maybe. The story follows the enslavement of one of the author's ancestors, a young mother named Nalla, who was kidnapped by slave traders. She lost her child, husband, family, everything."

"When?"

"Around 1760."

"How did she get to Dark Isle?"

"I don't know. I haven't gotten that far yet."

"Are you going to ignore me all the way across the Atlantic?"

"Probably, until I finish the book."

"I'm not sure I'm cut out for married life."

"Too late. The knot is tied. Go read your own book."

8.

Lovely took a curious turn with her narrative. Once Nalla was finally on the ship, the author paused and gave the reader some history to put the slave trade in perspective. Her research was impressive. She wrote:

The Venus was one of three slave ships owned by a Virginia planter named Melton Fancher. By the mid-1700s he was the largest landowner in the state with several tobacco plantations and hundreds of slaves. Most of the early slave trade was controlled by the Portuguese, Dutch, and British, but Mr. Fancher wanted into the business. He needed more labor for his tobacco farms and he could get it cheaper if he had his own ships. He loaded them with tobacco and whiskey and sent them to Africa to trade for slaves.

His slave ships were built in the shipyards at Norfolk, where hundreds were employed. They were financed and insured by banks and companies in New York, Boston, and Philadelphia. Since the slaves were considered to be nothing but chattel, same as livestock, they were insured too.

The slave trade was big business. Everybody made money. Except, of course, the slaves.

Since they were so valuable, careful records were kept by the trading companies. From 1737 to 1771, Mr. Fancher's three ships made 228 voyages across the Atlantic and delivered about 110,000 kidnapped slaves to American markets, primarily Norfolk, Charleston, Savannah. He was considered to be the largest American slave trader and became very rich.

Conditions aboard his ships were awful, like all slave ships. The suffering Nalla endured, described below, was common. It was standard procedure in those terrible days for other ships, small boats, fishermen, and dockworkers to clear the harbor when a slave ship approached port. The stench was toxic, nauseating, and carried for miles. It was said you could smell one coming before you saw the top of its sails.

9.

For three days Nalla waited with the others as the *Venus* slowly filled with more chained and shackled Africans, all naked and bewildered. Many of the men were belligerent and rebellious, and the slightest protests or cursing led to brutal whippings for all to see. Every lashing was done on the main deck with a full crowd of witnesses. The violence and gruesomeness was effective and muffled thoughts of fighting back. The sailors were heavily armed and aggressive, and acted as though the best way to maintain discipline was to beat any African who failed to quickly follow orders.

The men were attached at the ankles with iron cuffs that never came off. They were forced to walk, sit, and do everything in pairs. They were banished to the lowest deck, a stifling sweathouse with no windows, ventilation, light, nor place to urinate or defecate. They were packed together so tightly that they were forced to sleep elbow-to-elbow. The hold was as hot as an oven and breathing was difficult. Sweat poured from their skin and puddled and dripped through the cracks of the planks. The stench of sweat, urine, and feces hung like a thick fog that was almost visible. For a few hours each day the men were taken to the deck where they filled their lungs with air and ate gruel from a dirty porcelain bowl. They relieved themselves in one corner where the sailors had arranged a pipe-like chute to dump the waste into the ocean.

And they were still at anchor, still taking on more captives.

The women and children were housed in various rooms below the main deck and they were not shackled. Far fewer in number than the men, their conditions were slightly better, though they lived with the fear of sexual assault. They were allowed more time on deck and they constantly watched the men, hoping to find a lost husband or brother. It happened occasionally, though the women knew to stay quiet about it. It did not happen to Nalla. There was no sign of Mosi.

The sailors were a rough crew of derelicts, criminals, ex-prisoners, debtors, and drunks unable to find honest work at home. Working a slave ship was widely known to be the lowest job available, and they signed on only because they could find nothing else. They were not real sailors, with training and knowledge of the sea, but nothing more than a band of desperate men who often enjoyed the thuggery. Many were sadistic. The discipline came from the top and was driven down forcefully by the captain and his mates. They were harsh with the sailors so the sailors would be harsh to the slaves. Everyone feared a rebellion and the atmosphere was always tense.

After a week of waiting, the *Venus* finally set sail on April 12, 1760. It was bound for Savannah with 435 Africans on board.

Three hundred and ten were men, the rest women and children. There were forty-five sailors, ten mates, and a captain, Joshua Lankford, a veteran of many such voyages.

The ship never made it to Savannah.

10.

Roughly 20 percent of the Africans died en route. Three crew members died of smallpox; two of malaria. Sickness and disease were everywhere on the ship. Dysentery was widespread and virtually every slave, and most sailors, suffered some type of intestinal problem. The food was sparse and dreadful and resulted in scurvy and other afflictions. There were outbreaks of measles and smallpox that led to isolation in the deepest, foulest holds at the bottom of the ship. Given the levels of despair and depression, suicide was a common thought. Two men, chained together at the ankles, managed to scramble over the railing of the deck and go overboard. This inspired others, and more sentries were posted to prevent jumping. Nevertheless, a week later, two more Africans escaped gunfire and drowned themselves. A thirteen-year-old girl was severely beaten by two sailors when she fought them during a sexual assault. When they realized she was dead, they tossed her overboard to avoid punishment. It was not reported to the captain.

On Fancher ships, sexual contact with the female slaves was strictly prohibited. As with most rules, it was ignored and there was no punishment for the sailors. As captives, the women learned not to resist.

Nalla was tormented by a nasty ruffian nicknamed Monk, a burly black-bearded ex-criminal with scars on his neck. Each night she lay on the floor in the darkness, a friend on each side, praying the white men would not come. Often they did, and

Monk quickly became a regular. By the light of a candle, he led Nalla away and down through a maze of dark hallways to a dank, cramped little room where drinking water was stored. He latched the door for some privacy and had his pleasure. She did not resist. Sometimes other men were waiting. Many of the women were taken to the same room.

To show his good intentions, Mr. Fancher required a doctor on each of his slave ships. On the *Venus,* the doctor treated only sailors and preferred not to touch the Africans. He was quick to pronounce a desperately ill slave "dead" and order him thrown overboard. Only the captain could interfere with such a diagnosis, and Lankford was not one to second-guess the doctor. He dispensed a few pills and salves for the sailors but had nothing for the Africans.

The sighting of land caused a stir, and as it came into view the crew got busy. The lowly deckhands began scrubbing the deck in a futile effort to tidy up the ship. The women were brought on deck and given buckets of salt water and lye soap to bathe each other. Each was given a cheap burlap garment to wrap around her waist and cover her midsection. Their breasts would still be exposed, which meant nothing to the Africans but would be a source of curiosity on land. The men were not given soap and water but were instructed to cover their genitals with a strip of cloth.

Late in the afternoon, Captain Lankford made a rare appearance on deck. He inspected his men, a motley crew whose appearance had only deteriorated with the voyage, but he somehow managed to look impressed. He took a long look through his telescope, as if to verify that Savannah was indeed on course. He claimed to see the harbor, one he knew well, and said it was only two miles away. They would drop anchor at dark and make land early the next morning.

The *Venus* would get no closer.

The dark clouds and winds appeared in a rush from the north. The storm was so sudden, the crew did not have time to lower the sails and drop anchor. Within minutes the ship was being shoved southward and back out to sea. The waves were five feet, then ten, then crashing into the ship and spraying water across the deck. Everyone was ordered below. The gusts were stronger and louder and sustained for long periods of time.

Captain Lankford had survived hurricanes in the Caribbean, but he'd never seen such a storm come from the north. He found it impossible to steer the ship as the wind whipped it about. Though there was virtually no visibility, he could tell when the mainsail was ripped and began whipping the foresail and back sail. Larger waves were hitting broadside and drenching the deck. His ship was taking on enormous amounts of water. When the aft mast snapped and broke in two, the captain ordered his men to unlatch the lifeboats and begin lowering them. With the ship bouncing violently from side to side, it was an impossible task. Any fool who attempted to cross the deck was certain to be swept away. Lankford worried that the Africans might somehow break free from below, swarm the deck, and commandeer the lifeboats. He ordered the hold-hatches locked shut, entombing the 400-plus Africans and guaranteeing their deaths if the *Venus* went down. In a brief lull, the sailors scrambled over the deck and sealed off the holds.

Then the winds and waves were back, stronger than before, and the *Venus* rocked violently from side to side, almost capsizing several times. The captain told his men to jump if they wished, but to grab something that would float. He intended to go down with his ship.

Below deck, Nalla and the women clutched the children and tried to protect them from the fury of the storm. They held each other tightly as the ship rolled and pitched and seemed ready to break into pieces. They were tossed about and banged into walls and each other. They were crying and praying and often screaming when heavier waves hit. All candles were out and the holds were pitch-black. Below them they could hear the men yelling desperately. Above them, water was seeping through the cracks. They knew they were about to die.

The storm intensified after dark. Several women made it up the steps but couldn't open the hatch. They realized they were trapped below and would certainly drown. Water was a foot deep and rising.

A huge wave took the ship up and slammed it back down. It broke in half, spilling its cargo into the ocean. None of the Africans could swim. The men were doomed because they were shackled together. The women tried to grab the children but the storm was too fierce and it was too dark.

Nalla found herself clutching a jagged piece of a splintered mast. She and several other women clung desperately to it as the waves lifted them high then submerged them under the water. She urged them to hang on, to be strong. They had survived so far. They were away from the ship and they were not going to drown. Hang on. There were desperate voices everywhere, the last words of dying people, of anguished mothers, of sailors trying to save themselves. Their cries were lost in the howling winds, the crash of waves, the utter blackness of the ocean.

As if its mission had been to destroy the ship, the storm began to subside. The waves still rocked them along but they were not as fierce. The winds were losing their strength. Minutes were passing and Nalla was still alive. She held on and realized that the mast might just save her life. She kept talking to the other women, two of whom she could not see. Others were behind her, still desperately hanging on.

11.

The ocean was calm, still, flat as glass, with no trace of its fury only hours earlier. On the horizon a small orange ball appeared and began to grow as the sun rose for another day.

Nalla and five other women huddled around three children at the foot of a dune. The water was not far away and its quiet waves lapped at the sand. The beach stretched right and left as far as they could see.

They were cold and hoped the sun would rise quickly. They were naked again. The cheap burlap skirts they'd been given after they bathed were lost in the storm. They were starving and had not eaten in hours. The children whimpered in their discomfort but the women just stared at the ocean, too traumatized to think about their next move.

Somewhere out there, far beyond the horizon, was home. Nalla thought of her little boy and fought back tears. The dreadful ship that brought them here was gone. Could they ever find another to go back?

The splintered mast that saved their lives was wedged in the sand nearby. Nalla thought of the others who had clung desperately to it but had been swept away by the crushing waves. Their anguished cries rang in her ears. Were they all dead or had some managed to find the shore?

Death was everywhere. Nalla had seen so much of it since her village was raided, and she wondered if she was dead now. Finally dead and free of the nightmare. Finally dead and now on her journey to be reunited with Mosi and her little boy.

The women heard other voices and drew closer together, but they were the calm voices of men approaching. A group of Africans appeared down the beach, walking their way. Four men, one with a rifle, and three women from the ship. When they saw Nalla and her group, the women ran to greet one another with hugs and tears. There were other survivors. Perhaps there could be many more.

The men watched and smiled. They were shirtless and barefoot but they wore the same odd britches as the white men on the ship. They spoke in a tongue the women did not understand. But their message was clear: *You are safe here.*

They followed the men down the beach to a slight bend where the shore curved around a small bay. They slowed as they saw two dark objects in the surf ahead. Figures. Bodies. Two naked African men bound at the ankles, dead now for hours. They pulled them out of the water and across the sand to a dune where they would bury them later.

The sun was up now, and the women, elated to be safe for the moment, were mumbling among themselves about food and water. With hand and sign language, Nalla communicated with the leader, the man with the gun, and managed to convey the message that they needed food.

As they were leaving the beach, they stumbled upon three more women cowering near a dune. They hugged them and cried with them. At least they were alive.

The rescue party followed a trail around the dunes until it led to thick vegetation. Soon they were walking through a forest of old elms and oaks with moss hanging from the low branches. The forest grew thicker until the trees and moss blocked the sky and sun. The women smelled smoke. Moments later they walked into a settlement, a village with rows of neat houses made of wattle and mud and covered with thatched palm-leaf roofs.

The women, eleven in all with six children, were surrounded by their new friends. The men wore britches that fell to their knees. The women wore fabric dresses that flowed from their necks to their feet. They were all barefoot and wore broad, happy smiles of grace and pity. They reached out to their new sisters and their children from Africa.

They, too, had made the passage. They had endured the ships. And now they were free.

CHAPTER TWO
PANTHER CAY

1.

The Camino Island newspaper, *The Register,* was published three times a week and did a nice job of recording the milestones in the life of the community: funerals, weddings, births, arrests, and zoning applications. Its owner, Sid Larramore, had learned years earlier that the key to staying afloat, other than advertising, was to fill the pages with color photos of kids playing baseball, softball, T-ball, soccer, basketball, and every other possible game. Parents and grandparents snapped up the papers when the right kids were featured. Action shots of anglers proudly holding large grouper and wahoo were almost as popular.

Bruce read each edition from cover to cover, and Bay Books spent a thousand dollars a month on advertising. Touring authors could always expect a nice little story on page two, along with a photo.

Nothing, though, riled the island, and sold newspapers, like the gossip that yet another high-rolling developer from "down south" was gobbling up property and planning a million condos. "Down south" always meant Miami, a place famous not only for its drug traffickers but the legions of bankers and developers who laundered their money. For most Floridians, every project originating from down south was to be treated with great suspicion.

Because of an arbitrary decision made by a long-forgotten Spanish explorer centuries earlier, Dark Isle was considered to be under the jurisdiction of Camino Island, as was one other undeveloped spit of land near the Georgia state line. When Florida became a state in 1845, the name stuck and "Dark Isle" became official.

Bruce sat down at his desk with a stack of the morning's mail, a newspaper, and a cup of strong coffee. He was immediately greeted with the headline: "Tidal Breeze Announces Panther Cay Resort." Half the front page was a colorful artist's rendering of the planned overhaul of Dark Isle into Panther Cay, a fresh new name created by some clever folks in marketing. A giant casino was to sit in the middle of the island, with a music hall to seat five thousand and at least that many slot machines. Big-name bands and singers were virtually guaranteed, as were countless well-to-do gamblers. To the south of the casino was yet another 18-hole golf course for the deprived golfers of Florida, and for sure every fairway was lined with luxury homes and condos. To the north was a contrived village with stores, restaurants, and apartments. The sandy white beach on the Atlantic side was lined with hotels offering spectacular views of the ocean. On the bay side there were marinas with plenty of slips to accommodate all manner of boats, including, possibly, luxury yachts.

Something for everyone. Promises galore. The possibilities were endless. Tidal Breeze crowed about spending $600 million to bring Panther Cay to life. There was no mention of the projected profits from the development.

Missing from the slick art was the bridge to make it all possible, but a spokesman for Tidal Breeze said, "Our company stands ready to pay fifty percent of the total cost of the bridge, and we've been assured by the state of Florida that the legislature will appropriate the rest of the funds during its next session. When completed, Panther Cay will pay for the bridge with new taxes within five years."

Bruce had heard otherwise. The real gossip making the rounds was that Tidal Breeze was already in bed with some state senators and would get the bridge built without putting up a dime. It was promising to repay $50 million, about half the cost, over a thirty-year period with money saved from tax exemptions. It was a murky, complicated deal still being hammered out in bars around Tallahassee.

A much smaller story on page two offered some rebuttal from environmental groups. Needless to say, they were horrified at the project and vowed a tough fight. One of the more radical lawyers blasted Tidal Breeze for its long history of broken promises, failed projects, and environmental abuses.

The battle lines were quickly being drawn.

Bruce had been on the island for twenty-five years. He had opened Bay Books on a whim when he was only twenty-four years old and too young to be frightened. He had just nicked some rare books from his father's estate, sold most of them for around $200,000, and became enamored with the business. He bought the only bookstore on the island, renovated it, put in a café and coffee bar, changed its name, and opened the doors.

He loved Camino and wanted it to change slowly, if at all. Panther Cay was the most audacious attack yet on the laid-back, peaceful lifestyle enjoyed by those attracted to the island and the town of Santa Rosa. From its downtown harbor, Panther Cay would be a twenty-minute boat ride away. The bright, gaudy lights of the resort would ruin the views to the west.

Bruce was somewhat confident the county supervisors would block it. However, with that much money in play, nothing was certain. At least two of the five supervisors were constantly spouting pro-growth nonsense.

He chuckled at the new name. If there had been a panther sighting within a hundred miles of Dark Isle, he wasn't aware of it. There were only two hundred or so left in Florida. The species was highly endangered and lived near the Everglades. There was a beach called Panther Key on an island south of Naples.

But "Panther Cay" had a catchy ring to it and worked well in the promotional materials. There was already a website but it offered little.

His cell phone buzzed and he smiled at it. "Mercer, my dear, I was just thinking of you."

"I'm sure you were. Hello, Bruce. How's the island?"

"Still here. Miss me on your honeymoon?"

"Not at all. We're having a grand time. Right now we're on a train, the *Royal Scotsman*, somewhere near Dundee, headed for the Highlands."

"Sounds lovely. Nothing to report here, except that a rogue corporation from Miami just announced a six-hundred-million-dollar resort on Dark Isle, now known as Panther Cay, at least that's what the corporation is calling it. Other than that, things are quiet. There was a bar fight last Saturday at the Pirate's Saloon."

"I finished the book flying over. What an amazing story. Would it be possible to meet Lovely Jackson?"

"I can probably arrange that. As I said, she comes in twice a year and we have coffee. She's a real character, but kind of spooky."

"And you think she might cooperate if I write this story?"

"I don't know. That's the question. The only way to know is to ask her."

"Here's another question. How can this corporation develop Dark Isle if it's owned by Lovely? She still claims ownership, right?"

"Right. She says she's the last-known living heir to the property, but the paperwork is rather scarce. There has never been a grant from the throne or a property deed."

"Sounds like another chapter."

"Yes, it does. You'd better get busy. Is Thomas still around?"

"Sort of. He's got his nose stuck in the book now, completely ignoring me."

"What an idiot."

"I'll call when we get home."

2.

Steven Mahon had failed twice at retirement. For most of his illustrious career he was a top litigator for the Sierra Club and led assaults against all manner of environmental pollution and destruction. The lawsuits were long and brutal and after thirty years he burned out and retired to a small family farm in Vermont. There he lasted one winter, snowbound and bored, until his wife sent him to Boston to find work. He got a job with a small nonprofit, sued a few chemical companies, and survived a heart attack at the age of sixty-three. His wife was from Oregon, couldn't handle snow, and decided they needed sunshine. They moved to Santa Rosa and bought a beautiful Victorian three blocks off Main Street. She took over a garden club as he puttered around with the turtle-watchers guarding eggs on the beach. When boredom threatened their marriage, he founded the Barrier Island Legal Defense Fund, an aggressive-sounding outfit that consisted of himself and a part-time secretary crammed together in a tiny office above a dress shop, across the street from Bay Books.

Now seventy years old, he claimed he'd never been happier. Bruce liked him because their politics were similar, and also because he bought a lot of books at no discount. He was quoted on page three in the morning's paper as saying, "The proposed development of Dark Isle will be an environmental disaster like we've never seen in this part of Florida. We look forward to hauling Tidal Breeze into court."

Never one to mince words or run from a reporter, Steven was always quick with a colorful word or two and loved making threats. Trench warfare against rich, ruthless corporations had stripped him of any semblance of timidity or diplomacy.

He and Bruce met for lunch at least once a month, and seeing Steven's name in print prompted the invitation by Bruce. They found their favorite table on a waterside terrace at the main harbor, just as a shrimp boat chugged by loaded with the daily catch. Bruce, as always, ordered a bottle of Chablis. Steven said he would have only one glass. He was lean and in great health, but his doctors, and his wife, watched his numbers closely. Cardiac problems were hereditary.

"How's the book coming along?" Bruce asked.

The book was his memoir, his war stories, his greatest hits in taking on wolf poachers in Montana, nuclear waste leakers in New Mexico, coal strip miners in Kentucky, and Miami cruise operators who dumped tons of garbage in the ocean. The list was long and remarkable and Bruce had heard many of the tales over the years. Steven was a fine raconteur and a good writer as well, but the book required discipline. The author disliked desks and computer screens.

"Two hundred pages, with at least that much to go."

"When can I read some?"

"Later, not now." The waitress poured wine and they clinked glasses.

When it came to his writers, Bruce was famously nosy. He wanted to know what they were working on and pushed them to write more. A notoriously undisciplined bunch by nature, they usually lied and said they were making more progress than they really were. He was always ready to jump in and read their latest drafts, which, of course, meant they had to listen to his editorial comments. He wanted them to write hard and well, and get published, and enjoy the writing life. If necessary, he would call agents and editors and give his unsolicited opinions about the manuscripts. And they listened. He had built his store into a powerhouse on the independent bookstore circuit, and it sold a lot of books. He networked nonstop and could deliver as much in the way of gossip as in gross sales. He knew the writers, agents, editors, publishers, executives, book reviewers, critics, and many other booksellers, and he made certain they knew him.

He and Steven ordered seafood salads and sipped wine. It was June and the sun was hot, the tourists had arrived, and the harbor was busy with fishing boats and small craft.

And the bookstore was packed. The summer season was Bruce's favorite.

He said, "I saw where you popped off in the paper about Panther Cay."

Steven smiled and shrugged. "Popped off? I thought I offered my usual learned and reserved legal opinion."

"Well, it was certainly the usual. I assume you'll be involved."

"Not yet but we're watching closely. If Tidal Breeze gets approval, then all hell breaks loose."

"You file suit?"

"Oh yes. We'll unload all the heavy artillery, or as much as my little operation can handle. It'll be expensive, though."

Bruce and Noelle were generous to many local nonprofits and gave Steven's $5,000 a year. He operated on a tight budget and worked his contacts in the environmental world.

Bruce said, "I'm sure you can round up a nice litigation team. The big guys should be all over this."

"We'll see, but I'm worried. The big guys, especially in the Southeast, are stretched pretty thin right now. A lot of irons in the fire, a lot of development. Money has been so cheap for the past ten years that everybody is expanding. Theme parks, super-highways, offshore drilling, subdivisions. There are not enough tree-huggers like me who know how to litigate and win. It'll be a war."

"You've already done your homework?"

"Yes. We got word about a year ago that the developers were sniffing around. As you know, Leo changed the seascape. Dark Isle was there for centuries and nobody wanted it. Leo hits and within hours the reefs and currents are radically different. Suddenly, a bridge is feasible, and of course the highway boys are always looking for a new one to build."

"What about Lovely Jackson's claim of ownership?"

Steven shook his head and drank some wine. The waitress poured water and asked if they needed anything else. They did not.

Steven said, "I'm not a property lawyer, that's another specialty, but if she plans to fight the development, she has to go to court and prove ownership. Frankly, that's the easiest way to stop Tidal Breeze. I assume the company's legal squad will argue loud and long that she has no ownership interest. Therefore, the land belongs to the state, subject to local property taxes, and is wide open to development."

Bruce swallowed a fat shrimp, chased it with Chablis, and asked, "What's the legal principle called—'adverse possession'? Something like that?"

"That's it and it's pretty basic stuff we covered in the first year of law school. If you squat on property that's not yours for at least seven years, then you can claim ownership by adverse possession. According to Lovely's book, slaves settled Dark Isle almost three hundred years ago and kept it to themselves. By the 1950s they were all gone. She was the last one and she left when she was fifteen, if you can believe her story."

"You don't believe it?"

"I don't know. I'm not much for voodoo and black magic and such. But regardless, she needs a lawyer, Bruce, and now. Can you contact her?"

"I'll try. As I said, she likes to come to the store occasionally. I keep copies of her book up front on the 'Local Authors' shelf. We're selling about three a year. I get the impression that she rarely gets out."

"How's her health?"

"Not sure, but she appears to be in pretty good shape, very spry. I'll reach out."

"The sooner the better."

"I'll see what I can do."

3.

Two years earlier, in the aftermath of Hurricane Leo, a crew from the Florida Department of Natural Resources was probing the waters between Dark Isle and the mainland, a distance of roughly one mile. Satellite images revealed a remarkable shift in both the landscape and seascape due to the storm. The northern end of the island had been sliced off and now sat three hundred yards away by itself, even more secluded. The main section was still intact but long swaths of its Atlantic-side beaches were gone. The amount of sand that had been displaced was beyond estimation, and the crew was in the early stages of gathering information. The three scientists were taking hundreds of photographs and measurements. Using sophisticated underwater cameras, they were filming the reefs and currents and sending the data back in real time to their lab in Tallahassee. The day's weather forecast was typical for August—hot, humid, with an 80 percent chance of late afternoon thunderstorms, some possibly severe.

Their forty-foot vessel was a flat-bottomed floating lab the DNR had been using for many years and was not exactly seaworthy. It wasn't supposed to be because it was designed for beach and backwater research. The scientists were not concerned with the forecast because the dock on the mainland was within eyesight and easily reachable if a storm blew in.

Their work took them close to the bayside shore of Dark Isle, and, for some reason, they decided to have a look on land. The island was notorious for its slave history and old tales of trespassers who disappeared. However, it had been deserted for decades. The locals, especially the fishermen, stayed away from it. The scientists, though, were far too educated for ghost stories and scoffed at the legends of voodoo curses and savage animals. As they slid the boat to a stop in the sand, a strong wind rose from the sea. Lightning clapped nearby. Thunder boomed from the mainland. The sky quickly became dark and ominous. Since there was no shelter to be seen, the scientists made the decision to hop back onto the boat and head for the ramp. As they cast off, the winds began to gust and a thick, slicing rain began to fall. The boat was shoved away from the island. Heavy waves began slapping it around. The men were not wearing life jackets and couldn't find them in the chaos. The choppy water tossed them about. The boat was no match for the waves and finally capsized. All three men went under.

One managed to hang on to the boat for two hours as the storm raged and the winds howled. When it finally passed, a county rescue team pulled him to safety. The sound was dragged for hours and into the next day, but the two lost men were never found.

The usual inquiries were made but eventually went nowhere. It was a storm, an act of nature. The experienced scientists were doing their work properly. It was just bad luck.

Lost in the tragedy and its subsequent investigation was the fact that the two casualties were white. The survivor was black.

Dark Isle had claimed more victims.

4.

If the corporate suits who ran Tidal Breeze down in Miami were aware of the island's colorful legends, it was not evident. After suddenly becoming attracted to the island, and after preliminary conversations with the right politicians and bureaucrats, Tidal Breeze began a clandestine operation to inspect and monitor the property. It hired a firm to use satellites to photograph, chart, and record every possible square foot. It hired another firm to scour the island with drones and send back images. What was feared became a reality. The island was so densely packed with ancient trees and vegetation it was impossible to see what was really on the ground. Leo, a Category 4 with winds of 145 miles per hour and a storm surge of an estimated twenty-five feet, had knocked over thousands of mature trees and strewn their limbs and roots into massive piles of debris. Thousands of other trees stood their ground and were shading much of the interior of the island. The vegetation had grown back after the storm and was too thick and dense to walk through. There was no evidence of roads or trails, no signs of the ruins of old buildings. A slight ridge ran along the center of the island. Its height was estimated at twenty feet in places, but most of Dark Isle was at sea level.

Though they would never admit it, because of the inevitable backlash, the suits had already decided that the best way to develop the island was to turn loose the bulldozers. A scorched-earth approach, one that Tidal Breeze knew well. They would save some of the nicer trees, display them, make a fuss over them, and preen about the company's long-standing commitment to protecting the environment and natural habitats.

A third firm, called Harmon, was hired to send a team ashore. It consisted of four tough guys who'd once served in the army's Special Forces. Three had been dishonorably discharged. They were supposedly experts in the more demanding areas of corporate security and private, semi-military-style jobs. Scoping out a small deserted island would not be much of a challenge.

Swaney, the captain and leader, decided a nighttime landing would be the smarter move. They couldn't run the risk of being seen by police or sheriff's deputies. The Coast Guard patrolled the area around Camino Island and Cumberland Island, Georgia. The DNR was often seen poking around. There were dozens of fishing boats and pleasure craft in and out of the main harbor at Santa Rosa. Someone, it seemed, was always nearby.

Camping and picnicking on Dark Isle were not against the law. For the locals, the island was a no-man's-land that had never been developed and had never been owned, for all practical matters. It was just sitting there, three miles of deserted jungle surrounded by white beaches. Anyone could stop by for a swim, a picnic, or a hike.

But no one did. There were too many old stories of those who'd tried.

Moving quietly across the dark inlet, the team members sat low in their thirty-foot fixed-hull inflatable boat, a dinghy, and watched the lights of the Santa Rosa harbor grow distant. When the hull touched sand, Swaney lifted the motor and guided the boat onto the beach. The four pulled it out of the surf and secured it with stakes and ropes. High tide was four minutes after midnight, three hours away. Using night-vision goggles, they found the two large dunes they'd selected from the aerials and decided these provided the best cover for their camp. Each of the four had a small video camera mounted on top of his helmet, and the live feeds were sent to a control center in a brown, unmarked van—"the UPS truck" as it was known—parked in the lot of the Sheraton hotel on Camino Island. Each man also had a hot headset mike that allowed the two technicians in the van to talk in real time to the team. Everybody could communicate.

They set up camp by pitching four single rayon tents with fly screens. They unloaded coolers of food and drinks. The plan was to spend two full days exploring the island and two nights in the tents. They were not yet tired and decided to explore. They wore full military-style uniforms, minus the protective flak jackets. All were well armed with Glock 19 semi-automatic pistols and two carried M4 assault rifles. Each had a GPS monitor on his belt that allowed the technicians in the truck to follow his movements. The technicians were staring at the screen, following the four green dots as they moved along the beach, and trying to stay awake. No one on the team, and certainly no one in the van, expected excitement.

After an hour of walking the beach and finding no trail leading to the interior, Swaney said they would wait until daylight. By 11:30 the men were tucked away in their tents and falling asleep. They were all snoring an hour later when the first cat screeched at full volume and ruined their slumber. The animal was close by and its sound was a shrill, piercing call to action that ripped through the still night and caused the four to jump out of their skin. They instinctively grabbed weapons and looked out the fly screens. They waited, hearts pounding, lungs pulsing. The second scream seemed even closer, but that was probably because they were waiting for it.

The cry was not one of anguish. It was aggressive, as if warning the trespassers that they did not belong there.

Vince whispered loudly, "Hey, boss, what the hell's that?"

Swaney whispered back, "How am I supposed to know? Let's stay quiet."

"Let's get back in the boat."

"Nobody moves."

The cry seemed to come from the general direction of the south, either on the beach or close to it. A minute passed, and one to the north answered with his or her own version of a high-pitched growl that was distinguishable from the first.

There were at least two of them out there. Minutes passed and nothing was heard.

Swaney said, "Okay, get your lights and Glocks. On three we jump out and look around."

On three they scrambled out, bounced to their feet, flooded the area with lights, and saw nothing.

"Hey, boss, you ever heard a panther growl?" Roy asked.

Swaney said, "No, have you?"

"Not in real life, but I saw one in a movie."

"So you're the expert?"

"Didn't say that, but this boy sounded sort of like the one in the movie."

"It's either a panther or a bobcat," Marcus said with some authority. "Both are native to Florida, though the panthers went south a long time ago."

"Can you tell one from the other?" Swaney asked.

"Maybe. I'd bet it's a panther."

"Are they friendly?" Vince asked.

"Did they sound friendly?"

"Not exactly."

"No, they're not friendly at all. They're aggressive as hell when they feel threatened."

"I ain't threatened nobody," Vince said.

"Are you shittin' us again, Marcus?" Roy asked. "Always shittin' us."

Marcus said, "No I'm not. Panthers are known for their aggressiveness."

Swaney said, "All right, knock it off. We got food and supplies out here, so we'll take turns playing sentry. I'll take the first two hours. You guys get some sleep."

The other three returned to their tents as Swaney sat on a cooler with his M4. He smoked a cigarette and gazed at the distant lights of Camino Island. He listened carefully for the approach of something, though he knew the cats or whatever they were would not make a sound in the sand. There was no moon and the night was dark. Somewhere up there a satellite was watching them. An hour passed. Swaney smoked his third cigarette to stay awake. He walked silently around the campsite, holding his pistol. He heard no snores from the tents and figured the others were too rattled to relax.

They tag-teamed through the night, taking turns as lookouts, all armed and ready, and though there were no more screams or howls, they slept little. Roy was awake when dawn broke and made a pot of coffee over a burner. The aroma drew the others out of their tents.

After a breakfast of fruit and ham sandwiches, they dressed and prepared for a long day of exploring. All had their Glocks on their hips. Roy and Vince carried machetes to hack through the undergrowth while Swaney and Marcus were armed with their M4s. Swaney checked in with the boys in the UPS truck and all systems were go. A silver drone hummed into view about a hundred feet above them to act as their forward scout. Its 360-degree rotating scan gave the techs a clear view of the team on the ground and the intimidating job in front of them. Communication was clear and instant. The four on the ground talked to command at will, though Swaney wanted as little chatter as possible.

Using infrared images from satellite photos taken before Leo, Swaney chose a trail, or what he hoped would be a trail, off the beach, through some dunes and into a thicket of sea oats and hedge vines. For an hour they hacked with their machetes but made little progress. The drone was two hundred feet above them but could not penetrate the dense canopy of the oaks, elms, and Spanish moss. The techs in the UPS truck could see nothing but forest. The sun was high and hot, the forecast was for clear skies, temps in the eighties, and the chance of the usual late afternoon shower. After two hours the men were hot and tired, and Swaney signaled for a retreat. They had advanced perhaps fifty yards through the thick bushes, vines, trees, and storm debris. Back near the water and in the clear, the drone picked them up again and followed them as they hiked along the beach. At another slight opening, they found a trail covered with dead trees and made some progress, though every inch was contested. By noon, they were exhausted and fed up with the island. There was nothing there but dead trees and wild vegetation.

Their goal was to find nothing. If there were remnants of history, any signs of the lost slave colony, they were to destroy them. Tidal Breeze wanted a clean slate when it assaulted the island. Objections from historical societies and lawsuits from preservationists would only delay the beauty of Panther Cay.

The men were resting and eating sandwiches at the foot of a two-hundred-year-old elm when they lost contact. Their head-set mikes were suddenly dead. The boys in the UPS truck did not respond. Marcus, the tech expert, tried a cell phone but they were out of range. He tried a satellite phone but its batteries were dead. He said, "This is too weird. The batteries are brand-new, never been used. They can't be dead."

Swaney looked at his cell phone. It was dead. He looked at his handheld GPS monitor. The screen was black. The helmet cams were off. They listened for the drone but did not hear it.

Abandoned by the technology they took for granted, they said nothing as they ate and absorbed the reality of where they were. However, they were tough soldiers who'd been well trained years ago, and they were armed. After four hours of fighting their way through the forest, they were convinced that no other human was on the island. The only possible threat was those damned panthers, which would be dead the second they were spotted.

Swaney stood, stretched, picked up his backpack and his M4, and said, "Let's backtrack and head for the beach."

Shielded from the sun, the forest was cool and dark. As they moved slowly and searched for their trail, a thick cloud settled over the island and shut out even more light. Within minutes, Swaney stopped and looked for clues on the ground. All four scanned their surroundings. They were already lost.

5.

In the UPS truck, the technicians went through their emergency checklists and tried everything. After half an hour of futility, they finally called their Harmon supervisor in Atlanta. There was concern but no panic. The men had been in far more dangerous situations. They were experienced and armed and could take care of themselves. There was no discussion of a rescue.

6.

The first rattlesnake was resting on a limb three feet off the ground and showed no sign of alarm. He watched them as they froze and gawked at him. He did not coil as if to strike, nor did he bother to rattle his tail.

"Eastern diamondback," Marcus said softly, as if the snake might be upset at being identified. "The deadliest of all rattlers."

"Of course," Roy said under his breath. He no longer believed anything Marcus said.

Vince rubbed the handle of his pistol and said, "I can take him, boss."

Swaney lifted a hand and said, "No, let's just ease away."

To make matters worse, Marcus said, "These boys don't live alone. When you see one you know there are others."

"Shut up!" Roy said.

The second one was coiled and ready to strike, but gave the obligatory warning. When Swaney heard the unmistakable sound of the rattling, he stopped and took a step back. In the weeds, less than ten feet away, was a thick diamondback highly agitated.

"Take him, Vince!" Swaney said quickly.

Vince, a legendary marksman, fired four shots from his Glock and blew the snake in half. They watched him flip and jerk, his fangs still snapping as he died.

The gunshots echoed through the woods. When all was quiet and the snake was still, the four men realized how heavily they were breathing. No one spoke for a moment or two.

Marcus said, "This bad boy is over six feet long, very rare."

Swaney stepped back and looked around. "We came in from the southeast. I'm guessing west is that direction. Seems like the sun is brighter." He pointed and said, "Let's head this way. Mark the trees so we don't go in circles."

"We've been doing circles for the past hour," Roy mumbled.

"Shut up."

The third rattler hit Swaney at the top of his right boot and did not break the skin. Swaney jumped as he screamed and lost his footing. Vince fired away but the snake disappeared into a pile of wet leaves. Roy, the medic, examined Swaney's leg and pronounced him lucky. The vinyl layer of the boot had two deep fang marks.

They took a long break and had some water, but only a sip or two because they were running low. Each man gave his assessment of their situation and there was no consensus about which direction to try next. They had no idea if they were trekking closer to the shore or deeper into the jungle. Distant thunder did not lighten their mood. Marcus again tried the mikes, transmitters, and phones, with no luck. Even the compass on his watch was frozen.

It was a stretch to believe anyone would try to rescue them. The boys in the truck were geeks. Their bosses in Atlanta would not know what to do. They had sent in their best team for the job. Now that team was hopelessly lost. There was no backup.

They agreed that if they could manage to inch along in a straight line, more or less, they would eventually find the beach. Dark Isle was only three miles long and a mile wide. Surely they would find the ocean sooner or later.

They began moving, all eyes on the ground now, all ears waiting for the slightest rattle. Marking the trees as they moved along, Swaney tried to keep them in a straight line but it was difficult. There was no trail. Almost every step had to be cleared. They took a break at 5:00 p.m. and sat in a semicircle. Each took one sip of water from bottles that were almost empty. They had eaten everything in their backpacks.

Swaney said, "Okay, it'll be dark in a couple of hours."

"It's already dark," Roy blurted, and he was not wrong. The thick canopy above them kept the sunlight away.

Swaney went on, "I say we keep going for another hour and also look for a clear spot to bed down."

"We haven't seen a clear spot since this morning," Vince said. Tensions were smoldering and the men were losing confidence in Swaney's leadership.

"You wanna take the point?" Swaney shot back.

Vince did not reply. No one else volunteered. They picked up their equipment and began moving. There was more thunder and it seemed closer. When the rain began, dusk enveloped the jungle. They hacked out a small clearing and searched every log and burrow and pile of leaves for snakes. Roy and Vince had packed rain flys, and they strung them between two saplings for shelter. The rain, though, was kept away by the canopy. As it grew heavier it leaked down the trunks of the trees and began soaking the ground.

Swaney checked his watch at 8:00 p.m. Its dial gave the only faint light. The jungle was black, so dark and dense that the men could not see each other. They sat on the damp soil, backs to each other, watching the ground, trying to see signs of anything that might cause trouble. Swaney said he would pull the first hour of sentry duty. Exhausted, the other three finally nodded off. The thunder and rain faded as the storm moved away.

The jungle was eerily quiet. The only sounds were the rustling of tree limbs high above. Swaney fought to stay awake, and had nodded off himself when he heard panthers in the distance.

7.

Their second day on Dark Isle was beginning to look like their first, when they suddenly saw light. The canopy thinned ahead of them and the vegetation was not as dense. As weary as they were, they managed to shift to a faster walk and were soon on the beach. They had survived a nightmare, fought off poisonous snakes and avoided being mauled by panthers, and they were still in one piece. All four had numerous cuts and scratches but nothing serious.

They emerged at the far north end of the island, on the Atlantic side, about a mile from their camp. An hour later they saw their dinghy where they'd left it. Their tents were still pitched. The coolers had not been touched. They opened them and almost celebrated with cold water, ham sandwiches, and fruit. As they ate, they broke camp and tossed everything into the dinghy. A speedy exit from Dark Isle was underway. When they were in open water, their cell phones and GPS monitors suddenly had service.

Swaney avoided the harbor at Santa Rosa and navigated through the inlet to the Atlantic. At the southern tip of Camino Island, they puttered into a small marina. They moored the dinghy at the pier, unloaded it, then jumped into a waiting van. At the Sheraton, they showered, ate some more, and spent an hour on a conference call with headquarters in Atlanta.

By then, all four were complaining of fever and stomach cramps. They disbanded at the hotel, said quick goodbyes, and went separate ways. Vince, though, was too dizzy to drive and stayed in a hotel room. The small cuts on his arm were throbbing and blisters were forming on both wrists. His bowels were in turmoil and he sat on the commode for a long time. When he realized he could not walk without leaning against the walls, he called an ambulance and was taken to the hospital in Santa Rosa.

Swaney drove forty minutes to the airport in Jacksonville. His flight to Atlanta was two hours away, but he never made it. A violent case of diarrhea hit him in the terminal and he collapsed in the men's room. He had a high fever, severe chills, and blisters were popping up on his forearms. He was taken to a hospital in Jacksonville.

Roy lived in Ponte Vedra, ninety minutes south of Camino Island, and by the time he pulled into the driveway his wife was waiting. He had vomited on himself and was so dizzy he could barely see. He was delirious and kept saying he had no idea what was happening. His arms and legs were swollen and his hands were turning red. His wife was terrified and called 911.

Marcus died first. They found him the following day slumped in the front seat of his car at a rest area off Interstate 10 near Tallahassee. He had called his brother and reported that he was deathly ill, delirious, and suffering from acute diarrhea, among other things. His brother lived in Chicago and could not render aid at the moment. The state trooper who tapped on his window, saw his body, and finally opened the door, was nearly knocked out by the nauseous odor. Blisters and lesions covered his face and arms. First responders quickly realized it was too late and eventually hauled his body to the county morgue.

Swaney's doctors were the first to diagnose his condition—Vibrio vulnificus. Flesh-eating bacteria. It had apparently entered his body through one or more of the many nicks, scratches, and cuts he had incurred but largely ignored. Now they were so swollen and painful he had to be sedated. From there he went into a coma and never came out.

Vince died in the Santa Rosa hospital while his doctors were still scratching their heads. Roy lingered for a week in Ponte Vedra as his wife watched in horror as his skin rotted and turned black. When the doctor said it was time to turn off the machines, she did not object.

It took Harmon a couple of weeks to piece together the puzzle. All four men died of Vibrio vulnificus, which led to a condition called necrotizing fasciitis, type 3. It was a rare flesh-eating bacteria but not unheard of. In the United States there are about thirty such deaths each year, almost all in warm, tropical climates. Since the four deaths occurred in separate places, there was no way to link them to the job at Dark Isle. Indeed, that little project had been secretive, and Harmon wasn't about to divulge anything that was not required. The company had done nothing wrong, nor had anyone else. It would be difficult if not impossible to prove where and when the bacteria was encountered.

The report to Tidal Breeze did not mention the four deaths. It said nothing about the mysterious, temporary blackout of all communications. It certainly didn't mention the threat of wild animals—panthers and diamondbacks. It assured the client that there were no signs of ancient life on the island. No roads, trails, abandoned dwellings, fences, settlements, cemeteries. Nothing. Nothing but piles and mounds of fallen trees, broken limbs, and dead vegetation. Clearing the island for development would be a "substantial challenge," since so much would have to be hauled away, but it was possible.

The report was exactly what Tidal Breeze had in mind, and with it in hand the company pushed on with its aggressive plans to develop Panther Cay.

CHAPTER THREE

THE CURSE

1.

After two weeks of sightseeing, hiking, camping, pub-crawling, and loafing in the chilly air of the Highlands, Mercer and Thomas had returned to the heat and humidity of summer-time Florida. It was a rude reentry. The first morning back, they tried to enjoy coffee on the veranda but quickly surrendered to the heat and bugs. Their previous coffee had been on the terrace of a Scottish castle, wrapped in quilts.

But life goes on. It was now already July, and classes started at Ole Miss in late August. The summer was half over.

They were consumed with Lovely's history of Dark Isle. Mercer wanted it to be her next book but could not decide if it should be fiction or nonfiction. She could easily take the story, otherwise known as "stealing" in the trade and perfectly acceptable, and change the names and as many of the facts as she wanted. She would have complete literary license to create and fabricate. Thomas preferred nonfiction and wanted her to stick to the truth. He had sort of agreed to work as her researcher, though they had a long way to go. Being married would be enough of a challenge. They weren't sure if they could survive working together.

They went together to the Santa Rosa library and got lost in old newspapers, but didn't find much about Dark Isle. Lovely's story spanned over 250 years and had plenty of gaps. They didn't expect to verify any of it, but they had to dig anyway. Her story also stretched the imagination at times, almost to the point of disbelief.

Since Bruce Cable was the only person they knew who'd ever met Lovely, they were eager to talk to him. Mercer called and suggested lunch, always the best entrée with Bruce, and he responded predictably: *Lunch tomorrow!* And at his house, which, of course, meant a longer meal with a longer nap to follow, preferably in his hammock. He had someone they needed to meet.

Noelle was in France buying antiques, so Bruce, no slouch in the kitchen, cooked a tomato pie and served it with an arugula salad. They ate on the terrace with ancient ceiling fans swaying and creaking above. Bruce poured ice-cold Chablis and wanted to know all about Scotland.

Steven Mahon arrived fifteen minutes late, with apologies. He had met Mercer at the bookstore but she did not remember him. He had also just reread Lovely's book and was up to speed. "Bruce says you may want to write the story," he said.

Mercer frowned at Bruce and wanted to say, *Well, Bruce, as always, has a big mouth.* But she demurred with "We'll see. It's interesting."

"It's fascinating," Steven agreed. "And now the plot is getting really thick."

Mercer asked Bruce, "Do you think Lovely will talk to me? I'll have to tell her up front that I'm a writer and I'm thinking of borrowing her story."

"I have no idea. She's a pleasant person but very guarded.

I always get the impression she distrusts everyone and for that reason doesn't say much. I can call and find out. As I said, she refuses to talk on the phone."

"And she's here, on the island?" Steven asked.

"Yes, lives in The Docks, on the south end, outside the limits of Santa Rosa, an old neighborhood on the bay side where the oyster houses and canneries once operated. Many of the workers were black and they settled around the canneries. A hundred years ago The Docks was a bustling community with its own economy and churches. Even had an elementary school. It's still there, still busy. A lot of the blacks have scattered and a lot of hippies and artists have moved in. The housing is cheaper."

"Also known as Voodoo Village," Mercer said.

"That too. Years ago, when it was all black, white folks knew better than to go there after dark. There were stories about witch doctors and ghosts and such. African curses, rituals, and so on. But it's different now."

"So Lovely lives in Voodoo Village?" Steven asked, amused.

"The Docks. I haven't heard it called Voodoo Village in years. But, yes, she lives there as far as I know. I've never seen her house, never been invited. She told me at the bookstore one time that she lives in a small house with her neighbors just down the street. I got the impression they look after her."

"She has a friend, right?" Mercer asked.

"Yes, Miss Naomi, who is sort of her caretaker. When she visits the store, Miss Naomi is always driving."

"When did you move here, Bruce?" Thomas asked.

"Over twenty years ago."

"And you, Steven?"

"Just six years ago. Retirement."

"So none of us were here when Lovely tried to convince the state to preserve Dark Isle."

Bruce shook his head and said, "I've never heard that story."

"We found it this morning in the archives at the library. The story is dated in March of 1990. She claimed to be the owner of the island, the last descendant of the slaves, and she wanted to give it to the state of Florida if it would promise to protect it. Evidently, the state had little interest in doing so. It wasn't much of a story."

But Steven especially liked it. "That could be important evidence. It tends to prove that she was in fact the owner of the island. You see the problem here, right? A rather huge problem. In her own book, Lovely admits she left the island when she was fifteen years old. If we can believe that she was born in 1940, then she left in 1955. And she writes that she was the last person to leave. Everybody else was dead. Tidal Breeze will no doubt use her own words to drill home the point that the island was deserted then and has been so for decades now."

"How can she prove she was born there?"

"With no paperwork, no records, it will be difficult. She needs a lawyer, Bruce, and soon."

"Don't we all? I doubt she can afford one."

"What about a pro bono lawyer?" Mercer asked.

Steven laughed and said, "That's my specialty, right? Clients who can't pay."

"It's called a nonprofit for a reason," Bruce added.

"It has to be pro bono," Steven said. "No one can afford the fees it'll take to fight Tidal Breeze. I can do it to a point, but I'll have to find some help. Right now the first step is to talk to the client. That's up to you, Bruce."

"Okay, I'll give it a try. But no guarantees."

Mercer said, "There are some interesting stories about Dark Isle in the archives. Have you heard the one about the LSD boys?"

Bruce shrugged as if he hadn't a clue. "No."

"The story was dated May of 1970. These three teenage boys sailed out to Dark Isle to smoke pot. Figured they would have plenty of privacy. One took along some LSD, which I gather was rather new to the area in 1970. All three were tripping out and began making noises that attracted two large panthers. At first the kids thought they were just hallucinating, but when they realized the panthers were real, they jumped in the water and tried to escape. Two were rescued by a fisherman. The third one was never found, thus the headline and big story. His father was a well-known dentist on the island."

Thomas added, "They claimed they heard people screaming from the bush, but the police were skeptical. It was never clear what the boys really heard and saw. They were in another world."

They ate for a moment, savored the story, and sipped wine.

Thomas said, "And in 1933, during the Depression, there was a WPA project to record the oral histories of surviving slaves. There were still a few around then, and these two grad students were being paid by the government to find them. They knew about Dark Isle and decided to go find some descendants of former slaves. They were warned to stay away but insisted. When no one would take them to the island they rented a boat and went out anyway. They were never heard from again."

"Come on," Bruce said.

"I'm not making this up. It's in the newspaper, front-page headlines. November 1933."

"Was there a search party or something?" Steven asked.

"I don't know, but the sheriff is quoted saying he wasn't going out there looking for anybody. Said only fools and folks working for the federal government would set foot on Dark Isle."

Mercer and Thomas were enjoying the tag team. She took another sip of wine and said, "Right after the Second World War, a military plane was working the coast, taking aerial photos of everything. The navy was looking for a place to build a submarine base. The plane made a pass over Dark Isle and something happened."

"Must have flown too low," Thomas added.

"It crashed on the beach, killed the three men on board."

Steven held up his hands and said, "Okay, I get the message. I'm not going anywhere near that island."

2.

Miss Naomi Reed welcomed her two granddaughters, hugged their mom goodbye, and got them seated at the kitchen table with bowls of their favorite sugar cereal. She had not been raised on such junk food, but her upbringing was not important. Kids nowadays ate all kinds of bad food because it was sweet and delicious. Almost all of the grandmothers Naomi knew had given up on healthy diets for their young ones. They had lost all the food fights. The kids were already getting chubby. Let their parents worry about that.

Or their mother. Their father was seldom home. He drove a truck for a big corporation and the more he drove, the more money he made. Naomi was happy to keep the girls during the summer months. It was free babysitting for her daughter and precious time for Naomi.

She told them to stay in the house when they finished eating. As she did seven days a week, she left her modest home, walked off the porch and down the front sidewalk to a street called Rigg Road. It was a mix of asphalt and gravel, same as most streets in The Docks. She spoke to her neighbor across the street and waved at a kid on a bike.

This was her neighborhood, and each morning she asked God's help in guiding her to make it a better place. Two houses down, she turned in to a gravel alley, one barely wide enough for a small car, though she had never seen a vehicle going to Lovely's place. It was a small four-room home that had been built decades earlier for storage. Lovely had painted it bright yellow, her favorite color. The trim changed every three or four years. Now it was a royal blue, same as the boards on the narrow steps. Baskets of flowers—petunias, lilies, roses—hung in small clusters around the porch.

Naomi called out, "Say, Lovely, are you alive in there, girl?"

The reply came through the screen door. "Alive and kicking. Working on another lovely day." Naomi walked through the door and the two clasped hands. "Thanks so much for coming. Would you like coffee?"

"Of course."

Seven days a week she arrived at 8:00 a.m. The coffee was not only brewed but already poured and mixed with a little cream. They sat on the dusty sofa and took a drink.

"How are your girls?" Lovely asked.

"Bright and beautiful as always."

"I'd like to see them today."

"We'll go in a moment if you want."

Lovely had miscarried at the age of eighteen. After that, her husband lost interest in her and went to live in Jacksonville. After he died, she never remarried and, having no kids or grandchildren of her own, enjoyed doting on Naomi's granddaughters.

Then it was on to the weather, followed by a summary of the ailments currently afflicting their neighbors. Naomi grew more serious and said, "Mr. Cable from the bookstore called again yesterday, said he would like to see you."

"He's such a nice man."

"Yes he is."

"Did he say he's sold some more of my books?"

"Didn't mention that."

"Why is he calling?"

"I don't know, but he did say there were some people who wanted to meet you. Said there was something about Dark Isle."

One of their rituals was to read the island's newspaper together three times a week. They especially enjoyed the church news and obituaries. They had read the stories about the proposed development. "Tidal Breeze" was already a dirty word.

Gertrude lived two streets over and had been dying of cancer for years. Her illness had become so protracted that many in the village suspected she wasn't really that sick. Nevertheless, she was continually talked about and prayed over by her friends.

To move away from the unpleasantness of Dark Isle, Lovely asked about Gertrude and they spent a few worrisome minutes on that, which led to an update on Abe Croft, their former minister, who was nearing one hundred years old and definitely dying.

Miss Naomi said, "I need to check on the girls. Won't you stop by for lunch?"

"I'd like that. Thank you. And tell Mr. Cable I'll see him in the morning, if that's okay with you."

"Wonderful. The girls will be excited. They love the bookstore."

Lovely's two black cats eased into the room and eyed Naomi suspiciously. They kept their distance and perched themselves on a windowsill while watching the women. They didn't tolerate guests in the house and Naomi loathed them as well. It was time for her to leave.

"Thank you for the coffee. I'll call Mr. Cable and arrange a meeting."

Both women stood and walked through the screen door and onto the porch. They hugged tightly and said goodbye as if they might never see each other again.

3.

At dusk the heat began to break and Lovely needed her walk. As usual, she'd spent most of her day with her plants. She tended her flower beds in the front yard, and around back she grew more vegetables than she could ever consume. When the sun was high and she needed to rest, she retired to the front porch where she sat beside a window fan and read books from the library. And napped. At eighty, her naps were getting longer.

But so were her walks. Her favorite was a stroll through the streets to the harbor where the old canneries sat idle and neglected. She had worked there as a young woman, shucking oysters for ten cents an hour. She walked past two shrimp-packing plants that still ran all day and night and paid a lot more. At the end of the pier she gazed at the still water and enjoyed an orange sunset. In the distance the bridge to the mainland was busy with vehicles coming and going. Below it the Camino River moved slowly. When she was a child there was no bridge, only a ferry.

And far away, or as far as she could see at that moment, there was a dark speck of land. Dark Isle, the place of her birth, the resting place of her people, sacred ground for her. She owned it, as her people had for many years. They had fought off the white men with spears and clubs and then guns. They had shed tears and blood and never surrendered.

It was no surprise that the white men were back now, threatening once again. It would be her last stand. She was too old to fight much longer. And, if they were successful now, and they

flattened and paved the island and threw up buildings, there
would be nothing left for her, nothing to keep fighting for.

The fight would not be fair. They had the power and the
money.

She had nothing but the curse. Nalla's curse.

4.

After a rigorous day of loafing on the beach, the newlyweds
retired to the shade of their porch and a glass of lemonade.
The July sun was still white hot and had scattered most of the
beachcombers. It was time for either a nap or a swim in a pool.
Mercer's cottage had no pool, so she settled on the notion of a
nap. Thomas, after a month of matrimonial bliss, was worried
that being married might cause him to gain weight. They were
certainly burning their share of calories around the house and
they ate and drank as little as possible. Most of his married bud-
dies, though, had gradually chubbed-up over the years. Mercer
assured him he looked just fine. Nevertheless, he had bought a
new dirt bike and enjoyed riding in the surf at low tide. He said
he'd be back in an hour.

She dozed for moment, then had a thought. Nalla's story was
fixed in her mind and hard to shake. At random times, Mercer
would remember a scene and practically stop in her tracks. She
was working on a book proposal to send to her agent but it was
far from finished. In fact, she still wasn't sure how and where
to begin. Thomas had convinced her to tell the real story and
stay away from fiction. The truth was fascinating enough, and
the twist of a corporate land grab made it so compelling it was
almost irresistible.

One scene haunted her.

5.

Nalla and the other women and children were fed and clothed. One of the men was Joseph, who was slightly older and seemed to command the respect of the others. He was also from the Kongo and spoke Bantu.

Nalla told their story of the slave ship and the storm. The capture, kidnapping, and voyage across the ocean were experiences they knew well. How could they forget?

Nalla had plenty of questions of her own. Joseph explained that they, the only inhabitants of the island, were runaway slaves from Georgia, where slavery was legal. They were now in Florida, Spanish soil where slavery had not been legalized and runaways were safe. Nalla and the others from the *Venus* had been lucky enough to wash ashore on Spanish territory.

Will the white men find us here?

It's possible, Joseph said. The men who own the ship will most likely come looking for survivors. However, the Spanish don't like the British and they skirmish all the time along the border. Joseph spoke to a young man, one with a rifle. He pointed to it and explained that if the slave hunters set foot on their island there would be a bloody fight. They, the former slaves, were not going back. They would fight to the end and would die on their island.

Joseph had been captured and sold when he was seventeen years old. He came ashore in Savannah and was sold to a family that owned a large plantation where they grew rice, peanuts, and cotton. He lived and worked there for almost twenty years and learned to read and write and speak English. Compared to most owners, the master was a fair man who wanted his slaves to become Christians. He allowed an older slave to teach the children the basics. The overseer, though, was a cruel man who enjoyed using the whip. All the slaves in Georgia, especially in the southern part, dreamed of escaping to Florida. Joseph saw an opportunity and ran away. That was about ten years ago. He made it to the island, their island, and was welcomed by the others. There were about fifty then. Now, the number had doubled.

Joseph waved his hand at his people. *You are welcome here.*

There was a commotion at the trail. Half a dozen African men appeared and were dragging three white men, all of them dirty and bloodied. They were bound at the wrists with their hands behind them and a bamboo pole rammed between their bent elbows.

"We found them," one of the Africans said. "Hiding in the woods near the water. They are from the ship." The people surrounded the white men and waited for Joseph to inspect them. A boy handed him a heavy stick.

The men were unshaven, filthy, and shoeless. Their ragged clothes were stained with blood. Cuts, knots, and insect bites covered their arms and legs. "Stand up," Joseph said. They awkwardly struggled to their feet.

Nalla inched forward in the crowd for a closer look at the man in the middle. It was the one they called Monk, her rapist. She covered her mouth with her hands and gawked in disbelief. He saw her, made eye contact, then looked away.

"Where are you from?" Joseph demanded, toying with the stick.

"Virginia," one of them said.

"So you know English. You are colonists."

Two of them nodded. Monk stared at his gnarly feet.

Nalla stepped forward, took the stick from Joseph, and clubbed Monk three times on the head, each blow drawing blood and painful grunts. The villagers were startled by the attack.

Then she hit him again and again and he fell to the ground. Loosa, another woman from the ship, stepped forward, took the stick from Nalla, and began beating one of the other two. Nalla whispered to Joseph and explained that the men had repeatedly raped them on the ship. It was time for revenge.

Joseph explained this to the others. Some of the other women began crying because they too had suffered the same assaults on their voyages over.

Joseph began barking commands. Ropes made of aged tree vines and slumber grass were wrapped around the ankles of the three captives. They were hung by their feet from the same branch of elm tree in the center of the village. The younger mothers took the children to their homes.

Nalla began chanting in an unknown tongue and walking in tiny steps in circles around the men. Everyone else backed away. They recognized what was happening and gave her plenty of room. She began an odd little dance on her toes as she swayed and chanted and bounced around the men. Her eyes were closed and she was in another world.

A witch doctor stepped from the crowd and placed a wooden bowl and long knife on the ground. He said something to her and she nodded as if to say thanks. She continued her ritual, her dance, her curse. The voodoo was in her blood, passed down from her mother and grandmothers.

The three white men, upside down, were suffering intensely and watching Nalla as best they could. When it was time, she placed the wooden bowl under Monk's head, who squirmed but had no place to go. She held the knife high for all to see and kissed it. Then she squatted, grabbed his mangy hair, spat a curse in her African tongue, and sliced his throat.

When the bowl was filled with his blood, she lifted it and followed the witch doctor out of the village and back to the beach. With Joseph and the rest behind them and watching from a distance, she walked along the surf, dipping the bowl and leaving a trail of blood in the sand.

When the bowl was empty, the curse was complete. Woe to any white man who ventured onto their island.

By morning the other two were dead. Joseph ordered them cut down and dragged to the small dock hidden from the ocean. Using a boat they had confiscated from the last slave traders who'd paid a visit, they took the bodies out to sea and dumped them without ceremony.

The island had no place for a white man, dead or alive.

6.

The meeting was sure to be one of the more unusual ones in the history of Bay Books. Bruce tidied up his office, cleared away the debris from his desk, and straightened all of his first editions on the shelves. He had hundreds of them, but never enough.

Mercer and Thomas arrived first and took seats at the wine-tasting table Noelle had found in the village of Ménerbes, in Provence. Most of his furniture had been selected by his wife and came from the South of France. Her store next door was packed with fine antiques, so many that she often displayed the extras at the bookstore. It was not at all unusual for her to sell a beautiful table Bruce was using to display his bestsellers.

Steven Mahon was next and coffee was poured. Bruce cautioned them that the meeting might not go as planned. According to Miss Naomi, Lovely was hesitant about discussing important matters. "And, I'm not sure she really trusts white people," Bruce said.

"Can't blame her for that," Steven quipped.

"No, I'm serious. Several years ago Miss Naomi tried to convince her to prepare a will. Lovely has no blood heirs, supposedly, and no one knows what happens to Dark Isle when she dies."

"Could be a real mess," Steven said.

"No doubt. But she wouldn't do a will because there's not a black lawyer on the island."

"That's been a problem all over the South," Steven said. "It goes back generations, and it's the reason a lot of land owned by blacks has been foreclosed. No last will and testament, too many distant heirs, no clear title, so the land gets sold for unpaid taxes."

Thomas looked at Steven and asked, "You think she'll trust you?"

"What? Look at this face. The glow of complete honesty."

"Sorry I brought it up," Bruce mumbled as he stood. "They're here."

The kids' section of Bay Books took up half the ground floor and always had customers. Busy moms could drop off their kids for story time or just to browse and forget about them for an hour or so. The staff was always ready to read to the little ones and gently shove new releases to the older ones. Other than bestsellers, the kids' section was the most profitable in the store.

Miss Naomi's granddaughters loved the place and were excited to visit.

They were lost in books by the time she and Lovely entered Bruce's office and said hello. He introduced them to Mercer, Thomas, and Steven, and offered coffee. They politely declined and took seats at the table.

Lovely was stunning. She wore a bright yellow robe that flowed almost to the floor. On her head was a tall turban-style wrap that set high and was a mix of loud colors. Her necklace was a row of large shark's teeth.

Miss Naomi was stylish too, dressed for church or some gathering, but no match for her friend. Mercer guessed her age to be around sixty-five. Lovely claimed 1940 as her birth year, making her eighty, but she looked younger than Miss Naomi. Her eyes were a lighter shade, still brown but not dark. There was distant white blood in the family.

Around the table they struggled with the small talk. Bruce carried the ball and asked what the girls liked to read. Thankfully, Miss Naomi was a chatterbox and she and Bruce went back and forth. Steven, the lawyer, was hesitant to jump in. He was there to meet a potential client for a case he didn't really want, and there was an excellent chance the prospective client had no use for him. At some point, Mercer would be forced to tell Lovely that she wanted to write a book about her and her island, but she wasn't sure how to broach that subject.

Lovely sat regally in the leather chair and offered a tight smile, as if it was difficult. She seemed to be taking in everyone and everything and debating whether or not she liked what she was seeing. Her eyes glowed with a fierceness that did not spread to the rest of her face.

When Bruce began to flail, Mercer said, "I just read your book, Ms. Jackson. It's a great story."

The smile widened and she said, "Please call me Lovely. Everybody else does, including children. Jackson was the name given to my ancestors. They didn't ask for it, didn't like it, but they had no choice. For years I've thought about changing my name but, I'm told, that would force me to go to court."

"Court" was the opening Steven needed, but the timing seemed bad. He let it pass.

Lovely said, "I'm so glad you enjoyed my book." A careful voice, rich with a soft Southern accent. Mercer was floored when she said, "And I enjoyed yours. *Tessa.* I knew her, your grandmother, but not well. I met her once. I remember when she died. Just awful. I'm so sorry."

"Thank you," Mercer said. It seemed odd receiving condolences from a person whose family had suffered as much as Lovely's, but that was ancient history now. Or was it?

Mercer continued, "If possible, I'd like to talk to you about writing your story. I find it fascinating."

"But I've already written it. And we've sold how many copies, Bruce?"

Twenty-seven to be exact, but he wasn't about to embarrass her. "Don't know for sure. I'll have to check."

Lovely smiled again and said, "Not very many. Stories about old slaves are a dime a dozen."

Mercer said, "Maybe, but the story is not over. Your island is about to be in the center of another storm."

"Yes, so they say. Naomi and I have read every word in the newspaper. I don't know why they can't just leave us alone. The island is mine. My ancestors are buried there. I would live there if I could, but I was forced to leave many years ago. You know the story. It's in my book."

"I do. But I'd like to tell the rest of the story."

"Is there a happy ending?" she asked with a smile.

"I don't know. Maybe Steven could answer that."

Lovely glared at Steven and the smile vanished. She had been warned that a lawyer might be present. He made eye contact, could not maintain it, glanced away, and said, "I'm not your typical lawyer, Lovely. I don't get paid. I work for a nonprofit foundation based here on the island, and we try to protect the environment. The developer who wants your island will hire a thousand lawyers if it has to, and it will be a tough case to win. My nonprofit is willing to go to court and fight to keep these bad guys away from Dark Isle."

"You need my permission?"

"Not really. We can join any effort to stop developers and protect natural areas, but it would be nice to have you sign a contract and hire us to protect your rights."

"So I would have to pay you?"

"There would be a small fee up front."

"How much?"

"I don't know, say five dollars."

Everyone needed a laugh and enjoyed one. Steven felt like he was on a roll and kept going, "The first step is to beat them to the courthouse and file a lawsuit to get a good title. It's called an action to quiet a title. Legal jargon. That will start a big fight in the court and it will drag on for some time. You will be named as the plaintiff, another legal term, which means you're the person bringing the lawsuit."

Steven had an easy manner and talked like a layman. Bruce had never seen him in action before but had heard that he was smooth in the courtroom. He'd also found old articles that described some of his Sierra Club brawls. In his day, he had owned the courtroom.

"And there's no way around this?" Lovely asked.

"I'm afraid not if you want to keep your island and protect it. This company, Tidal Breeze, has a long history of big developments, primarily in Florida. It plays hardball and usually wins. Unfortunately for you, and I suppose for all of us who want to preserve nature, the company has now discovered Dark Isle and is coming after it."

"Why?"

"Because they smell money, and lots of it. This is just what they do."

Lovely looked at Bruce, a man she trusted because he had

never wanted anything from her. It was the other way around. They met when she came to his store and needed his advice about selling her self-published book. He showed her respect, spent time with her, and cautioned that such books were hard to sell. He put hers in the front window, under the "Local Authors" section, and treated her like a real writer.

"What do you think about it, Bruce?" she asked.

"It depends on how hard you're willing to fight. Lawsuits are no fun, regardless of how strong you believe in your case."

"If you were in my shoes?"

"I'd pay Steven here the five dollars and tell him to start the war over the title. And I would spend time with Mercer and let her describe the book she wants to write."

She looked at Steven and said, "I'm an old woman without much time left. I don't want to spend my final days all knotted up in a court fight. How long will this take?"

Steven smiled and scratched his gray beard. "There are two issues here, both equally important. The first is who owns Dark Isle. That will be a local fight in the courthouse just down the street and it should take about a year. If you win, the company, Tidal Breeze, will appeal to the state Supreme Court. That's another year or so. If you lose, then we'll appeal. So in about two years we should know who has the title to the property, who's the true owner. If it's you, then everything is finished, no more court fights. However, if you lose and Tidal Breeze gets title to the island, then the bigger fight will be over its development. That will be in federal court and could easily take five to ten years. But you will not be a party to that litigation."

Her shoulders sagged and she suddenly seemed tired and older. She shook her head and said, "I just don't understand all this. How can someone else claim our island? It's mine because

I'm the last one of my people. Nobody ever wanted Dark Isle. Nobody built schools or roads or even put in electricity. Nobody cared about us. So, we took care of ourselves and we certainly took care of our island. It was the only home we knew. Now, all the rightful owners are gone but me. Everybody else has passed. I'm the true owner of my island and it's wrong for somebody else to say otherwise."

Her eyes were moist and her voice cracked. The room was perfectly still.

Steven, the trial lawyer, suppressed a smile as he envisioned her in a courtroom, explaining her views on ownership to a judge. Mercer, the writer, wanted to start scribbling to capture every word.

Finally, Thomas said, "May I ask a question?"

"Of course," Steven said.

"Do you expect Tidal Breeze to file a lawsuit to clear the title?"

"Yes, certainly. In fact, I'm surprised the company has not already done so. I know it has filed some preliminary notices with the Department of Natural Resources and, immediately, there was a question about ownership. The company has been snooping around the island for at least a year or so."

Bruce asked, "Is there an advantage in being the first to file a lawsuit?"

"Perhaps a slight advantage, but all interested parties will have plenty of time to jump in."

"And it has to be decided by a court in this county?"

"Yes, same as all title disputes. The company can't run to federal court or anywhere else."

"And you know the local judges?"

"Sure, but it won't matter. Tidal Breeze will hire a bunch of local lawyers to get in the way. We have good judges here and they'll do what's right."

Lovely folded her hands in her lap and looked at Miss Naomi, who said, "Well, we certainly have a lot to think about, don't we? I'm sure the girls have picked out ten books each."

"I sure hope so," Bruce quipped.

CHAPTER FOUR
THE CONTRACT

1.

Gifford's idea of a book tour was to sail his yacht from its home port near Charleston down to St. Augustine in Florida, then up to the Outer Banks of North Carolina for a stop in the coastal town of Manteo. He liked the bookstore there because it drew crowds when he was in town, and also because its owner was an old girlfriend he was still fond of. He finished a book every three years and usually got a new wife once he turned in a fresh manuscript. He'd had so many, books and wives. They, the exes, came and went because they inevitably got bored living on a boat in Charleston's harbor.

On each tour he visited the same thirteen bookstores and was never in a hurry. His signings went on for hours as his fans waited patiently for a word and an autograph. The exploits of his protagonist, Bake Boudreau, had been entertaining readers for over twenty years and Gifford couldn't write fast enough. Not for his fans, anyway. However, his pace suited him perfectly since he could hammer one out in six months, then travel and play golf the rest of the year. Truth was, he was quite lazy and needed plenty of down time between tours.

He was a son of the Low Country. He spoke the language and knew the culture and cared deeply about its preservation. A lot of his money was spent fighting those who wanted to disrupt his land. He held a passionate hatred of developers. He gave speeches, wrote op-ed pieces and nice checks, and in doing so managed to attract a lot of attention for himself. He even funded a documentary film about the fight to protect a swamp in Georgia. In it, he made his acting debut and loved being on camera. Like most documentaries, it was an hour too long and failed to find an audience.

When his boat, a sixty-foot beauty, slipped into the Santa Rosa harbor, Bruce was waiting. Gifford yelled an obscene greeting when he saw him, then bounded off the boat before his deckhand had time to moor it. They hugged on the pier like long-lost frat brothers and made their way to the dockside café, both talking at once. Lunch would last at least two hours.

The current wife was rarely invited on a book tour. Gifford didn't want the restraints, so he sent them to Europe or California. At that moment, Bruce couldn't think of the current one's name. They ordered wine and seafood and caught up with the publishing gossip. Gifford took pride in the fact that he had not been to New York in ten years. He loathed his publisher and was convinced he was being cheated out of royalties.

"Bought any more stolen manuscripts lately?" he asked. A bit too loud.

"Of course not. I've gone straight."

Among a handful of friends it was believed that Bruce had made a killing years earlier when he brokered a deal to return the stolen manuscripts of F. Scott Fitzgerald, a rumor that he strenuously denied. The FBI had snooped around and he assumed their file was still open. The Princeton library had the manuscripts back in its vault. Everyone was happy. Let it go.

Bruce said, "You've heard the latest about Dark Isle?"

Gifford chewed a mouthful, offered a blank look, and shook his head.

Bruce pointed across the water and said, "It's about two miles over there, you can barely see it."

"The old slave island."

"That's it. Deserted years ago. Now it's been discovered by some real estate swingers from South Florida. Ever hear of Tidal Breeze?"

"Maybe."

"Big private company with plenty of projects under its belt. Resorts, casinos, golf, the works. Now they've renamed it Panther Cay and printed up all the usual brochures. Got a fancy website. Lots for sale in due course."

"That's awful."

"That's Florida."

"Can we stop them?"

Gifford was never shy about jumping into the fray. He'd even been arrested several times while staring down bulldozers. Each arrest, of course, was well documented by the news crews who'd been tipped off. The fact that he had already adopted a "we" posture was no surprise.

"Oh, it'll be a fight. We might need you to lean on some of your tree-hugger groups for support. I gave you a book called *Tessa*. Ring a bell?"

"Afraid not." Unlike most writers, Gifford didn't read much. Nor did he pretend to. "Who wrote it?"

"A lady named Mercer Mann, sort of a local, got a cottage on the beach and spends her summers here."

"Who summers in Florida? Thought you were supposed to go to the mountains."

"Ask her tonight. She'll be at dinner, along with her new husband. She just got married last month here on the beach, so hands off."

"If you say so."

"Anyway, she's considering a book about Dark Isle, its history and so forth, and the fight to preserve it. She's given me a ten-page rough draft of a book proposal which I think is excellent. Care to take a look?"

"Not really. I'm not much of an editor."

"Come on. It's a favor. You know these stories better than anyone. It'll take fifteen minutes to read."

"And what if I don't like it?"

"You will."

"Okay, what if I do like it? What am I supposed to do?"

"Enjoy it, and file it away. I want you to open some doors with your environmental crowd. You know every group from here to Washington, even beyond, and we'll need plenty of help."

"Sounds like fun. I'm always ready for a fight."

"That's one of the few things I like about you."

"Fair enough. And no one expects me to call my publisher and gush about this proposal."

"No one. Mercer has her own publisher."

"Good. I'm thinking about suing mine."

"Don't do that. They're paying you plenty. What's the first printing this time out?"

Gifford could not suppress a proud smile. He drank some wine, savored the moment, and said, "Bruce, I'm now officially over half a million in hardback. Same for ebooks. I'm in the top ten, buddy. Can you believe it?"

Bruce smiled too and they clinked glasses. "Congratulations, Gifford. You deserve it. I devoured your latest book in one night. Great stuff."

"Thanks."

"Don't mention it."

"No, Bruce, I'm sincere. I owe you a lot. We were sitting right here almost twenty years ago when you, rather bluntly, told me I was wasting my time with literary fiction. Said I wasn't complicated enough, as I recall."

"You still aren't and that's why you have a million fans."

"And you convinced me that the route to success, at least for me, was to create a great character and use him over and over. It's working. Here's to Bake."

They clinked glasses again. "Love that guy," Bruce said.

2.

They drove to Bruce's home where Gifford spent two hours in a hammock snoring off his lunch. At 5:00 p.m. they went to the bookstore where a line had already formed out the front door and down the sidewalk along Main Street. The star kicked into high gear and spent hours autographing his novels, posing for photographs, greeting old friends, hitting on attractive women, chatting with local journalists, and all the while sipping his favorite Chardonnay that Bruce was required to furnish. At 8:00, he left with apologies but promised to return at noon the following day for round two, then he would do a reading at 5:00 p.m. and take questions.

The literary crowd reconvened on Bruce's patio. Gifford hugged and kissed Leigh and Myra, squeezed a bit too hard on young Amy Slater, swapped insults with Bob Cobb, practically fondled Noelle, who had just returned from France, and gushed over Mercer and Thomas. Over another glass of wine, he confided in her that her proposal was brilliant and had all the makings of an important work of nonfiction. He would be happy to help in any way, except speak to his publisher. They were not on speaking terms and any communication had to go through his lawyer.

Most participants in polite dinner conversation are aware of their floor time and limit what they say. They deem it important to make sure everyone at the table is engaged. Not Gifford. Half drunk and getting louder, he hogged the spotlight and drowned out all other voices. At other times he might have been an obnoxious bore, but his stories were so outlandish, and told with such colorful language, that the other guests were often laughing so hard they couldn't eat. They loved the one about his last arrest, the prior year, when he and some other activists chained themselves to a gate in a national park to disrupt a logging operation. Before the police arrived, an angry logger with a large pistol stood very close to them and fired shots in the air. Gifford's ears rang for a week. The activists next to him started crying. The local sheriff refused them bail and they were locked up for a week. It was their finest hour.

When his bladder was finally full, he excused himself and staggered away. Myra was quick to say, "Thank God he only publishes every three years. I couldn't take many more of these dinners."

"Now Myra," Leigh chided.

They were all shaking their heads and enjoying a brief respite. Mercer said, "This guy's insane. I assume these stories are true."

Bruce shook his head. "I have no idea. He spends a lot of time and money with environmental groups. Check out his website. He rants and raves and features a montage of photos of his arrests. I told him about the new plans for Dark Isle and he went ballistic. He'll be an ally when we need him."

Mercer frowned as if she wasn't so sure.

Amy Slater asked, "Are they serious about putting a casino on that island?"

Steven Mahon answered, "Dead serious."

Myra said softly, "Here he comes."

They took a collective deep breath as Gifford found his seat. He was quiet for a few minutes as they passed around a platter of grilled grouper. Myra asked loudly, "So who's coming next week, Bruce?"

Bay Books maintained an endless schedule of signings, and Bruce expected his gang to show up for most of the events. Myra and Leigh especially enjoyed meeting the touring writers and seldom missed a signing.

Bruce said, "A young man from Kentucky with a debut novel. Rick Barber is his name. We need a crowd, next Tuesday."

"What kind of book?" Bob Cobb asked.

"A collection of stories about tough times in rural Kentucky."

"It's not grit-lit, is it, Bruce?" Myra asked.

"Well, it's not called that officially, but it has the elements."

"I can't take any more of that shit, Bruce. They're all the same. My beer's hot. My girl's cold. My dog's dead. My truck won't start. I need a job but I'd rather drink. Mama's on pills. Daddy's in prison. Come on, Bruce. Give us a break. Grit-lit is out of control."

"I'm not the author, Myra. I'm just the bookseller. If you don't like it then don't read it."

Thomas said, "I saw a review in the *Post*. Very positive, said Barber has a distinctive new Southern voice."

"Great, just what we need," Myra said. "A dazzling new grit-lit star. I'll bet he won't sell five thousand copies, hardback and paper. Mind if I skip it, Bruce?"

"I'm not sure I want you there."

Gifford said, "I met Barber last month at a book festival in Savannah. Nice guy."

"Is he cute?" Myra asked.

"Now Myra."

"You don't do guys," Bob Cobb said.

"I can look, you know? I might need a new character. A handsome new author who writes about roadkill and such. You like it, Bruce?"

"No."

"I don't either."

Gifford had been quiet long enough. He asked, "Has anyone been to Dark Isle?"

For the first time in hours the room was instantly quiet. Total silence, then some squirming. Bruce looked around the table and said, "I suppose I've lived here longer than anyone else, and I've never heard of anyone going to the island."

"Why not?"

"Well, for one, it's uninhabitable. There's nothing there but thick woods and wildlife. Hurricane Leo did a lot of damage, I'm told."

Bob Cobb said, "Plus there's plenty of sand around here. If you want a beach, they're not hard to find."

Gifford said, "I want to go see it. I may sail out day after tomorrow and have a look. Anybody up for a boat ride?"

More silence. Bruce finally said, "A sailboat won't get there. It's too shallow."

"Okay. I'll find another rig. Nobody wants to go?"

"That's not a good idea, Gifford," Mercer said. "There are a lot of bad stories about people who ventured onto the island. Few, if any, returned. You should read Lovely Jackson's book about Dark Isle. It's frightening."

"And this is the book you want to write too?"

"I'm seriously considering it, from a different angle, of course."

"Okay. Here's my offer. When you are ready to explore the island, let me know. I'm not afraid of ghosts and spirits and legends and stuff like that. We'll put together a little patrol, boat out to the island, and have a look around. Deal?"

"I don't know. We'll see. Until then, read Lovely's book. It's fascinating."

3.

The first obstacle was cajoling a "yes" out of Lovely. For two weeks she was not responsive to the invitation to sit down and talk. And since all communications had to go through Miss Naomi, progress was slow.

The second obstacle was where to meet. Mercer was quick to offer the hospitality of her beach cottage. She would be delighted to welcome Lovely for a long conversation and maybe even lunch, with complete privacy. Two days later the answer came back—no thanks. She suggested the bookstore, since Lovely seemed to be comfortable there. Two days later there was another no. Mercer really wanted to see Lovely's home in The Docks. She dropped a few hints and waited for the invitation, but it never came. What about the county library, where there was plenty of room and privacy? Two days later Miss Naomi called to report that Lovely wouldn't go there. She had been turned away from the library when she was a teenager, back when it was for whites only.

After three strikes, Mercer was out of suggestions and wondering if they would ever meet again. She was also mildly discouraged that their collaboration, or whatever it was to be called, was off to such a labored start. Given what had already been written, and what was brewing over Dark Isle now, she could certainly write the story in 100,000 words and publish a compelling work of nonfiction. But she would not do that. It would put her in the position of being accused of exploiting Lovely's past. If Lovely chose not to cooperate, Mercer would move on.

Miss Naomi finally called with the news that Lovely would agree to have a brief chat at a church in The Docks—the World Harvest Tabernacle Temple. With such a spectacular name, Mercer envisioned a sprawling megachurch with thousands of members. A glance at the website, though, revealed a modest redbrick building with a leaning steeple and two converted school buses in the parking lot. It was the domain of Reverend Samuel and his wife, Reverend Betty. In the photo they wore matching burgundy robes with gold trim and offered matching kilowatt smiles.

Robeless, they greeted Mercer and Thomas at the door to the Fellowship Center, an aging metal building stuck to the rear of the church. "Welcome to Harvest," Reverend Samuel beamed. Everyone shook hands warmly and went inside to a long dining room next to a kitchen. Reverend Betty frowned when Mercer and Thomas declined beverages. She said, "In this weather, you must have some sweet tea."

They acquiesced and she served them tea in quart fruit jars. One sip, and Mercer knew that she held in her hand more calories than a chocolate milkshake. As they waited for Lovely, they talked about the church—"Harvest"—and its ministries in the community. Trolling for details, Mercer asked how long Lovely had been a member. The two Reverends glanced at each other before he said, "Well, she's not officially a member, you see. But she comes occasionally."

It was obvious she rarely came at all and that this was possibly a sore subject. Then she arrived with her entourage—Miss Naomi and the granddaughters. Lovely wore a long flowing

dress that was bright orange and topped it off with a matching orange turban wrapped fiercely on top of her head. Mercer,
in jeans, sandals, and a loose cotton blouse, wondered if Lovely
ever left the house dressed as anything but an African queen.
She looked spectacular, with bangles on both wrists and over-
sized necklaces around her neck.

They settled into folding chairs at the end of a long table
and everyone sipped sweet tea. It quickly became apparent that
both Reverends, along with Miss Naomi and her granddaughters, planned to participate in, or at least listen to, whatever
conversation was to follow. The room was muggy and not well
air-conditioned. Miss Naomi commented on the current heat
wave and the weather was batted around. Everyone agreed that
it was indeed hot. Lovely said nothing. She smiled and listened
and seemed to ignore the meaningless prattling around her.

Conversation lagged and things grew even more awkward.
Mercer was not going to start asking serious questions with an
audience, but as a guest herself, she was not in position to ask
anyone to leave.

Thomas finally took the hint and asked Reverend Samuel if
he would show him the sanctuary, said he was fascinated by the
architecture of small Southern churches. It was a lame effort—
one glance at the building and you knew its builders had not
bothered to fool with an architect—but it worked. Though it was
an unusual request, both Reverends stood and left the room
with Thomas.

Lovely asked Mercer, "How long do you want to talk today?"

Mercer looked at Miss Naomi and said, "Oh, we should wrap
things up in about an hour." It was almost a direct command to
leave and return in an hour, but Miss Naomi didn't take it that
way. She and the girls hung around as Mercer fiddled with her
recorder, then her pen and notebook.

"What's that?" Lovely asked, nodding at the table.

"It's a small recorder. I hope to use it if you don't mind."

"I've never been recorded."

Mercer almost said it was a first for her too. She was a novelist, not a journalist. "It's a good way to remember everything that's said. But if you don't want to use it, then no problem."

"I still don't know why you want to write this book."

"I'm fascinated by your story, Lovely. The history of your people and their survival on the island. And now a new threat that will destroy it."

The girls were suddenly bored and giggled at something. Lovely glared at them and they froze. She said to Miss Naomi, "We'll be right here for an hour. If you make it to town, please see Henry at the nursing home."

Miss Naomi gathered her purse and nodded at the girls.

When they were finally alone, Lovely said, "I already wrote that story."

"Yes you have, and I enjoyed it, as I said. But there's more to it now. I want to take the past, with all its complexities, and tie it to the present, with all its conflicts."

"Sounds like a lot of work just to sell a few books."

"Oh, it will sell, Lovely. I'm almost finished with a book proposal that I'll send to my agent in New York. If she likes it, and I know she will, then she'll try to sell the idea to a big publisher. Maybe we'll get a book deal."

"You mean a real book, like those in Bruce's store?"

"Sure."

"Like *Tessa*?"

"Exactly. That's what I have in mind."

Lovely smiled and asked, "How much money are we gonna make?"

Mercer was anticipating this. "It's too early to talk about

money. Let's wait and see if we find a publisher, then we'll nego-
tiate the deal."

"So I get some of the money?"

"That's only fair, Lovely, but I have no idea how much at this
point."

Lovely stopped smiling and gazed at a window in the distance. The glow was back in her eyes and her thoughts had left
the room. Mercer almost said something, but decided to wait.
If these long pauses were normal, she needed to learn to adjust.

Finally, Lovely said, "Seems to me the best course is to wait
and see if you get a deal up in New York. No sense doing a lot of
talking now if it ain't going nowhere. You agree?"

Mercer preferred to work now. In three weeks she would leave
the island and return to Ole Miss for the fall semester. Since
Lovely avoided the telephone, the interviews would be difficult.
Now, though, they could talk and record for hours. Her impulse
was to push a bit and start asking questions; she had pages of
them.

Lovely, though, projected the aura of someone who reacted
badly when pushed. All of her words and motions were delib-
erate. And she was right. Why waste time if there was no book
deal?

"I suppose," Mercer said, shrugging. "I'll send the proposal
to New York this afternoon. I have a copy for you."

"That'd be nice."

"Since we have a few minutes, could I ask a question?"

"Of course you can, dear."

"How much of the story did you leave out of your book?"

Lovely flashed a wide smile. "Why do you ask that?"

"Because I got the feeling that some things were left out."

"Such as?"

"Was Nalla pregnant when she landed on Dark Isle?"

Lovely thought about it for a long time, then said, "Yes she was. It was not at all unusual for young women to be raped on the slave ships. Six weeks at sea, and a lot of them were pregnant when they got to this country."

"Who was the father?"

"The child was half white."

"Monk?"

Her eyes narrowed and flashed hot. She said, "She sliced his throat, didn't she?" The word "sliced" was uttered with a touch of satisfaction.

4.

One of Mercer's more pliable rules for writing fiction was to keep quiet about your work. She had long since tired of windy writers going on and on about their current projects, most of which were never finished. Writers, especially when drinking, which was most of the time it seemed, liked to try out their new material over dinner or cocktails, as if they needed the approval of their captive audience. She knew of many novels that had been described for years, yet not a word had been seen on paper. "Don't talk about it, just do it," she told her students. "Once the story is finished, then you have something to talk about." Her students found it ironic that she made them discuss their ideas in class before writing their stories.

Like her other rules, she often violated this one. Now she found herself in the middle of a major violation. After showing her proposal to Thomas, Bruce, Steven Mahon, and Lovely, she felt as though she had been blabbing about it all summer. So she spent two days trimming it—Bruce in particular thought it too long for a simple proposal—and sent it, all five pages, to Etta Shuttleworth, her agent in New York.

It was the first of August, a month in which no one in New York publishing would be caught dead actually working. Etta was "summering" in Sag Harbor and reading, of course, nonstop. August reading was not considered working, and everyone—editors, agents, publishers—worked hard to give the impression that they read many hours each day. One was supposed to believe that they had little time for swimming, sailing, fishing, beachcombing, partying, or porch-sitting due to the stacks of books they were devouring.

At any rate, Etta managed to open her laptop a few minutes each day to take a peek at who might be looking for her. Mercer called and said the proposal was on the way and it was imperative that Etta read it immediately. It was only five pages.

Remarkably, within the hour the agent was on the phone gushing. Once she'd waded through the avalanche of superlatives, she said, "We should send it to Lana right now."

"Hang on," Mercer said. Lana Gallagher was her patient editor at Viking who had been waiting far too long for the next idea. "Are you sure it's for her? It is nonfiction."

"I know, but we have to start with Lana. She may decide to hand it off to a colleague, but your contract requires a first look for her."

Mercer said, "It's August. Have you ever sold a book in August?"

"No, don't think so, but there's always a first."

"Where is Lana?"

"She has a place in Maine. I'm sure she has plenty of time to read, especially something this quick. I'll send it to her and pester her to take a look."

"What's it worth?"

"That's a tough one. Let's wait until we hear from Lana. If she likes it then we'll talk about money."

"And if she doesn't?"

"She will, Mercer. Trust me. This is a great proposal for a great book, fiction or otherwise."

"Thank you, Etta, but it's not my idea. The story was lived by other people. I'm just an observer."

"It's brilliant, Mercer."

"You really think so?"

"Yes I do. When are you leaving the island?"

"In two weeks. Classes start at the end of the month. I'd like to spend some time with Lovely but she is hesitant. She's not convinced there's going to be a real book."

"Okay, look Mercer. I'm your agent and you need to trust me here. I'll call Lana right now, tell her I'm sending your proposal for a brilliant work of nonfiction, and insist that she read it immediately."

"Okay."

Evidently, Lana was having a slow day in Maine. An hour later, Etta called, gushing again. "Mercer! She loves it! She wants to buy it now and publish as soon as possible."

"Well, that may be a bit down the road since I haven't started writing it yet. "

"There is one problem, though, and it's rather obvious."

"The lawsuit?"

"The lawsuit. In your proposal you write that the lawsuit could take years to resolve, especially if it turns into a huge environmental fight. Viking doesn't want to sit on the sidelines for a few years waiting for the litigation to end."

"I know. Believe me, I've thought about that. Thomas and I have discussed it for hours and we have an idea. I write the book now, starting with Nalla and the slave story, and cover two hundred years of history. Basically the same material Lovely has in her book but with a lot of extras. She's already told me that there are stories and twists and turns that she left out. Good stuff. I'll end the book with the court's ruling on the title to the land. If Lovely wins, then the story is over and everybody's happy."

"Except Tidal Breeze."

"Except Tidal Breeze, of course, but who cares. If Lovely loses the title fight and the island ends up in the hands of Tidal Breeze, then the other lawsuits will rage. I'll be there and write about that too. Maybe a sequel."

"I love it. You haven't written the first word and you're already thinking about the sequel."

"You're an agent. You're supposed to love sequels."

"I do. Sounds like a plan. I'll explain this to Lana."

"Do that. And when do we get around to the issue of compensation?"

There was a long pause on the other end as this delicate issue rattled around. Publishing contracts were all about advances—how much could the writer get up front? How much should the publisher offer and still protect itself from a flop? *Tessa* sold 90,000 in hardback and ebook combined and spent four weeks on the *New York Times* bestseller lists. In paperback its sales had slowed considerably but were inching close to 200,000. Since its publication three years earlier, Mercer had netted roughly $375,000. Nice money and all, and most of it was still in the bank, but she wasn't ready to retire yet. What Mercer desperately needed was another big book. Two of them, back to back, and she could ditch the teaching gig and join the slim ranks of the lucky writers who didn't have real jobs.

That was her dream, anyway.

Etta said, "If it were a novel, I would ask for seven-fifty. The nonfiction angle will cause Lana to offer less, I suppose. It usually works that way. You have no track record with nonfiction.

Plus, there is the complication of the litigation. That could really slow down the project."

Mercer said, "Four hundred thousand is a fair number, Etta. Spread over several years, it's not much. I'll need all of it to survive and do my research. Plus, there is another complication. Lovely deserves some of the money."

"Oh dear."

"Yes. We've had a preliminary chat about the money and I'm certain she'll want some of it."

"Okay. I'll run this by Lana and see how generous she feels."

After the call, Mercer and Thomas went for a sunset walk on the beach. As she kicked water in the surf, she couldn't help but laugh.

"Okay, what's so funny?" he asked.

"Life. Five years ago a budget got cut and I was the lowest form of life on the English faculty. My job disappeared. I came here to get away and to spy on Bruce. Then *Tessa* hit and everything changed. Now I'm telling my agent that I think four hundred thousand dollars is a fair price for my next book. Who do I think I am?"

Thomas saw the humor and said, "You're Mercer Mann, bestselling writer, rising literary star, author of a great novel that a lot of people enjoyed. This is where you are in life, dear, and those are the numbers that go along with it. Savor the moment because it may not last."

She stopped laughing and bent to pick up a shell. She studied it, then tossed it back into the water. "So true. Think of all the writers we know who found success before the age of forty and can't find a publisher at fifty. The mid-list group. They sold enough to barely get by and showed a lot of promise, now they're practically forgotten. It's such a brutal business."

"We know writers who've quit."

"Yes, and the ones who can't even find a job on a campus. They give up and find another calling."

"That's not going to happen to you, Mercer. Believe me."

"Thank you, sweetheart. No, I'm going to write this book and make enough money to survive on, but I'm still searching for the great American novel, Thomas."

"I know, and you'll find it. It's out there somewhere, just waiting for you."

"You really believe that?"

"I do. And so do a lot of people."

She grabbed him and held him close, and for a long time they stood in the surf as the warm water rose and fell while the sun dipped behind the clouds.

5.

The lawsuit was filed in the Camino County courthouse, five blocks east of Bay Books on Main Street. It was a beautiful old courthouse dating back to the 1870s and had been carefully renovated through the years. The formal courtroom was on the second floor and the judges kept their offices nearby. The clerks tended to their business on the ground floor, and it was there that Steven Mahon walked in with his lawsuit and filed it in chancery court. He could have done so online, but he still enjoyed the ritual of "filing" by presenting it to a clerk, who stamped several copies and gave one back to him.

Thus the battle began, but without the drama that often surrounded big cases. The lawsuit itself was rather bland reading and did not seek a fortune in damages. It did not contain the usual allegations of bad or reckless behavior. It did not demand

punitive damages. It did not insist that the judge step in immediately with an injunction to stop something. Though it was
destined to mushroom into a larger brawl, it began as a simple
petition to "quiet a title."

As far as lawsuits go, it was rather brief, only four pages. In
broad strokes, Steven laid out the history of Dark Isle, beginning
with the Franco-Spanish struggle dating back to 1565 and leading up to 1740 when the Spanish claimed sovereignty over the
region after ruling it for two hundred years. Dark Isle was considered part of Camino Island, and it first appeared on a map in
1764 when the British seized the territory. Then they lost it to
the French, who in turn lost it again to the Spanish. The three
countries sparred for a few decades, each winning land and then
losing it, often making individual land ownership impossible to
determine. Native tribes still occupied most of the land, but that
would soon change. In 1821, America cut a deal with the Spanish and got all of Florida. By then, Dark Isle had been a refuge
for runaway slaves for almost a hundred years and no one else
really wanted it. Florida was admitted to the Union as a slave
state in 1845.

The plaintiff, Lovely Jackson, claimed to be a direct descendant of slaves who'd lived on Dark Isle since the early 1700s.
She was born there in 1940, to Jeremiah and Ruth Jackson. Her
father died in 1948 of typhoid, leaving Ruth and Lovely as the
only two survivors on the island. They barely managed to survive for a few years, then left for Santa Rosa in 1955, the last
residents of Dark Isle.

Like those before her, there was no official record of her
birth. She had been delivered by a midwife, same as everyone
else. There were no records of the births and deaths of her parents, or grandparents.

Her claim of ownership was based on the legal principle of adverse possession. She and her ancestors had lived on the island "openly" and "notoriously" and without interference or interruption for over two hundred years. Florida law required only seven. Though she was forced to leave in 1955, she did not abandon her ancestral home. For decades, she and a friend or two traveled by boat to the island several times each year to tend to the graves of her people. They walked the island from north to south looking for trespassers and squatters. They found none. Then Hurricane Leo did enormous damage to Dark Isle. It destroyed what was left of the settlement where she and her ancestors lived. It washed away centuries' worth of artifacts and ruins.

Attorney Mahon requested a hearing within thirty days, as required by the statute, though he knew it would take months. As a courtesy, he sent a copy of the petition to the in-house counsel for Tidal Breeze in Miami. He also sent a copy to a contact in the Attorney General's office in Tallahassee. The state of Florida would be party to the lawsuit.

One of many rumors swirling around the Panther Cay project was that the state would claim ownership, as it had for hundreds of other uninhabited islands, and then, once cleared, quickly sell it to Tidal Breeze for a fair price and get out of the way. The skids had been greased in Tallahassee. The politicians and bureaucrats were in line.

Steven walked up the stairs to say hello to Judge Lydia Salazar, the presiding chancellor. He'd met her once at a bar lunch but rarely appeared before her. Steven's cases kept him in federal court and he seldom ventured into local courthouses. However, under Florida law, land and title disputes were the sole jurisdiction of chancery court, to be decided without juries. Thus, Judge Salazar would have enormous power over the future of Dark Isle.

She enjoyed a solid reputation as a firm and fair jurist, though one lawyer had told Steven over coffee that she was known to talk too much about her cases. Out of school. Over drinks at cocktail parties. Loose lips sink ships and all that.

Steven just wanted to say hello, but her secretary said she had the day off.

His downtown stroll continued to the offices of *The Register*, the island's newspaper. He paid for a legal notice that would advertise the filing of the petition and the hearing in thirty days. The owner/editor, Sid Larramore, was an acquaintance and they enjoyed an occasional coffee. Steven handed him a copy of the petition and waited as he read through it. They had already discussed its contents.

Sid was also a transplant from the D.C. area. He had retired to Santa Rosa for health reasons but, like Steven, had found retirement to be unhealthy. So he started writing for *The Register* and bought it when the owner died and no one else wanted it. In his opinion, one that he rarely shared with his readers, the island's rebound after Leo was creating enough work for everyone. The comeback was strong. Traffic was heavy enough. The last thing they needed was a huge resort and casino. Sid was also fascinated with the legend of Dark Isle. He'd read Lovely's book years earlier, had even tried to do a feature but got nowhere. He'd heard the rumor, probably from Bruce Cable, who often started them just to see how fast they would travel, that Mercer Mann was interested in writing about Dark Isle and the upcoming battle over its future. He had interviewed Mercer twice and was a fan.

"She'll slay this story," Sid said.

"I think so too. Bruce told me her publisher likes it."

"She and Thomas have been digging through our archives for a month. They know more of the history of this place than

anyone. They told me last week that they cannot find any refer-
ence to a white person who has ventured onto the island and
lived to talk about it. Several have tried. Mercer thinks there's an
old voodoo curse still hovering over the island."

"I'm not going over there."

"I suppose you'd like this on the front page as soon as
possible."

"I'm a lawyer. Of course I want the front page."

"I'll see what I can do."

"You're the owner, editor, publisher, and only full-time
reporter. You can do anything you want."

They shared a laugh and Sid promised to find room on the
front page.

6.

Another late afternoon thunderstorm had blown through,
drenching the island and breaking the humidity. It was now
pleasant enough to eat outdoors on the veranda, Bruce's preferred spot in the rear of his cherished Victorian home. When
the table was cleared they moved to the side and settled into
cushioned wicker rockers. Frogs and crickets began a loud cho-
rus. The old rattan ceiling fans rattled above and kept the air
moving. Bruce fired up a cigar and offered one to Thomas, who
waved him off. They were finishing a bottle of Chablis.

The topic of the evening was the quandary over Mercer's book
proposal. Etta, always the agent, had suggested the amount of
$500,000 for an advance against royalties. It was an aggressive
opening and she justified it by the performance of Mercer's last
book, *Tessa*. The success of that novel, plus the compelling story
at hand, was more than enough to support such an advance.
Mercer was thirty-six, an accomplished writer with three books

to her credit and many more to come. As usual, Etta had implied that if Viking couldn't handle such up-front money, then Mercer might be forced to shop around.

The vague threat went nowhere. Lana Gallagher was a tough editor who gently deflected such warnings as just another part of the agent's routine. She countered with $200,000, and showed barely enough enthusiasm to placate the author. Viking had two major concerns: nonfiction was something new for Mercer and, in the broadest of terms, paid less than popular fiction; and the near certainty of protracted litigation could delay the project for years.

To make the offer even less attractive, Viking proposed to string out the payments over the next several years: one-fourth at signing, one-fourth upon delivery of the manuscript, one-fourth upon hardback publication, and the last check when the paperback came out. If the book sold as well as hoped, and the advance "earned out," the prospect of royalties might kick in even further down the road.

Mercer was disappointed with the offer but did manage to find humor in the fact that she was disappointed with a contract worth $200,000. She still had the fresh memories of being the impoverished grad student, then the adjunct professor with a one-year contract. Her future was far from certain. She did not have tenure at Ole Miss. Her salary was a wonderful cushion but budget cuts were always hovering. She dreamed of writing books for the rest of her life but lived with the fear of not having the next story. Only a few years ago she would have fainted if Etta had called with a $200,000 offer.

Bruce commiserated with her and, as always, sided with his writer. But he knew the offer was reasonable. He also remembered that four years earlier, Mercer had been delighted with the $50,000 advance she had received for *Tessa*. He also knew from years of observation that new writers needed two or three best-sellers in a row to establish themselves and expect bigger contracts. Mercer wasn't quite there yet.

She said, "Etta wants to shop it around. What do you think about that?"

Since most of the writers on the island confided in Bruce, he knew the ins and outs of the business. They trusted his advice and spoke openly to him about money. He was discreet and fiercely protective of their business.

He replied, "That always sounds good, but the problem is that it could damage your relationship with Viking, and the bigger danger is further rejections. What if you shop around and get less, or nothing, from other publishers? Lana will be ticked off, and she'll also be proven correct. Don't run from happiness, Mercer. If you're happy at Viking, stay there. I've seen so many writers hurt themselves by hopping from one publisher to the next chasing a few extra bucks. You don't want that reputation. Lana is a great editor and Viking is, well, it's Viking. One of the legendary houses."

"What would you do?" Thomas asked.

"Counter at three hundred and push hard. Tighten up the schedule and get more money sooner. One-third at contract, same at delivery, same at hardback publication."

They pondered this for a moment as Bruce poured more wine. Noelle excused herself and retired for the evening.

Mercer asked, "And what about Lovely?"

Along with the disappointment of Viking's offer was the complicating and quite sticky issue of Lovely's expectations.

"How much does she want?" Bruce asked.

"We didn't get that far, but it was obvious she expects to be compensated. And I'm fine with that, to a point."

"Ten percent?" Bruce said.

"That seems low. I don't want to insult her and I don't want to give the impression that us white folks are once again taking advantage. On the other hand, I could reach a threshold where I ask myself if the whole project is worth it. If she wants too much and I walk away, then she gets nothing."

Thomas said, "We've talked about this endlessly. Mercer is basically taking her story and relying on her memory and history. Let's say that's half the book, and much of the work has already been done. The other half is the fight to save the island. There, Mercer will do all the heavy lifting."

"You'll help," she said.

"Of course I will."

Bruce blew a cloud of smoke at the creaky fans and said, "Look, why not just talk to Lovely and see what she wants? She's never had a dime. She spent her life working here on the island, first in the canneries, then in the hotels, cleaning rooms and doing laundry. Now she lives on Social Security. She has no family to support, and as far as we know there's no one looking for a handout. It's hard to believe she's expecting a big windfall. Keep in mind she knows something about publishing and selling books, although hers has yet to top a hundred copies."

Mercer said, "I know. I just want to be fair."

"Then talk to her. Meet her at the store tomorrow. Use my office. I'll make sure you have some privacy."

"Thanks, Bruce."

"And when are you guys leaving? Myra wants to have a proper send-off, a small dinner, one final booze-up before you have to go back to work."

"Saturday. She called today and said she and Leigh are having a party. Didn't ask if we wanted to be included, just assumed so."

"I'm sure you agreed."

"Of course. Who says no to Myra?"

"No one in this town."

7.

Since the first two meetings with Lovely took over a week to arrange, Mercer was surprised when Miss Naomi called back and said they would be at the bookstore at ten o'clock the following morning. Mercer suspected the granddaughters wanted some more books. A clerk welcomed them to the kids' section and showed them some new arrivals. Thomas managed to occupy Miss Naomi in the cookbook section with a discussion about Low Country recipes. Bruce turned off his desk phone and locked the doors.

When they were alone, Mercer explained what was happening with the book proposal in New York. Etta had wrangled $250,000 out of Viking as an advance. Miss Lovely absorbed this figure without a reaction.

Mercer was saying, "This sounds like a lot of money, but it's really not. Fifteen percent goes off the top to the literary agent, then about thirty percent goes for taxes. The money will be spread over four years, maybe five, depending on how long it takes me to write it."

"How long will it take?" Lovely asked.

"It's hard to say. A lot depends on what happens to the island now, and that's tied up in court. With court cases, it's difficult to predict anything."

"But you have an idea."

"Yes, in two years I should be finished with a draft that is publishable. How long did it take you to write your book?"

"Oh Lord, Mercer, I worked on that book forever. I have

some old notebooks that go way back to when I was a kid in high school. I did finish school, you know? Wasn't easy but I was determined to finish. We went to the colored school back then. It's gone now. Been gone."

Mercer smiled as she listened to her soft, slow voice, one that seemed to reach back for centuries. They were sitting knee to knee, almost touching, almost to the point where they could talk about anything.

Mercer said, "It's only fair that you get some of the money. It's the story of you and your people. I'll need to spend a lot of time with you to get all of the details and background. It's not going to be easy, writing is never easy."

"Hardest thing I ever did."

Mercer chuckled and wanted to say her book was far more interesting than most of what she read. She knew Lovely was not experienced in deal-making, so she cut to the chase. "I think fifty percent of the advance is too much, and ten percent is too little. What do you have in mind?"

"I had nothing in mind, until now. If I say twenty-five percent, how much will I get?"

"About fifty thousand dollars, before taxes, spread over the next three or four years."

She closed her eyes and thought for a long time. Mercer took the opportunity to examine her turban of the day, a lime green and bright yellow headdress wrapped as tight as always. Her robe was a lively blue and red floral pattern. Yielding to the modern world, on her feet she wore a pair of brown sandals with a small Nike swoosh along the side.

She opened her eyes and said, "That sounds good to me. If I get some money I want to clean up the island and fix up the cemetery."

"It's still there?"

"Oh yes, honey. I know where it is but nobody else can find it. My parents, grandparents, lot of great-grandparents are buried there. I know where they are. Can't nobody else find 'em, but I can."

Mercer took a deep breath and said, "We have so much to talk about."

CHAPTER FIVE
THE DEFENDERS

1.

The ten-hour drive home was scheduled to begin around 8:00 a.m., or at least that's what they had tentatively agreed upon the day before. But the farewell party at Myra and Leigh's had gone on later than anticipated, which was exactly what they should have expected, and Saturday was off to a slow start. By 9:00 they were barely awake and guzzling black coffee. By 10:00, the Jeep Cherokee was half loaded with luggage and boxes and other stuff they had accumulated during their two months on the island and felt compelled, for some reason, to take with them. Mercer filled a picnic basket with sandwiches, fruit, cookies, and bottled water, as if they would not be able to find food between Camino Island and Oxford, Mississippi. At 11:00, Thomas finally locked the cottage, wedged the dog into the backseat, and started the engine.

"Only three hours late," he mumbled. She ignored him. Things were somewhat tense but within minutes both were breathing normally and beginning the transition from beach to campus. The truth was that they were both writers and accustomed to a life that was somewhat unstructured. Punctuality was not that important. Who cared if they arrived in Oxford at 6:00 p.m. or 9:00 p.m. on a Saturday in mid-August, with the temperature there at least ninety-five and the humidity even higher?

It was a summer they would always remember and treasure: the wedding on the beach; the honeymoon to Scotland, a trip they still talked about and relived through photographs and vowed to do again; the excitement of finding the story for the next book, and an impressive advance with which to write it. After two months of marriage—two months that followed two years of living together—Mercer knew she was in love with the right guy. They were compatible and shared the same interests. They laughed a lot, at each other and especially at everyone else. They shared the irresistible dream of writing full-time and traveling the world in search of great stories. The issue of children was still being ignored.

"You want to drive?" he asked.

"What? We're not even off the island yet."

"I know but I'm yawning."

"Drink some more coffee."

He was kidding, of course, and breaking the ice to let her know he was no longer irritated because they were three hours late. He smiled at her, rubbed her bare and beautifully tanned thigh, and kept driving.

High on the bridge over the Camino River, Mercer looked to the north and saw the distant tree line of Dark Isle. She was curious about how it must have looked on the horizon three hundred years earlier.

2.

Being from an inland village, Nalla was not familiar with seafood and had never tasted an oyster or a shrimp. In her new home, though, the food came out of the sea, and there was an abundance of it. She and the other new arrivals were fed as often as they wanted to eat. Their stomachs had not been so full in months.

Communication was initially a challenge, though they were motivated to learn a new language. An older woman was also from the Kongo and spoke Bantu, and she became the English teacher. All the runaway slaves were from plantations in Georgia and spoke English along with a variety of African tongues.

They lived in small mud huts with thatched palm roofs. There were twenty of the homes in a perfect square around a central common. The entire settlement was heavily shaded by massive oaks and elms. The women cooked at night so the smoke from their fires would not be seen. They lived in fear and with the constant threat of being captured. Slavery had been forced upon them once. It would not happen again, not without a fight. Joseph, the unquestioned leader, explained to the new arrivals that the white men would likely return in search of survivors from the *Venus*. Therefore they must remain vigilant at all hours. The older boys and younger men watched the beaches day and night in a coordinated system of surveillance. If a boat approached, the men and some of the women would take up arms, a collection of homemade knives and spears, but their arsenal also included three rifles they had robbed from an earlier band of intruders.

The warning finally came early one morning, about two weeks after Nalla landed on the beach. A small ship was spotted and it was approaching. It anchored a half mile off the island, and by then Joseph and his men were watching it from deep in the trees. A rowboat about thirty feet long was lowered, and four white men got on board. Four black men, slaves in all likelihood, also boarded and took up the oars. Slowly, the boat left the ship and picked up speed with the incoming tide. Joseph moved his men into position. The rowboat grounded in three feet of water. The slaves jumped out and tugged it onto the beach. The white men, each with a rifle, pointed here and there and gave orders to the slaves, who picked up packs of supplies. It was clear they planned to stay a few days as they looked for survivors from the *Venus*. One of the four black men stayed behind with the rowboat.

Because they knew nothing of the island, the white men landed to the far north, away from the settlement. Joseph tracked them throughout the first day and waited for darkness. The men walked across the island, found nothing, and turned south. Trekking through the dense forest was difficult and they stopped to rest often. As the sun began to set, the white men ordered the slaves to set up camp. Then they wanted dinner.

The slave left behind on the beach to guard the rowboat was napping in it when he was jolted to life by two strangers with dark skin. They explained that he was no longer a slave, but now a free man. They shoved the boat into deeper water, then rowed into a bay where other vessels were moored and hidden. Over the years, the men of Dark Isle had collected other boats from curious slave hunters and fishermen.

Long after the white men had finished their rum and fallen asleep, Joseph and his warriors eased into the camp. They seized the three slaves, who were horrified and thought they were seeing ghosts. They settled down soon enough when they were granted immediate freedom. They were given knives and offered the chance to kill their masters. They sneaked into the tents and slit four white throats. Their bodies would be dumped in the ocean.

At sunrise, the ship's captain scanned the beach with his spyglass and did not see the rowboat. It had vanished and he suspected trouble. There was no conceivable reason for the crew to move it during the night. Something had gone wrong, but what was he to do about it? He had only two men and one slave left on his little ship. They wasted the day waiting and watching the beach.

Joseph and his men were watching them. The ship did not move throughout the day or during the night. The following morning, a smaller boat with two white men left the ship and rowed to the beach. The men appeared nervous and kept their rifles close at hand. They carried backpacks too small for tents. After trudging through the forest for a few hours and finding no one, they decided to leave before dark. But they were ambushed by Joseph and his men, taken prisoner, and tied to trees. After a severe lashing they told everything. There was only one white man left on the ship, the captain, and one slave. They were from Savannah and had been hired by the owner of the *Venus* to recapture slaves lost in the storm. A few had been found alive on Cumberland and Jekyll islands and up the coast to Savannah, but none in Florida.

Joseph threatened to shoot them with their own weapons, then decided to save ammunition. He cut their throats and left their bodies for the panthers to devour.

After dark, Joseph and his men loaded into the two stolen boats and rowed silently through the still water to the ship. They boarded with ropes, surprised the slave who was sleeping on the deck, and dragged the captain out of his bed. When he staggered onto the deck he was shocked at the sight of a dozen armed Africans waiting to kill him.

He asked about his men. Joseph told a lie that would become part of the legend of Dark Isle, one that he had contemplated for a long time. It was outrageous, sensational, yet utterly believable, and it spread like the gospel truth up and down the coast, all the way to Savannah and Charleston. The lie hung over the island for a century, and long after Joseph was dead those who ventured to within five miles of his island knew and believed the legend.

He told the captain he and his people were descendants of cannibals from the jungles of Africa. His men were being prepared for a feast.

He, though, would be spared. Joseph tossed him overboard and gave him the smaller boat, with one paddle. They watched with great amusement as the captain flipped it twice as he scrambled to get in. When he finally managed to keep it upright, he took the paddle and rowed furiously in the general direction of Camino Island.

The ship was taken to the bay and stripped of all supplies. There were medicines, smoked meats, barrels of rum, log books, and a small arsenal of guns and ammo. The five former slaves from the ship had worked in the shipyards and harbors and knew how to sail. They quickly taught the others everything they knew. They had wives and children back in Savannah and they wanted to rescue them. Joseph was not convinced.

3.

A month after Steven Mahon started the battle over the ownership of Dark Isle, the state of Florida filed its answer in chancery court. It was nothing unusual or creative, just the standard textbook denials from the Attorney General's office. The state denied that Lovely Jackson was entitled to ownership because she had not adversely possessed the property for the past seven years. Overall, the response was tepid and predictable.

A week later, some heavier artillery entered the fray. Tidal Breeze, through its $1,000-an-hour lawyers in downtown Miami, politely asked Judge Salazar to allow it to intervene as an interested party, then went on for ten nasty pages setting forth all the reasons Lovely Jackson should not be awarded title to the property. In great detail, and obviously the work of some serious lawyers and paralegals, the response laid out the history of the island as gleaned from official records, of which there were so few. No records of births or deaths. No census data. No property tax assessments and no tax collections. No records of electrical or telephone service. Camino County had never built a school on the island and there was no evidence of any child from there attending an existing school. No health department records. No voters registered from Dark Isle. It was as if no one had ever lived there.

As for Lovely's claim, Tidal Breeze made much of the fact that she admitted in her memoir that she had left the island in 1955, as a fifteen-year-old girl, and that she was the last living descendant. Thus, the island had been deserted for almost seventy years. This was not at all unusual in Florida, the response added helpfully in one of its many superfluous asides, because, according to official records (attached thereto), there were at least eight hundred deserted or uninhabited islands in Florida. And, every single one was considered the property of the state.

Tidal Breeze went even further by questioning whether Lovely had been born on the island, as she claimed, or even lived there at all. There was simply no proof of any of it.

Taken as a whole, the response was a masterful denial of the legend of Dark Isle. Where, in 2020, was the proof? Other than Lovely, where were the witnesses? Where were the records? Where was the evidence of ownership?

4.

Steven Mahon read the response twice and each time felt worse. Tidal Breeze was obviously committed to the long game and would spend any amount to gain title. He did not look forward to the inevitable discussion with his client. Lovely would not take kindly to being called a liar and having her entire ancestry challenged.

He emailed a copy of the response to Mercer.

5.

Like her students, Mercer preferred classes later in the day, certainly nothing before 10:00 a.m., and such a schedule allowed her to write in the mornings. Thomas was a night owl and they seldom crawled out of bed before 8:00. She brewed coffee, took a mug to her little workroom, and shut the door. Thomas read the morning paper online, went for a jog, and made sure she got off in time for class. Both enjoyed early solitude. They had the rest of the day to catch up with the gossip.

Mercer was writing every morning for at least an hour. With Lovely's memoir as her guide, she was reliving Nalla's story and often had trouble thinking of anything else.

The death of the slave hunters. The birth of Nalla's child, a little girl with lighter skin. The death of Joseph's wife and his desire for Nalla. Their three children together. The sporadic arrival of other runaways. The growth of the settlement. Its culture—language, food, customs, rituals, and fears, always the fear of being invaded and recaptured. The religion became a mix of the Christianity that had been forced upon the slaves by their white masters and the African mysticism they clung to. Joseph's attempts to teach everyone, adults and children alike, the basics of reading, writing, and math. He had been fortunate enough to have received some education on the plantation. A few resisted his efforts, just as they rejected Christianity. His death from a disease that killed a dozen others in their settlement. Nalla's heartbreak at his loss. The power struggles to take his place. The harshness of life on the island. The heat, mosquitoes, insects, panthers, snakes, storms, disease. The constant struggle for self-sufficiency by a people determined to avoid contact with the world and too afraid to venture off the island. Life expectancy was about fifty years. Half the children died at birth.

Mercer was consumed with her story and longed to hear Lovely's voice. She wanted to spend hours on the phone with a million questions, but Miss Naomi could not convince her. Lovely had no phone, no television.

The more Mercer wrote, the more she disliked her job. She was in her third year at Ole Miss, her third teaching position, and she was tiring of the departmental politics. She assumed they were present on every campus and Ole Miss was no exception. With a master's degree but no doctorate, and no plans to get one, she was deemed a lesser academic and one probably not worthy of tenure. What she did have was a publishing career that now included two novels and a collection of stories. Adding insult to envy was the fact that *Tessa* had spent four weeks on the *New York Times* bestseller list. At that moment, no one else on campus could make that claim. Indeed, according to Thomas's meticulous research, it had been over thirty years since an Ole Miss professor had "hit the list."

In spite of her misgivings, and she kept most of them to herself, the fall semester was clicking right along, with SEC football the main focus and academics somewhere down the list. Mercer and Thomas lived in a rented condo on University Avenue, fifteen minutes from campus on foot. Heading east in the other direction, they often walked to the picturesque town square for dinner with friends or drinks in one of the many student hangouts.

Six weeks passed before Etta emailed with the news that the contract with Viking was on the way. Mercer should sign immediately and maybe the money would arrive by Christmas. Publishers were notorious for taking their time with contracts and payments.

When Mercer received the emails from Steven Mahon with the responses from the state of Florida and Tidal Breeze, she read them twice and felt uncomfortable. She called him and they talked for half an hour.

"What is discovery?" she asked.

"Both sides get to poke around in the other's case. Live depositions, written interrogatories, document swaps, the like. It's one of the more unpleasant aspects of litigation but a necessary evil."

"So Lovely will have to give a deposition?"

"Oh yes. I've explained this to her. She was less than enthusiastic. It's gonna take some work and preparation, but she's our only witness."

"Has she told you about her notebooks?"

A long pause on Steven's end. Then, "What notebooks?"

"She told me that she has a box full of notebooks that date back many years. When you read her book and you see all of those names and dates, you realize that someone had to write them down."

"Well, I asked her about that. She said it all came from memory."

A long pause on Mercer's end. Then, "Okay, so what happens if she does in fact have notebooks?"

"The other side gets to look at them, and given the resources they have, you can bet they'll go through everything with a magnifying glass."

"She might not like that."

"No one likes that, but it's part of the litigation process."

"Okay, but if she has extensive notes that date back years, wouldn't that tend to support her story?"

"One would think so."

"So what's your next move, Counselor?"

"You're watching too much television. I'll do some interrogatories, same for the other side. We'll slog through a document swap and so on. Nothing much will happen until they take her deposition."

"We'll be down for fall break early in October. I'd like to be around for the deposition."

"A good idea. I'll try but no promises."

"Any word from Judge Salazar?"

"Not a peep. She's known to lay low during the preliminary matters."

"All right. Keep in touch."

6.

The early stage of the lawsuit generated only passing media coverage.

The Register and the Jacksonville daily ran stories when it was filed but had not revisited the controversy. The only letter

to the editor of *The Register* was from a noted crank who habitu-
ally griped about property taxes and welcomed any new development that would generate revenues elsewhere. Around town, the
sentiment was that Dark Isle had been forgotten for so long it
wasn't worth discussing.

The quiet was shattered by an op-ed piece penned by Gifford Knox, fresh off his latest book tour and obviously looking
for trouble. He began with a brief history of Dark Isle, poked
endless fun at its gimmicky new name of Panther Cay, a "slick
marketing creation," and tore into Tidal Breeze for its attempt
at the "outright theft" of the island. Showing some impressive
research, he described two other Tidal Breeze projects in the
past ten years that involved the company's "swiping" of public
land by cozying up to politicians and bureaucrats in Tallahassee. He lamented the environmental destruction of even more of
Florida's natural beauty, blasted the idea that more gaming was
needed to shore up someone's tax base, and railed against yet
another "chemically drenched" golf course.

His closing paragraph was a beauty: "Eighty years ago white
people wrecked the ecosystem of Dark Isle by building a paper
mill upstream on the Camino River. The pollution wiped out the
oyster beds and abundant fish. Faced with starvation, the longtime black owners of the island were forced to flee. Now another
white corporation intends to steal the island from its last owner
and turn it into another gaudy resort for white people."

7.

For reasons she kept to herself, Lovely refused to meet with
her lawyer anywhere other than Bruce Cable's office on the
ground floor of Bay Books. And since Bruce was always on the
prowl for local gossip, or even regional, he welcomed Steven and

his client whenever they wanted to meet. He offered them coffee and made sure they had plenty of privacy, then busied himself with some first editions in a narrow hallway where he could eavesdrop at will.

Only later did Miss Naomi reveal the secret to Bruce. Steven Mahon's office was in a building that had once been a restaurant, which, decades earlier, had refused to serve black customers. Steven had no way of knowing this, and would have never known if Bruce had not whispered it to him.

Lovely had a long memory and carried many grudges.

With her granddaughters in school, Miss Naomi was as free and eager to take Lovely anywhere she wanted. Both women loved the bookstore because they felt welcome there. Bruce kept a long table near the front for African American writers and invited the ladies to the store whenever one was passing through. At Mercer's request, he also kept Miss Naomi occupied elsewhere when Lovely was in his office.

Lovely assumed her position in her favorite chair, an old French chaise that Noelle had hauled back from Provence. Miss Naomi and Steven exchanged pleasantries as Bruce poured coffee. After a few minutes he left and closed the door. Steven placed his iPhone on the corner of the desk and said, "I like to record my client conferences, if that's okay."

Lovely glared at the phone, then looked at Steven. "Why you doing that?"

"It's standard procedure. My memory is not what it used to be and I like to have a record. It's no big deal."

His memory was fine and he seldom recorded conversations with his clients. With Lovely, though, there was plenty of room for misunderstanding and he wanted to take precautions. She looked at Miss Naomi, who shrugged as if she had no idea.

Lovely said, "I suppose."

"If it makes you uncomfortable, then I won't do it."

"No, that's okay. Just treat me like you treat the rest of your clients."

"I promise I am." He picked up a stack of papers and said, "This is the answer, or response, to our lawsuit that has been filed. Two of them actually, one by the state and one by Tidal Breeze. As expected, both deny your claim of ownership. The one filed by Tidal Breeze may be a bit hard to swallow because they make a lot of allegations that are not true."

"Such as?"

"Such as, well, the most blatant is a claim that you cannot prove you were even born on the island."

Her face contorted and her eyes burned at him like lasers. Her bottom lip quivered and she bit it. "Who said that?"

"The lawyers for Tidal Breeze."

"I know where I was born and I know the name of the midwife who birthed me. She birthed my mama and daddy. I know where they were born and where he was buried, same place I hope to be buried. How can you let people like that say such things?"

"Lawyers say a lot of things that aren't true, I'm afraid. It's just an allegation, that's all. Just part of the lawsuit. Don't take it personally."

"So they can lie all they want?"

"No, they have to believe what they say, and since there are no records of your birth, they can claim you weren't born there. Again, there will be other allegations and you cannot take them personally."

"I don't like this lawsuit business."

Steven offered a smile, one that was not returned. "I don't blame you, Lovely. Lawsuits are unpleasant business, but they are necessary. If you want to prove ownership of the island, then you have no choice but to go to court."

She absorbed this without seeming to accept it. After a pause she asked, "Are those lawyers going to be in court?"

"Sure, that's their job."

"Don't expect me to be nice to them."

"You don't have to, but they're not bad people. They're just doing their job."

"And lying's part of their job?"

Steven took a deep breath and let it pass. "I need to ask you about records, notes, memos, stuff like that. Paperwork. The other side is asking for all of our paperwork, especially any and all notes you relied on when you wrote your book."

Lovely gazed at a shelf of Bruce's first editions and seemed to get lost in them. A long minute passed, then another. Steven was learning that huge gaps in the conversation did not bother her at all. She talked and moved at her own pace.

Finally, "Who says I have papers and notes?"

"Well, do you have papers and notes?"

"If I say yes, then those bad lawyers get to look at them, right? If I say no, then there's nothing for them to see. Right?"

"I suppose that's correct. Do you have notes?"

"I did, but I lost them."

She was not convincing, but Steven knew better than to push. In her world survival was more important than honesty. There would be ample time and many opportunities to discuss her source materials later. He said, "You must have an amazing memory."

"I do. So did my parents and grandparents. We told stories, Mr. Steven. You see, way back in the early days most of my people could not read or write. A few could and they tried to teach the others. I got lucky because my grandparents could read. I clearly recall my grandmother teaching me to write my name. It was very important to them, but not to all the others. There was even a little school on our island and I went there as a child. Some of the other children did not go. We relied on stories, long colorful stories told by my parents and grandparents, the same stories they had been told by their parents and grandparents. The stories were important and they were kept like gifts to be passed down. Not everybody could read but everybody could tell a story. And the stories were true and accurate because if you told one and got something wrong, then there was always somebody to correct you. That's how I heard the story of Nalla, the slave girl, my great-grandmother six times over. She landed on the island in 1760 and died there in 1801."

"How do you know it was 1801?"

"Because every story happened in a certain year. That's how we kept up with the time and the history. We always knew the year."

"But how do you know it was accurate?"

"How do you know it wasn't?"

"I'm just asking because the lawyers on the other side will ask you."

"I don't care. They can ask all they want. I know my history, Mr. Steven. They don't."

"Did you ever see any part of the history written down? Anywhere?"

She frowned at him as if he were an idiot. "No, didn't need to write it down. We kept it all up here." She tapped her left temple. "That's what I'm telling you. The stories were kept alive by the telling because we couldn't write them down. Long before I was born they didn't have pencils and papers and books and such. But they had words and stories and imaginations. When I was a girl and heard stories about Nalla, I could just see her in my visions. I could feel her suffering, her pain of being led away in chains, taken from her family, her little boy, her village, and sold to the slave traders. I knew all of Nalla's life's story when I was ten years old, Mr. Steven."

The lawyer smiled at the thought of his client taking the witness stand and giving her testimony. No lawyer in the country could cross-examine her, because she alone knew the stories and owned the facts.

However, the case was far from over. The law preferred hard evidence, such as birth and death certificates, marriage licenses, land surveys, deeds, and property tax rolls. Tidal Breeze and its horde of lawyers would have a fine time poking holes in evidence based on old stories, legends, and folklore.

8.

Later that afternoon, Steven met a friend, Mayes Barrow, for coffee at a café on the waterfront. Mayes was one of two Santa Rosa lawyers hired by Tidal Breeze. He was a popular young lawyer with a growing practice and a well-earned reputation as a fine courtroom advocate. Since money was no object, the company used many lawyers and always associated a few local ones to help navigate politics and curry favor with the judges.

Mayes said, "The company has asked me to explore the possibility of a settlement."

Steven was not at all surprised. Tidal Breeze could save a fortune in legal fees by simply buying off Lovely Jackson. It had much bigger court battles ahead. And for a company planning to spend at least a half a billion, a few bucks tossed to Lovely would be nothing but a rounding error.

"You want to pay Lovely to drop her suit and go away?"

"Yes."

"She's not going to settle."

"You won't know until you ask her."

"The answer is no, Mayes. Why would I ask her? She doesn't need or want money. She's never had it and knows it will only complicate her life. And if she settles and gives your client a clear title to the island, then we go to war over the development. Our best strategy is to win the first round, clear the title for Lovely Jackson, and tell your client to kiss our ass all the way back to Miami. Surely you understand this."

Mayes chuckled and nodded his head in agreement. "Makes perfect sense to me."

"I know. You're just doing what your client tells you to do."

"Yes, and they pay very well, Steven."

"So does my client. My retainer was five bucks, less than these two cups of coffee."

"They're offering a hundred thousand bucks right now."

"That's insulting. I will not take that to my client."

"Do you have a figure?"

"No. And I don't plan to discuss one with Lovely. She won't budge, I assure you. The trial will be a lot of fun, Mayes, especially when I put Lovely Jackson on the witness stand. It will be something we remember for a long time."

9.

For the third semester in a row, Thomas was shelving his studies in creative writing and pursuing other projects, namely research for his wife. He had begun his master's three years earlier and had been making progress until he found himself in a classroom with Ms. Mercer Mann as his teacher. He immediately lost interest in writing fiction and began studying her.

One lovely autumn afternoon he arrived at their condo with an expensive bottle of champagne and in fine spirits. *The Atlantic* had just bought his proposal for a long story about a missing Soviet submarine. The pay was $20,000, a record for him, with all expenses covered. The submarine, a nuclear job as long as a football field, had gone silent in the South Pacific, about five hundred miles north of Australia.

There were at least two hundred men on board. Not a trace of the sub had surfaced, and there were enough rumors to fill half a dozen books. His first research would take him to Washington, then on to Sydney. He would be gone for a month, their longest separation yet.

They were looking forward to a break. Mercer especially needed some time alone to jump-start her book. Thomas, who had seen far more of the world than his wife, was eager to travel again. He still saw himself as the adventuresome journalist dashing all over the globe looking for the next great story, and always with a possible book in mind. Mercer encouraged this because she loved him and wanted him to succeed, but she also cherished long stretches of solitude. After almost three years together, including four months of marriage, they liked their routines, solo and together, and they almost never fought. They were, at least so far, wonderfully compatible, and the sensual side of the union was only growing more intense.

They drained the bottle on the patio as they celebrated and talked about the damned submarine. Mercer had already heard so much of the story that she was almost dreading another six months of it, but she gamely hung on. A successful writer needed a sounding board, a first reader, a cheerleader, a person who loved them and wanted them to succeed. Thomas loved her work and couldn't wait to read her next chapter. Likewise, she listened to his ideas for projects and read his early drafts.

He said, "I'll finish my last Florida story tonight."

"Which one?" He was working on several. Thomas was a dogged researcher who could dig deeper into the internet than anyone Mercer knew.

"General Dunleavy. Another story that Lovely did not include."

"She probably never heard it."

"That, or it was too gruesome."

"Do you often wonder how accurate her stories are? We're talking about oral histories handed down for almost two hundred years. There had to be some embellishment along the way."

"Sure, and that makes your job easier, Mercer. With no one to check the facts, you can embellish all you want. You do write fiction."

"Thank goodness."

10.

Florida was admitted to the United States as a slave state in 1845. Florida had been a territory since 1821 and slavery was widespread, especially in the north, on cotton plantations and citrus farms around St. Augustine. One of the largest landowners was Stuart Dunleavy, a roguish politician who had once been a soldier and still fancied himself a military man. He would later get shot at Gettysburg and lose an arm. Using bribes and connections, he had amassed huge swaths of land east of Tallahassee and grew cotton on four thousand acres. When Florida joined the Union, he owned more slaves than anyone else in the new state and boasted of having a thousand Africans toiling in his fields.

Like most plantation owners, he was plagued by runaways and angered that many of his slaves were escaping to Dark Isle. Its legend continued to grow, and it was widely believed that hundreds if not thousands of slaves were hiding there, flouting the law.

In 1850, General Dunleavy, as he insisted on being called, decided to do something about it. He badly needed more labor and was fed up with the idea that the slaves were living on Florida soil as free men and women. He decided to capture them, keep all of them for himself, convert them to Christianity, put them to work in the fields, and in general improve their lives. He leaned on the governor, who, for some cash, agreed to "rent" General Dunleavy an old steamer that had been converted into a gunboat by the navy. He rounded up some troops, a motley mix of white farm laborers, common criminals, mercenaries, and a handful of real soldiers, gathered them on Camino Island, and spent a few days trying to train them, but finally gave up.

At dawn one morning they launched from the main harbor at Santa Rosa, with Dark Isle in sight. A quarter mile from shore they dropped anchor, positioned eight of the ship's cannons, and began bombing away. Dunleavy's brilliant battle plan was to bombard the island with the cannons, terrify the savages into surrendering, and send in his "troops" to capture them on the beaches.

The bombardment continued nonstop through the morning. By noon, there was no sign of the Africans, so the general and his men broke for lunch. After a meal and a nap, he gave orders to recommence the attack. At 3:00 p.m. his gunners reported that they were running out of cannonballs. Still, no sign of any terrified slaves waving white flags on the beaches. At 5:00 p.m. the cannons went quiet because there was no more ammunition. With an eye on the island, Dunleavy waited until dark, then retreated to their camp on Camino Island where they spent the night. The next morning, they reloaded and sailed to the southern end of Dark Isle where there had allegedly been signs of human activity in the past. They shelled the hell out of a thick forest, but saw no Africans.

After lunch, the general gave the dreaded orders. Two thirty-five-foot rowboats were lowered into the water and a dozen men boarded each. No one had volunteered for the little assault. Indeed, it was widely whispered on the gunship that there could be a mutiny if the troops were ordered to go ashore. The legend of Dark Isle and its cannibals was well known.

The men hit the beach and tied off their rowboats. One squad went north, one south. All of the men were armed with rifles and long knives, but they were moving far too slow and timidly in the general's opinion. He watched intently with his field glasses atop the wheelhouse. Finally, they left the safety of the beach and disappeared into the dense woods. An hour passed, then another. Late in the afternoon, gunfire erupted at the southern end of the island, and this pleased the men on the boat. Part of the legend was that the slaves had only spears and darts and such, the weapons of their ancestors. How could they possibly have modern weapons? The gunfire meant they had been found and captured after a quick skirmish. Then there was more gunfire. It was comforting to hear but Dunleavy began to worry about casualties. He needed to capture the slaves, not slaughter them.

But the slaughter was on.

He had given his men strict orders to return to the gunboat by dark. However, as nightfall came there was no sign of the men on the beach. Their two rowboats had not moved. They had no food or supplies for the night. As the hours passed, a sense of fear and dread engulfed the gunboat. The general wasn't sure what to do next. He couldn't abandon his men on the ground and return to Santa Rosa. He gave orders to pass around whatever food could be found on the gunboat and stand guard. A long night was ahead of them.

At the first hint of dawn, the lookout began yelling. The men woke up and scurried to the deck. The two rowboats had been cast off the island and were drifting with the tide. At first glance, they seemed to be empty. Dunleavy ordered his captain to start the steam engines and move close to the rowboats.

The horror revealed itself slowly. The rowboats were not empty. Lying in their hulls was a ghastly collection of bloodied and mangled corpses. The men had been shot, hacked, cut, and gouged—several were practically decapitated. Whole limbs were missing. Some had been gutted and their entrails ran down their legs.

Several of the men on the gunboat vomited. Most gawked for a moment then turned away. Little was said, and the word "cannibal" was never used.

They managed to capsize the rowboats and watched one sink slowly, then the other. Twenty-three men buried at sea. Twenty-one more safely on deck with no desire to do anything but go home.

The general's slave-hunting expedition was over. If he wanted more slaves he'd have to pay for them. He turned his gunboat around and retreated to Camino Island.

11.

Mercer was shaking her head. "And where did you find that little gem?"

"Dunleavy lived a long, interesting life and decided to share it by writing his memoirs, which he completed at the age of ninety. He lived eight more years. The book was copyrighted in

1895, and it probably sold about as many copies as Lovely's. I saw it listed in some obscure bibliography and skimmed it online. When I saw the story about Dark Isle, I perked up."

"You're a genius."

"No, but close."

"Do you find it odd that Lovely did not mention this story? I mean, it had to be one of the most memorable events in the island's history. An outright attack, two days of cannon fire, the ambush by armed soldiers and their killings. How was it forgotten?"

"Maybe it wasn't. Maybe Lovely heard the story a hundred years later and didn't want to include it. It's pretty gruesome."

"It's also pretty great. The ex-slaves who were thought to have nothing but spears, yet had more guns than the slave traders, and the general thought his men had been cannibalized."

"So you'll use it?"

"I don't know what I'll use. I can't get started. I need to spend time with Lovely."

"When is fall break?"

"Two weeks. I'm thinking of driving down."

"I'll be in Australia."

"I know. I might miss you by then."

CHAPTER SIX
THE INTERN

1.

The Tidal Breeze Corporation had been built over fifty years by the Larney family of Miami. Rex Larney got things started in 1970 when he bought at foreclosure a low-end motel in Fort Lauderdale. He was thirty-one years old, selling real estate, and the closing of a couple of nice deals had whetted his desire for money. He wasn't afraid to borrow money and take chances, and before long he was buying more small lots close to the beaches. His buildings got taller, along with his debts and his ambitions. By 1980 he was one of many high-flying property developers riding the wave of frenetic growth in South Florida.

His son Wilson grew up in the business and happily took over when Rex died of cancer in 1992. He inherited his father's appetite for risk and serious toys. He bought Thoroughbreds. and racing boats. He loved to gamble at the tracks and shrewdly foresaw the boom in casino gaming. He partnered with the Seminoles and built four splashy resorts around the state. The Feds almost nailed him twice on dodgy deals, but he proved too slick to pin down. His closest friend was his lawyer, J. Dudley Nash, otherwise known simply as Dud, a nickname Wilson stuck him with decades earlier. Dud's law firm grew almost as fast as Tidal Breeze and became a prominent Miami player in the commercial real estate world.

Tidal Breeze barely survived the Great Recession of 2008. When the dust settled, and the company was still standing, Wilson surveyed the wreckage and rolled up his sleeves. It was time to play the vulture. When the Fed slashed interest rates to almost zero, Tidal Breeze gorged on cheap debt and scooped up shopping centers, hotels, golf courses, and condos by the thousands.

In 2012, Wilson found himself in hot water again with the law after he forced another real estate swinger into bankruptcy. Once again, Dud navigated a deal that required him to pay a fine but nothing else. Wilson got his photo in the newspaper, something he detested. He was fiercely private and never talked to reporters. Tidal Breeze had only one shareholder—himself.

The jewel of his empire was a fifty-story office building in downtown Miami that Rex had snagged from a bankrupt savings-and-loan in 1985 during that crisis. Over the years, Wilson had refinanced it twice to lower rates and squeezed out over $50 million in cash. It was still heavily mortgaged, but then so was everything else the company owned, including its jet.

For Panther Cay, Wilson planned to borrow every dime the banks would loan for the project, though there was the usual concern about rising rates. Wilson never worried about the cost of borrowing. As Rex always said, "The rates go up and the rates come down."

From his splendid office on the fiftieth floor, Wilson had a view like few others. Looking east, the azure blue Atlantic stretched to eternity beyond the beaches; to the north, to Boca and Fort Lauderdale and even further, the shoreline was packed with clusters of beautiful high-rises, some owned by Tidal Breeze, but not nearly enough.

The view was always there, though Wilson had little time for it. He lived and played hard, and when he wasn't playing he was working many hours a day with each hour jam-packed with meetings and ideas and schemes to build and develop even more. In his plush, private conference room next to his office he sat at the end of a table covered with papers, plats, and drawings. To his right was Donnie Armano, the VP in charge of Panther Cay. To his left was Pete Riddle, a lawyer from the firm that Dud built, Nash & Cortez.

J. Dudley Nash was just as ambitious as Wilson and wanted to build the biggest law firm in Florida. They golfed and fished together and had once tried to buy the Miami Dolphins, but Wilson's debt-heavy balance sheet had, oddly, frightened the other NFL owners. As the law firm grew and added offices, Dud's hourly rate also increased impressively. Wilson chirped when it hit $1,000 but Dud said he was worth that and more. Wilson continued to chirp, and two years later when Dud whispered that he was the first lawyer in town to bill at $2,000 an hour, Wilson said, "Okay, you win. Send me a junior partner."

Pete Riddle was Dud's replacement. He was saying, "We're in discovery and not much is happening right now. The judge is expected to give us a schedule any day now."

"What about settlement?" Wilson asked. "Surely we can buy off this old woman. Hell, she's never had a dime."

"Her lawyer says no."

"And he's one of those environmental pricks?"

"Right. He knows the quickest way to protect the island is to win the title dispute. And he says his client will not settle under any circumstances."

"There's always a way to settle. Offer half a million."

"Okay, if that's what you want."

"And we're still on solid ground with the case, the title dispute?"

"Nothing has changed, nothing can change. The plaintiff herself, Miss Jackson, wrote in her own book that she left the island in 1955 and she was the last person there. Everyone else was dead. We've searched high and low and found no official record that anyone has lived there since 1955."

"And her book is admissible in court?"

"That's up to the judge, but there's no way to exclude it. And, Miss Jackson has to testify because there's no one else to support her claim of ownership."

"When's the trial?"

"Who knows? My best guess is early spring."

"And there's no jury right, just a bench trial?"

"That's correct."

"Any clout with the judge?"

"Maybe." Pete looked at Donnie Armano, who took the handoff and said, "We're still digging around and might have found something. Judge Salazar has a son in Jacksonville, married with two kids, her only grandkids at the moment. Got a daughter in Pensacola. The son owns a little company that builds cheap government houses and apartments. He does okay but he ain't getting rich by any means. We can approach him one of two ways, straight-up or behind the back. Straight-up we go through a shell company and get the kid some nicer houses in better parts of town, make sure he's busy and getting paid. We'll eventually dangle the carrot, let him know that he might strike gold in the boom on Panther Cay. Or, we can get him a big contract for subsidized apartments, riches galore, but first he has to bribe a federal inspector."

Wilson wasn't bothered by either plan. "Let's start off by giving the boy some business and see how it goes, nothing out of line, nothing to arouse suspicions. God knows we have enough companies to hide behind."

"Sixty at last count," Pete said with a grin.

"And I can think of three in the Jacksonville area. Get him sucked in for now and let's see how it goes. As usual, I'd like to keep the Feds out of it."

"Please do," Pete said.

"What about the rest of her family? The judge?"

"Single, divorced a long time ago. Sort of estranged from the daughter in Pensacola, all wrapped up in the two grandkids."

"How about previous rulings in title cases?"

"We've found only one, a few years back. Nothing helpful. She's been on the bench for six years so there's not much of a record."

"Okay," Wilson said, sticking his pen in a pocket, his way of saying enough of this. "We'll review it again next week."

2.

October was Mercer's favorite month on the island. The suffocating summer heat was gone, as were the tourists, though they seldom got in the way. The beach, ten miles long and rarely crowded, was even more deserted. She loved the long slow walks in the cool mornings. She missed Thomas, but not that much.

About half the beachfront houses were lived in year-round, and she often saw familiar faces as she walked. She even recognized some of the dogs, a friendly bunch as a rule. Stopping for a quick hello and a chat about the weather was not unusual, but Mercer did not want long conversations in the sand. She was there for a purpose, a walk to clear her head and, occasionally, give her inspiration. A story, a name, a place, perhaps even a subplot. As a writer she was always on the prowl for material, which had been sparse lately. Nor did she want to get close to her neighbors, most of whom were retired and usually eager to drop whatever they were doing for some gossip or maybe even a glass of wine. She wasn't looking for new friends. Her cottage, one that she owned with her sister, was a second home, a getaway and a refuge where she craved quietness and solitude.

But the damned thing was also becoming expensive. Upkeep on a house at the beach was never-ending. Thomas wasn't much with a hammer or a paintbrush, nor was Connie's sorry husband. So the two owners split the costs of all repairs and renovations, and the bills were getting bigger. They had never discussed the idea of selling it, though Connie had dropped a few hints. Her husband rarely came to the beach and her family was using the cottage less and less. It had been built by Tessa fifty years earlier and meant far more to Mercer than to Connie.

Fifty years of salt air and storms were eating away at the wood, tiles, and paint.

Mercer was on the back porch, ignoring the blank screen of her laptop, sipping green tea, and instead of writing she was staring at the ocean and listening to the waves, her favorite sound. In October she left the windows open at night and fell asleep to the sounds of the sea. The happiest moments of her childhood had been at the cottage with Tessa, who regardless of the heat didn't like air-conditioning. When the humidity was down, Tessa opened all the windows and they listened to the waves in the dark as they talked in bed.

Once again, a memory of Tessa came and went. She smiled, tried to shake it off, and looked at the blank screen. She had written the first chapter twice and tossed both drafts. She needed more time with Lovely, whom she would meet with tomorrow, at Bay Books, of course.

The paint was peeling. Everywhere she looked around the porch, the deck, the doors and windows, even the pine flooring, there was old paint either peeling or fading. Larry, her part-time landscaper and handyman, got an estimate from a lower-end painting contractor. The thief wanted $20,000 to repaint and seal the exterior, but Larry said that was about right. Mercer had to giggle at the thought of asking Thomas for his entire check from *The Atlantic* to spruce up the beach cottage. She thought of her sister and the smile went away. Not too many years ago Connie and her husband were flying high with his company and buying whatever they wanted. Then something happened. Mercer had no idea what, and she would never know because Connie would never tell, but the business wasn't booming anymore and they were tightening their belts. The sisters had never been close and it was too late to make the effort now.

She forgot about her laptop, and her unwritten manuscript, and walked around the cottage. A fresh coat of paint was desperately needed, so she made a decision. A firm one. An unpopular one. She and Thomas would spend their Christmas break on Camino painting the cottage. If he couldn't figure out a paintbrush and a roller, then she would be more than happy to give lessons.

Her phone was ringing on the porch. She was expecting a call from Thomas but instead got one from Bruce Cable. "Hello, dear," he began in his usual hyper, chipper way. "When did you get on the island?"

"Yesterday, Bruce, and how are you?"

"Swell. Books are selling. Someone saw your car in the driveway. Guess you drove down."

She was always amazed at how little he missed on the island. He had spies everywhere. "Yes, got in last night."

"How's Thomas?"

"He's not here."

"Left him already?"

"He's in Australia these days, on assignment for *The Atlantic*."

"Awesome. Finally got the boy to work. Look, Noelle's up for a light dinner, on the early side. Just the three of us. Catch up on the gossip, you know."

"I'm sorry, Bruce, but I'm tucking in. Got a good book. Give me a rain check."

A long pause on the other end, because no one said no to dinner with Bruce and Noelle. "Okay. Fair enough. See you tomorrow."

3.

The following morning at ten, the team gathered at Bay Books and enjoyed doughnuts and coffee in Bruce's office. Lovely was adorned in her usual African splendor—an orange robe, matching turban, with an assortment of bangles and baubles rattling whenever she took a sip of coffee. As always, Miss Naomi was by her side. Steven Mahon flipped through paperwork as they listened to Bruce talk about an upcoming autograph party for a hot new mystery writer. After a few minutes of greetings and chitchat, Bruce left his office and closed the door.

Steven held a document and said, "This is fairly straightforward." He looked at Lovely. "It's called a 'collaboration agreement' between you and Mercer that gives her and her publisher the exclusive right to your story. For your cooperation you are to receive twenty-five percent of the total advance, minus the agent's commission."

Lovely smiled and said, "I've read it. Looks good to me. When do I get a check?"

Mercer smiled and slid another document across the table to Steven, who examined it and removed a check. "Right now. The contract with Viking provides one hundred thousand dollars upon signing, which Mercer has already done, and one hundred thousand upon delivery of the manuscript, which I understand has not been done."

Mercer laughed and said, "I haven't finished the first chapter." Everyone enjoyed the moment.

Steven continued, "And a final payment of fifty thousand upon hardback publication, whenever that might be. So, here's a check for twenty-one thousand two hundred and fifty dollars."

He handed it to Lovely who took it gently and smiled. After a thorough examination, she held it so Miss Naomi could have a look. She approved too.

Miss Lovely said, "I'm going to use this to fix up the island, you know. I think I'll start with the cemetery where my people are buried. What do you think about that, Steven?"

"I think you should wait until this lawsuit is over. As I have explained, there is always the chance that we might lose, and if so the entire island will be changed completely."

She was shaking her head. "That's not going to happen."

"No, I don't think so either, but let's go slow."

"All right, all right. Do you want some more money?"

Steven chuckled at this and shook his head. "No, Lovely, you've paid me a five-dollar retainer and that's what we agreed on. I'm paid through my nonprofit."

Mercer said, "I'm making a donation to your foundation, Steven."

"Well, thanks."

"I'll make one too then," Lovely said. "How much do I give?"

Steven held up his hands and said, "Let's postpone that too.

We can talk about it later. There is another money matter we need to discuss. Mercer, this is confidential, for now anyway, and I'm not sure I want it written about."

"Shall I leave the room?"

"No, just keep it confidential. Miss Lovely, Tidal Breeze is offering you more money to dismiss your lawsuit and give up all claims of title in the island."

She absorbed it slowly. "I don't care how much they offer. It's my island, belongs to me and my people."

"Do you want to know how much?"

"Don't matter. I ain't giving up."

"Okay. As your lawyer, I have to tell you that Tidal Breeze will pay you half a million dollars to walk away."

It could have been five or five million, it didn't matter. The only reaction was a slight nodding of the head to acknowledge the amount and let it pass. Steven was delighted with the non-response.

"I take it your answer is no."

"Already said no."

"Good. As I understand things, now that the contract is signed and all, you and Mercer will want to spend a couple of hours going through the past. If you don't mind, I'd like to sit in on the session and take some notes myself. I need to know as much as possible. Discovery will start soon."

"Fine with me," Mercer said.

Lovely shrugged and said, "You're my lawyer. Got you for five dollars."

4.

The Barrier Island Legal Defense Fund's budget was so thin that Steven Mahon preferred to avoid interns. Fortunately, there was never a shortage of young, bright, idealistic college grads planning to go to law school, to be followed by a career in the trenches saving the environment. He received letters and résumés every week, and dutifully answered all of them, but rarely took the next step. The office "suite" he and his secretary occupied was barely large enough for the two of them. He had tried interns over the years but they were usually more trouble than they were worth.

Diane Krug, though, would not take no for an answer. Two years earlier, she had driven from Knoxville to Camino Island with her bags packed and ready to go to work, for no salary if necessary. She was fresh out of college, reeling from a bad romance, and had just inherited an unexpected $15,000 from an aunt she had neglected but suddenly wished she'd spent more time with. Like most folks, Steven was charmed before he could say no, and Diane entered his world. After two weeks, he began to wonder if she would ever leave it. She commandeered the small, cheap card table in the kitchen and began squatting there. If she needed real privacy, she went to the county library. The secretary was divorced and lived alone in a small home with an extra bedroom. Diane moved in there too and immediately began washing dishes and windows.

As a legendary litigator, Steven had no time and little patience with the drudgery of investigating. He happily dumped those chores upon Diane, who relished the challenge and volunteered for more. Late at night she read Steven's briefs and began editing them. After six months she knew more environmental law than most of the attorneys Steven had partnered with over the years.

After she dissected Lovely's memoir for the third time, Diane had a list of potential witnesses, a short one. Given Lovely's age, and especially considering the time frame of her story, real witnesses were scarce. An important one could be a man named Herschel Landry, a native of the area who had moved away. According to the final chapter of *The Dark History of Dark Isle*, Lovely was forced to leave her home in 1955 with her mother, who died not long thereafter. There was no one left on the island. All of her kinfolks had scattered and most of them were dead. When she was in her twenties, she began returning to the island periodically to tend to the cemetery, primarily the graves of her father and grandparents.

Herschel Landry had been one of the few black men on Camino Island who owned a boat. Decades earlier, there were many black fishermen, but they, too, had scattered. Herschel was married with children. Lovely was separated from her husband and still grieving the death of her only child. In her book she vaguely suggested a bit of a romance with Herschel, but regardless of how he was compensated he volunteered to ferry Lovely to Dark Isle for a few hours once or twice a year. Occasionally, a kid called Carp went too. Lovely paid him a dollar to help pull weeds in the cemetery.

Carp, whose last name was not mentioned in the book, and was still forgotten to Lovely, could not be found. Herschel, though, was ninety-three years old and living in a nursing home in New Bern, North Carolina. Diane found him there with an arduous internet search. According to his son Loyd, who also lived in New Bern, he was in a wheelchair and, typical for a person of his age, had good days and bad ones. The son had left Camino Island as a child when his parents divorced, and he had no recollection of his father's days on the water.

The defendants would hit hard at Lovely's assertion that she had never abandoned the island. Her book admitted that she did leave, at least as a resident. Her lawsuit claims she never left, but instead maintained close contact with the past, her people, and her heritage. Other than her own testimony, though, that would be difficult to prove, and the other side would label it completely self-serving.

Diane flew to Raleigh and rented a car for the two-hour drive to New Bern, on the Neuse River Sound. She met Loyd at the front door of the nursing home and they had a cup of coffee while waiting for a nurse to roll Herschel to the front lobby. He was napping when he arrived and looked every bit of his ninety-three years. The nurse hurried away and they spoke in hushed tones as they waited for him to come to life. Loyd said, gravely, that as of late his bad days were outnumbering his good ones.

Diane had low expectations for this potential star witness and her first impression was deflating. She and Steven never expected Herschel to be able to travel to Santa Rosa to testify. The best they could hope for was a video deposition at the nursing home, with poor Herschel surrounded by a dozen lawyers, that could be replayed in court for the judge. As they watched him snooze peacefully, though, she doubted such a deposition would ever take place.

Loyd gently shook Herschel's leg and he woke up. Loyd chatted with him, got his mind to work, and he became somewhat conversational. He did not know what day or month it was and could not remember what he did the day before, though in all fairness it was safe to assume one day in a nursing home was the same as the others.

Diane asked about his youth, those long-ago days on Camino Island, when he fished with his father and hung around the shrimp boats. The old man came to life. He smiled more, flashed his dentures, and had a sparkle to his eye. She asked if he remembered a young woman named Lovely Jackson and he thought about it for a long time. Then he nodded off.

Not exactly ready to be deposed, Diane thought as she waited patiently.

When his eyes opened she quizzed him again and got nothing. Digging through the island's historical registers, church rolls, and cemetery records, Diane had a list of African Americans who had lived on Camino Island during Herschel's lifetime. She mentioned a name, got a blank stare, gave a bit of background if she had it, and waited for something to register. He tried but just shook his head.

Loyd leaned over and whispered, "Not a good day."

After a long hour, Diane was ready to surrender and Herschel was ready for another nap. Her last question was, "Do you remember a kid everybody called Carp?"

He scratched his chin and nodded and finally smiled. "Oh yes, I remember that boy," he said softly. "Carp, yes."

"And he worked on your boat?"

"He hung around the docks, like a lot of the boys. A good boy."

"Did he go with you out to Dark Isle?"

"To where? He rode with me, yes. He cleaned fish and cleaned boats. A good boy."

Diane took a deep breath and asked, "Do you remember his full name?"

"Carp."

"And his last name?"

"One of Marvin's boys."

"And who was Marvin?"

A long expectant pause, then "Marvin Fizbee. A buddy of mine. Now I remember."

Somewhere in the depths of the historical records Diane had dug through, she had seen the unusual last name of Fizbee. She scribbled it down, as if she might forget it, and asked, "This Carp kid was a son of Marvin's?"

"Who's Marvin?"

Oh boy. This poor old guy would never get near a deposition. "You said Marvin Fizbee was a buddy of yours."

"Yes, he was. And he had a several boys. Carp was one of them."

"And Carp sometimes worked on your boat?"

"That's right."

"Do you remember Carp's full name?" A wasted question but one she had to ask.

He shook his head and fell asleep.

5.

On the flight back to Jacksonville, Diane worked the internet and found a nest of Fizbees in Lake City, Florida, an hour to the west of Camino Island. There were no records of anyone with that surname closer. None were named Marvin, and, not surprisingly, none went by Carp. After landing, she drove straight to Lake City, found the nearest Fizbee, and knocked on the front door. The neighborhood appeared to be white. So was the Mrs. Fizbee who answered the door. Diane fed her a line about working for a lawyer and looking for a witness in a case, and with her smile and charm she talked her way inside for a glass of tea. Mrs. Fizbee led her through the family tree, at least as far as the living relatives were concerned, but the friendly chat yielded nothing. Quite diplomatically, Diane explained that there were some black Fizbees around Camino Island who went back for decades. Mrs. Fizbee wasn't surprised but claimed she had never met one.

In the days that followed, Diane doggedly chased every possible lead in her search for black folks named Fizbee. She found some near Columbus, Georgia, but there was no connection to Camino Island. She was also quickly learning that black folks did not warm to the idea of talking to a white person working for a white lawyer, regardless of the circumstances.

The trail led to another family near Huntsville, Alabama, but they were just as disinterested.

If there had once been a kid called Carp, he was now at least seventy years old and it would take a miracle to find him.

6.

After giving plenty of notice, Judge Lydia Salazar convened the lawyers for what she described as an "informal status meeting." It was the first time the lawyers had met in the same room. So far, all communications had been cordial, which was usually the case when Judge Salazar was in charge. Steven Mahon was old-school, and though he had slugged it out with some of the largest corporations in the country in tough lawsuits, he took great pride in playing by the rules and treating his opponents with respect. He'd seen enough bad behavior by other lawyers. Mayes Barrow was the local lawyer for Tidal Breeze and had good manners. He also knew Judge Salazar frowned on bad ones. His co-counsel from Miami, Monty Martin, was surprisingly down-to-earth for a big-firm type and seemed to enjoy the bucolic setting of the old courtroom. The Attorney General's office sent three lawyers, though only one was needed. They appeared confident, primarily because they felt as though the state's claim of ownership was the strongest.

Seated behind all the lawyers were their associates and clerks. Diane Krug had already ingratiated herself with Judge

Salazar, and came and went as she pleased. She took a ringside seat in the jury box, a move no other underling would dare to try. Beyond the bar, several spectators waited. Sid Larramore of *The Register* was in the front row flipping through a newspaper, not his. A bailiff napped in one corner. The court reporter's desk was empty because no official record of the proceedings was necessary.

Because it would be a bench trial with no jury, the atmosphere was more relaxed. Scheduling would be far less complicated. Judge Salazar entered from behind the bench, without a robe, and greeted everyone. She asked each lawyer, all six of them, to remain seated, turn off their phones, and introduce themselves. She welcomed them and made them feel at home.

The first matter was a discussion of discovery and how it was progressing. There were no complaints, so far. The usual pile of interrogatories and requests for documents were making the rounds. Depositions had yet to start. Mayes Barrow said, "Your Honor, we would like to begin with the deposition of the plaintiff, Lovely Jackson. It seems only fitting that she goes first."

"I agree. Mr. Mahon?"

"Sure, Judge. May I suggest next Thursday at nine a.m.?"

Everyone lurched for their calendars. Busy people. Soon they were all nodding, primarily because a quick resolution to the title fight was wanted all around. If Tidal Breeze was getting sued, which happened all the time, its lawyers wrote the book on stalling and delaying. Monty Martin, though, was under strict orders from Wilson Larney to push hard for a trial.

Steven watched them for a moment and said, "And Your Honor, I'd like to borrow the courtroom for Ms. Jackson's deposition. My office is on the second floor and not that, shall I say, spacious."

"I see no problem, Mr. Mahon. The courtroom has been used before for depositions. There's plenty of room and I'll arrange security. Any objections?"

There were none.

Judge Salazar surprised them with the idea of a trial date. Discovery was just beginning. A trial seemed too distant. However, she had a one-week opening beginning on Monday, May 18, and set aside three days. Since they had plenty of time, she would not tolerate delays and requests for more time. In other words, get busy and let's get it over with.

7.

After the hearing, Diane drove to The Docks and parked on the street in front of Miss Naomi's. She and Lovely were waiting on the porch, enjoying a beautiful day and a gentle breeze. It was time for tea.

From a brown bag, Diane removed a plastic bottle of herbal tea, with sugar, and three large coconut cookies from a downtown bakery. She cracked the seal and poured it into three tin cups, the same ones every time. Lovely really liked coconut cookies, and the bigger the better.

Lovely knew the lawyers were meeting with the judge that morning and was eager to hear what happened. Diane covered the status meeting from top to bottom, said things went well, and that her deposition was set for Thursday next week. Diane had already explained the purpose, formality, and importance of depositions—sworn testimony from potential witnesses that allowed the lawyers to learn more about the case. They could, and would, ask almost anything, regardless of the relevance. Depositions were often fishing expeditions, but they were nothing to worry about. Preparation was important, and Lovely would be ready. Steven would be there by her side. He'd sat through a thousand of them and would keep the opposing lawyers in line.

"Can we talk some more?" Diane asked.

"We're talking now," Lovely said with a smile.

"With the recorder on?"

"I suppose. You do ask a lot of questions."

"That's my job. We're preparing you for the deposition and all those lawyers. That in turn will prepare you for the trial, which Judge Salazar wants to have next May."

Lovely bit her cookie and kept smiling. She nodded and said, "Go ahead, dear."

Diane pulled out a slim digital recorder and placed it on the small round table. "Now, last time, we were discussing your grandparents. You remember all four of them."

"Oh yes. My father's parents were Odell and Mavis Jackson. My mother's were Yulie and Essie Monroe. Their people came from a big farm in Georgia called the Monroe plantation."

"And they were slaves who'd escaped?"

Her shoulders sagged a bit as she frowned, as if they had already covered this territory. "You see, Diane, all the people who ever lived on Dark Isle were slaves or their descendants. Nobody ever moved there because they wanted to live there, and my people didn't want anybody new. There was not always enough food to go around as it was. Life was hard on the island. The women took care of the kids and raised vegetables and cleaned and such, and the men fished the water and watched for trouble. They was always watching. From the time a boy was ten years old he was trained to watch the water. They lived with the fear that the white men would return one day and cause trouble."

"Did that change after slavery ended?"

"Took a long time. News was slow getting out there to the island. Some of the men traded with black men down at the docks on Camino and also on the other side at Wolf Harbor, on the mainland, but there wasn't much contact."

"Why not?"

"Why not. Because they were afraid of disease. White people got all sorts of diseases that black folk don't need and can't handle. There was always the fear of catching something."

"Even when you were a child?"

"Not so much by then, in the forties and fifties. But around the turn of the century smallpox got to the island and killed half the people. The population went from a hundred to about fifty. Everybody lost somebody. I remember my parents and grandparents talking about it."

Diane scribbled some notes. Not for the first time, she wondered how much had been forgotten, and how much had been fabricated.

CHAPTER SEVEN
OLD DUNES

1.

Across the Camino River and headed west away from the island, the busy highway was lined with shopping centers, fast food restaurants, car dealerships, car washes, churches, and big-box retailers, the typical American sprawl. Billboards advertised cheap loans, scowling lawyers, and plenty of subdivisions. Construction was in the air. New developments, new "neighborhoods," new retirement villages were going up seemingly overnight. Realtors' signs clogged the intersections. Every other truck belonged to a plumber, an electrician, a roofer, or an HVAC specialist advertising a deep concern for your comfort and quality of life.

Off the main highway and near a quiet bay, another bustling development was springing to life. The Old Dunes Yacht and Golf Club had been approved by the county a year earlier, and, as they say in the trade, "the money had hit the ground." Luxury homes were being built by the water. The 18-hole golf course was half finished. Rows of expensive condos were in the framing phase. A marina with fifty slips for small boats was being assembled. The air buzzed with sounds of hammers, drills, diesel engines, and the shouts and laughter of hundreds of well-paid laborers.

Old Dunes was a new Florida corporation with a registered agent in a law office in Jacksonville. Its front man was a CEO from Orlando who reported to the home office in Houston. In late October, the private company in Texas sold Old Dunes to a Bahamian shell company that in turn flipped it to another faceless entity registered in the tiny Caribbean territory of Montserrat. Such financial gymnastics were nothing unusual for Tidal Breeze. Wilson Larney and his super-aggressive tax lawyers had long since perfected the game of Slip & Flip, a barely legal maneuver that involved offshore companies and willing bankers. Whatever profits Tidal Breeze ultimately netted from Old Dunes would remain beyond the reach of the IRS. Indeed, the IRS would never know the identity of the true owner.

The shuffling and filing of papers in faraway places went unnoticed in Camino County. All the proper fees were paid, everything was above the table. Developers bought, sold, and flipped properties with their morning coffee and all was well. A microscopic legal notice might appear in *The Register* or the county weekly, but no one would read it. Old Dunes was just one of many new projects underway in North Florida.

2.

Lenny Salazar, the son of the judge, was thirty-three years old, married with two small children. His family lived in one of the many communities sprawling out from Jacksonville. For the past four years he had worked hard building a company that mass-produced small homes. There was a ton of competition and profit margins were thin. Lenny's dream was to gradually move up to custom building, which was more lucrative. Unfortunately, it was the same dream of every other small contractor, along with every two-bit builder with a pickup truck and a claw hammer.

Lenny was making money because he was at every job, every day. He arrived early to greet the subs and worked late to clean up the sites. Within the trades, his reputation was growing because he delivered on time and paid his bills. He was attracting better subs, the key to success in the business.

His brick supplier was a sales rep named Joe Root, a veteran in the business. Root had seen a thousand builders come and go with the ups and downs of Florida real estate, and he believed Lenny had the smarts to rise above the competition. He found him on a ladder working with a framing crew and said hello. Root dropped in from time to time to check on his customers. Lenny followed him to the curb and they sat in the shade of the only tree in sight.

Root was saying, "Just got back from Camino, got a big order for eight tons of Florida white. You heard of the Old Dunes project?"

"Maybe," Lenny replied. There were so many developments.

"High-dollar stuff, million-dollar homes, a golf course, the works. On a bay just off the bridge, near the old Harbortown."

"I know the area."

"They're looking for builders. Company out of Texas, I think. Good reputation so far. All of my bills have been paid on time."

"Building what?"

"Condos, two to three thousand square feet. Lots of them."

Lenny was all ears. "Can you get me in?"

"Maybe I know the guy to talk to. Here's his card." Root handed over a business card for DONNIE ARMANO, PROJECT MANAGER, OLD DUNES. Address in Jacksonville. A phone number.

Root said, "Let me know and I'll put in a good word for you. They're building like crazy and it's not the run-of-the-mill crap like you got here."

The conversation quickly shifted to college football. Lenny was a proud graduate of UF. Root was an FSU man. Both teams were struggling but would meet in the season finale. Neither liked the teams at Georgia or Alabama so they trashed both schools for a while.

After Root drove off, Lenny called Donnie Armano with Old Dunes. He threw in Joe Root's name and Donnie could not have been nicer. That afternoon, Lenny left the subdivision early, drove thirty minutes to Old Dunes, and had an off-duty beer with Armano in his comfortable trailer office. They shook hands on a deal. A week later they signed contracts. Two weeks later Lenny's foundation crew arrived on-site to prepare the first slab.

He worked hard to temper his excitement and enthusiasm. His little company was taking a huge leap upward and he was not about to screw up the opportunity. With a bit of luck to go along with his formidable work ethic, he just might be developing his own projects in a few years.

3.

Mercer and her twelve students were enjoying a class outdoors in The Grove at Ole Miss, under the shade of two-hundred-year-old oaks, on a perfect fall day. The temperature was in the sixties. The golden leaves were falling. Scattered about were other classes with professors who had also succumbed to the weather and abandoned the buildings. They took over picnic tables, gazebos, stages, a pavilion, and lounged about under the old trees. The Grove was bracing for another football weekend when 20,000 fans would crowd into it for another epic party. Ole Miss might lose on the scoreboard but it never lost the pregame tailgate.

The literary challenge of the day was to look around at the setting, as peaceful and lovely as it was, and create a plot with serious conflict in less than 1,000 words. A beginning and an ending were required. Mercer wanted serious drama, perhaps even some violence. She was tired of the boring navel-gazing and self-pity that dominated their fiction.

As they pecked away on their laptops, Mercer studied hers. Diane was in the courtroom in Santa Rosa, preparing for Lovely's deposition. Mercer wanted to be there. And Thomas was home from his submarine-hunting adventures and wanted to spend time with his bride. He had not found the Russian sub but was getting closer, in his opinion.

Mercer was at 18,000 words, stalled again, and seriously considering deleting everything she had already written. Thomas was reading it that morning and she did not look forward to his comments.

At ten o'clock, eleven in Santa Rosa, Diane emailed: "Lovely's here and we're getting ready. So long for now. Will check in when it's over."

4.

She walked into the courtroom smiling, adorned from neck to toe in a bright red flowing robe. The mandatory turban was lime green and somehow wrapped into a tight cone that spiraled upward from the top of her head.

No judge in Florida allowed hats or caps in courtrooms, and Steven Mahon was already thinking about the trial. He planned to discuss her attire with Judge Salazar long before it started.

What could be the harm in allowing Lovely to wear one of her many turbans during the trial? In his forty-plus years as a bare-knuckle litigator he had never had a fight over headwear.

He'd worry about that later.

He directed Lovely to a chair at a long table that had been arranged in front of the bench. Normally, he would have introduced his client to the opposing attorneys, but she had made it clear she did not want to meet them. They had told lies about her and her island and she would not be nice. She assumed her seat at the end of the table, nodded politely at the court reporter next to her, and glared at the enemy lawyers. A court clerk offered coffee from a large pot. Judge Salazar entered, without a robe, and said hello to everyone.

Beyond the bar and seated in the front row was Sid Larramore of *The Register*. Depositions are not usually open to the public, and Judge Salazar did not approve of his presence. They knew each other well and spent a few moments in whispered conversation. Sid smiled and nodded and reluctantly left the courtroom. A deputy was posted in the hallway outside to keep away unwanted visitors.

Diane sat alone in the jury box and worked on her laptop. She was tracking yet another old ghost from The Docks, the alleged son of a fisherman who spent his life on the shrimp boats and got his photo on the front page in 1951. She had been through every edition of *The Register* since it began ninety years earlier, and she knew more about the history of the island's people, black and white, than the lady who ran the historical society. But she had yet to find the kid called Carp. They had to find either him or another witness who could walk into that very courtroom in a few months and verify Lovely's story that she routinely visited the island for years. The issue of abandonment was looming larger and larger.

After Judge Salazar had made her rounds she said, "I will be in my office if there is an issue. As agreed, you will go until twelve-thirty, then break for lunch, then resume at two p.m. After that, the deposition will continue as long as Ms. Jackson wants it to. If you do not finish today, we will resume at ten in the morning."

Steven was being overly cautious because of his client's age. He had warned the other lawyers that she might tire easily, and that he would not tolerate rough questioning or even badgering. Not that he was worried. Four months into the lawsuit he knew his opponents well enough to know that they were pros who played by the rules.

Finally, when everyone was in place, and the coffee was poured, and the door was secured, and the witness was ready to the point of looking bored, Steven said, "Okay, I guess we can get started."

Lovely took a deep breath and stared at her audience. Steven Mahon, close by; next to him was Mayes Barrow, then Monty Martin from Miami. Across the table sat three lawyers from the Florida Attorney General's office. Behind the lawyers were various paralegals and assistants. Miss Naomi sat in the front row. Quite the audience.

The witness was sworn to tell the truth. Steven made a few preliminary comments and turned her over to Mayes Barrow, who began with an earnest smile, "Miss Jackson, when were you born?"

"April the seventh, 1940."

"And where?"

"On Dark Isle, just over yonder."

"Do you have a birth certificate?"

"No."

"May I ask why not?"

"I was a baby. I wasn't in charge of the paperwork."

The answer was so beautiful, everyone had to enjoy it. The ice wasn't just broken—it was thoroughly melted. The enemy lawyers got the first hint that they might have their hands full with this witness.

Mayes, a good sport, collected himself and said, "Okay, who was your mother?"

"Ruth Jackson."

"How many children did she have?"

"Two. I was the first. Then there was a little brother who died when he was about three years old. I don't remember him. Name was Malachi."

"Do you know when your mother was born?"

"I do."

"When was that?"

"She was born in 1916. The third day of January."

"Where was she born?"

"Same place the rest of 'em was born."

"Where?"

"On Dark Isle."

"When did she die?"

"Nineteen seventy-one, fourteenth of June."

"You seem pretty certain about these dates."

"What's your mama's birthday?"

Mayes smiled, took another one on the chin, and reminded himself to stick to the questions. "Right, well, now, so she was only forty-two when she died."

"That's right."

"Where did she die?"

"Here in Santa Rosa, at the hospital."

"May I ask the cause of her death?"

"You're asking me if you can ask me a question?"

"No, sorry. What was the cause of Ruth's death?"

"She caught cancer."

"Where were you living when she died?"

"Down in The Docks, same place I live now. Round the corner with a friend who took us in when we left the island."

"And when did you leave the island?"

"When I was fifteen. Summer of 1955."

"And why did you leave the island?"

Lovely paused for a moment and looked down at her robe. Without looking up she said, "We were the last two. Everybody else had died. Life was just too hard and we couldn't live there anymore. One day Jimmy Ray Bone came out to the island, he had a boat and checked on us now and then, and he said it was time for us to leave, said he'd found a place for us to stay in town, said he was tired of checking on us and everybody who knew us thought it was time to let go of the island. And so me and Mama got our clothes and things together, wasn't much, and he helped us pack up and load it all in his boat. And then he waited while we went up to the cemetery and said goodbye to our people. It was terrible, after so many years. We were upset and crying and Mama began speaking in tongues but I could understand. She was saying goodbye to her parents and grandparents and all the way back to Nalla, one of my great-grandmothers. They were all buried there, still are." She stopped, looked up, and said, "I'm sorry, Mr. Barrow. I wasn't answering your question."

Her lawyer had told her more than once that she should not volunteer anything. Answer the questions directly, if possible, but give them nothing extra. If you don't understand the question, say nothing. Steven would step in and clear things up.

"That's okay," Mayes said. "You did answer it. Let's talk about your father."

5.

The genealogy consumed the first two hours. Without notes, Lovely recalled the names of many of her ancestors, along with the approximate spans of their lives. She could not remember all the dates of their births and deaths, but then who could?

Her memory was remarkable and Mr. Barrow asked if she had refreshed it with notes of any type. She explained that she once had some notebooks and diaries, and she had used them when she wrote her book, but they had been misplaced, or lost.

For lunch, Bruce hosted her, Miss Naomi, and Steven and Diane in the upstairs café at Bay Books. He gave them a corner table and left them alone so they could debrief. Steven whispered that Lovely was a fine witness so far—collected, certain, and believable. But she was showing signs of fatigue.

6.

Back in the old days, a deposition was "taken" by a court reporter using either the really old method of rapid shorthand or the more modern stenographic machine. Once it was taken, the court reporter would then translate the language into a readable form by typing every word. Lawyers would sometimes wait weeks to get a copy of the deposition or a court proceeding.

Nowadays, though, the technology was so advanced that the voices of the witnesses and the lawyers were captured and printed in real time. A deposition was not official until reviewed and signed by the witness, but it was not unusual for a lawyer to get an unofficial copy of, say, a 100-page depo emailed to him by the court reporter within hours of the testimony.

Diane had a copy before 5:00 p.m. the day of Lovely's deposition, and though she was technically not supposed to share it with anyone until it became official, she sent it to Mercer anyway. Late that night they compared notes. The more they talked, the more they worried. There were plenty of discrepancies between Lovely's book and her deposition; wrong dates, names, and events.

Steven and Diane had urged Lovely to reread her book to refresh her memory, but they did not know whether she had. Evidently not. She had self-published the book ten years earlier, at least fifty years after leaving the island as a young teenager, and her memory was obviously clouded. But what eighty-year-old could recall the names of her great-great-great-ancestors without notes? Lovely had tried, but there were too many mistakes.

Late in her deposition, Lovely described the cemetery where the dead were buried on Dark Isle. It was a big square area on the "high ground" and enclosed with a fence of heavy logs lashed together with ropes and vines. There were many graves there, some dating back to the 1700s. Where else were the people supposed to be buried, she asked? Since there were no rocks or stones on the island, the only markers were small wooden crosses with the names carved into them. Over time, these faded and rotted and disappeared, but the bones were still in the ground. As a child she had watched the men build a simple casket for her grandfather and cried as it was lowered into the ground. She knew exactly where it was located. Every person on the island attended each burial, even the small children. She and the others were taught about death from early on. In Africa, death was not to be feared and the dead often rose again as spirits, even ghosts.

At trial, the state, along with Tidal Breeze, would attempt to discredit her story and claim that there was simply no proof of anything she had said in either her book or her lawsuit. There was no record of anyone ever having lived on Dark Isle. No proof of a settlement, buildings, roads, cemetery, of anything, other than the suspicious stories of an old woman.

In their view, Lovely was an opportunist being used by others to litigate a false claim. The attorneys for Tidal Breeze had made enough off-the-record comments for Steven Mahon to know that they suspected he and his organization had latched on to Lovely's claims as the easiest way to block the resort.

By the time Mercer read the deposition for the second time, she had a knot in her stomach. There were too many conflicts between what Lovely wrote and what she was now remembering. At trial, the lawyers would pick her apart.

7.

One advantage to teaching creative writing was the avoidance of final exams. If Mercer so chose, and she always did, she could require one last short story of, say, 3,000 words to be turned in before December 1. After then, she had little to do but read the damned things and give grades. On December 2, she and Thomas left Oxford for a month's holiday at the beach. She was still determined to paint the cottage and save the $20,000, but her husband seemed to be hedging.

Thomas really couldn't see himself on a ladder, on the wrong end of a paintbrush, in the sun, for a month. He'd had little experience with contract labor, if that's what it was called, and had been scheming of ways to avoid the work. He had yet to find the Russian submarine, but there were some records at the Naval Institute in Annapolis that might need to be reviewed.

His article had gotten off to a slow start and things had not picked up.

Thankfully, the rains set in as soon as they arrived on Camino Island, and painting was out of the question. The cottage had not been decorated for Christmas in many years, and Mercer insisted they put up a tree, a few lights, and some garlands. They hosted Myra, Leigh, Bruce, and Noelle for a long dinner party, and two nights later went to one at the fine home of Amy Slater. They visited the bookstore every day and drank lattes as they read Mercer's final batch of stories from her students.

When the skies cleared, she announced it was time to start painting the cottage. She dragged Thomas to the hardware store and spent two hours choosing the right color. "Why not just keep it white?" he asked more than once, and when he finally got the hard frown he shut up and found some rat traps to study. She eventually settled on "chalk blue," which, in his opinion, looked very white, but he let it pass. She bought six gallons from stock and ordered six more. The salesman said two coats would be needed because of the salt air, and Thomas wondered how often he had used that line to sell more paint. But again, he bit his tongue and began hauling supplies to the car: paint, brushes, rollers, roller pans, extension poles, sandpaper, a sander, caulk, caulking gun, scrapers, drop cloths, and two stepladders. He had never used such tools and materials and doubted his wife had either.

The bill for their first load was almost $3,000, and Thomas asked himself, again, if it was really cheaper to do it themselves.

The following morning they woke early to clear skies and temps in the fifties. Perfect for painting, according to Mercer, who finally admitted that her only experience with a brush was touching up a crappy apartment she once had in Chapel Hill.

Now, though, she had somehow become an expert. She decided they would start on the front side facing the street and away from the morning sun. Thomas just grunted and began fetching supplies.

8.

The island was decorated for Christmas and the cooler temperatures helped the holiday spirit. When the weatherman in Jacksonville predicted a slight chance of flurries in two days, the entire island went wild and braced for a blizzard. Grocery stores were packed with frantic people afraid they might miss a meal. A retired couple from Minnesota unpacked their old snowblower, called a reporter from *The Register,* and got themselves on the front page.

Bay Books hosted an afternoon party each Christmas Eve, with plenty of drinks and food for all ages. Santa was there taking requests, posing for photos, and worrying about hustling off to get ready for his big night. The kids were giddy as they grabbed one book after another for their mothers to buy. Bruce, Noelle, and the staff wore festive sweaters and elf caps and worked the crowd. With snow on the way and the first white Christmas in history virtually guaranteed, the customers were bundled in layers suitable for skiing in Vermont.

Were they really in Florida?

The highlight was a 4:00 p.m. reading upstairs in the café where the autographing parties took place. Bruce shoved all the tables to the walls and packed in two hundred chairs. Three local writers and two high school students read original holiday stories.

Mercer, the best known of the bunch and the crowd's favorite, read a story she had been writing for many years. It was called

"Almost a White Christmas," and she promised it was true. In the story, she spent each summer on the island with her beloved grandmother, Tessa, who lived there year-round, and alone, except when Mercer was visiting. For various reasons, her childhood was not always pleasant, and when she was in school she dreamed of the next summer with Tessa. Without a doubt her happiest moments as a kid were on the beach with her grandmother. One Christmas, her mother was ill and hospitalized and the house was quite gloomy. Mercer and her sister prevailed upon their father to drive them to Camino Island for the holidays. Tessa welcomed them warmly and they immediately began decorating a tree and going through the usual rituals. Two days before Christmas, the weather turned cold and windy, and, suddenly, there was a chance of snow, something Tessa, a longtime resident, had never experienced on the island.

"Just like now," Mercer said, teasing her audience. Now in Santa Rosa it was forty-five degrees and windy, with the chance of snow fading quickly, but no one believed it.

Back to her story. On Christmas Eve, Tessa took the girls to church for the early evening service. When they came out, they looked to the dark sky and saw no snow. At bedtime, they read stories, opened gifts, and even put out cookies and milk for Santa. Early Christmas morning, they peeked out the window, praying for a blanket of snow, but saw none.

Over pancakes and sausage, Tessa said that, according to the old-timers on the island, a measurable snowfall happened about once every fifty years, and there had never been a white Christmas. The girls were disappointed, but they lived in Memphis and were accustomed to mild winters. After breakfast, they bundled up and followed Tessa down the boardwalk to the beach. She had to check on turtle eggs. When they arrived, they saw something unusual. The ocean was at high tide with strong winds pushing the waves onto the beach. Long ridges of thick, white foam from the surf covered the sand and blew into the first row of dunes. The wind whipped the foam into small clouds and swirls as it covered the beach. The girls squealed as they kicked the foam and tried in vain to grab it. As far as they could see in both directions, the beach was covered with foam.

Tessa stopped, spread her arms, and said, "Look, girls, it's almost a white Christmas after all."

The turtle eggs would have to wait. They hustled back to the cottage where Tessa got her camera.

Thomas handed Mercer an enlarged black and white photo of her and her sister knee-deep in what appeared to be snow. She showed it to the audience and said, "Christmas Day 1997. Believe it or not, that's our beach just down the road."

The audience admired the photo and passed it around. Bruce cracked, "How long did the snow last?"

"About two hours," Mercer said and everyone laughed.

She said, "Now, I have proof that there was a big snowstorm here many years ago. In fact, a young girl who lived in this area back then is still with us and she told me the snow was almost up to her knees."

She paused and looked around. It was obvious no one believed her. She motioned for Lovely to leave her seat in the front row and join her at the front. Mercer said, "Folks, this is Lovely Jackson, who lives in The Docks. Some of you know her because she published a book about her life ten years ago. She has a story for you."

Lovely smiled and looked around calmly as if she appeared onstage every night. "Thank you, Mercer, for inviting me, and thank you, Bruce Cable, for hosting this fine party." She spoke slowly, eloquently, with every syllable getting its due. She looked from face to face, carefully making eye contact with everyone. She smiled at Diane, seated in the third row.

"I was born on Dark Isle in 1940, so that means I'm eighty years old, probably the oldest person in the room. When I was about five, a big storm blew over the island. It was wintertime and, as you know, it occasionally gets cold here. We didn't have radios, never heard of televisions in 1945. There was no electricity on my island. So, we had never heard of a weather forecast, we simply didn't worry about the weather. We just took things as they came. Late one afternoon, it was really cold, and it started snowing. My parents, who were about thirty years old, had never seen snow. We were all excited, same way we are now, just waiting for it to start, but this snow was serious. It got heavier and heavier, the snowflakes bigger and bigger. Soon the ground was covered and it began to pile up. We were very poor and never wore shoes, so we had no choice but to go inside where our parents and grandparents were tending the fireplace and making dinner. My grandfather was named Odell Jackson, and he told us the story of his first and only snow. It happened when he was about fifteen years old, so somewhere around 1890. It snowed just enough to cover the ground, and the next morning the sun was out. The snow melted fast. He didn't like snow, none of my people did, because they were descendants of African slaves and there is no snow over there."

The crowd sat silent and absorbed every word. Mercer was amazed at Lovely's presence and poise. It was doubtful she had ever spoken to such a large audience, yet she was at ease, unruffled, and completely unintimidated.

She continued, "The next morning when we got up and looked out the window we were amazed at the snow. It had stopped falling and the sky was clear, but everything was covered in a beautiful white layer, like a big thick cloud had settled on the island. We stepped outside. It was still very cold. As I said, I was a little girl, only five years old, so the snow was almost up to my knees. It was probably the biggest snow ever around here."

She smiled at Mercer, nodded to the audience, and said, "Thank you for listening to my story. And thank you for inviting me here. May you have a Merry Christmas."

An eager ten-year-old boy raised his hand and Lovely smiled at him. "Did Santa Claus come that year?" he asked.

Lovely chuckled and flashed a broad smile. "Well, we didn't have a Santa Claus over there on Dark Isle. Though it's not too far from here, it was a different world. It was settled by former slaves, most of them from the plantations of Georgia. They had learned the English language and some of them were Christians, so we had a little Christmas ceremony each year in our chapel. But, as I said, we were very poor and didn't give gifts and things like that."

The children looked at each other in disbelief. Mercer stepped forward and said, "If you want to know the rest of Lovely's story, I suggest you read her book. It's a fascinating history of her life on her island."

9.

After the party, Mercer, Thomas, and Diane retired to a wine bar two blocks down Main Street. Diane didn't want to go home to Tennessee for the holidays and was hanging around the island. Mercer had invited her to dinner later in the evening at her cottage where she had a pot of gumbo on the stove.

Thomas bought a bottle of wine from the bar and poured three glasses.

Diane said, "We may have a problem."

"The snowstorm," Mercer said.

"Yes. A great story but I'm not sure it holds up. Snow around here is a big deal, right? According to *The Register*, the last measurable snowfall here was in 1997. There was a photo of it on the front page. The story went on to recap the other major snowfalls on Camino Island. The record was set in 1932—eight years before Lovely says she was born. The weather bureau officially recorded it at five inches, probably not up to the knees of a child. Of course, it was front-page news then as well, and *The Register* had this great photo of the drifts along the east wall of the train depot. Renfrow's Café still has the photo enlarged on its back wall, near the kitchen. It's also included in several of the local history books."

Mercer said, "And I don't recall this story in Lovely's memoir."

"Another problem. It's not there, not that it has to be. As the author, the memoirist, she can include anything or nothing. There are no rules, right?"

"I suppose."

"But, you'd think she would have included such a good story."

Thomas said, "Maybe she forgot it."

"Yes, and that would be okay, except Lovely is forgetting a lot of things. I've studied her deposition, word for word, and compared it to her memoir. I have flowcharts, spreadsheets, and timelines, and so far I've found at least a dozen inconsistencies, or discrepancies, or whatever you want to call them. Names, dates, events."

"Are you doubting her story?" Mercer asked.

"Some of it, yes. Plus, she's eighty and slipping. It's only natural. The problem, and it's rather significant, is that the lawyers on the other side will find, if they haven't already done so, the same inconsistencies. And, Lovely can't produce the notes she relied on when she wrote the damned book. Her memoir could really hurt her case."

Mercer asked, "You don't doubt her history on Dark Isle, do you?"

"No. That part of the story is believable, if the judge wants to believe it. The problem is that she admits she left, or abandoned, the island in 1955. And so far we have been unable to find anyone to verify her story that she returned periodically to tend to the graves."

Thomas said, "To me, as the non-lawyer, the biggest problem is that she did nothing for almost seventy years until the developers showed up and wanted the island. Suddenly she ran to court claiming ownership. Why didn't she do that decades ago if she was so concerned with the property?"

"Maybe she wasn't threatened," Mercer said.

"Maybe, but why does she care now? I'm not being cruel, but her days on this earth are numbered. She has a nice, quiet life in The Docks. Why should she care what happens to the island?"

Diane said, "Well, her people are buried there."

"Are you sure? If they were, they're probably gone now. What Leo didn't level it washed out to sea."

Mercer's eyebrows were raised and aimed at her husband. "Don't you care what happens to the island?"

"Of course I do. I don't want it developed. I'd like to see it preserved as it is, with maybe a memorial to the slaves."

Diane said, "Right. Fat chance of that these days here in Florida."

All three took a sip and a deep breath. Another group of revelers rolled in from the street and a gush of cold air filled the wine bar. Thomas, from Ohio, wearing sandals with no socks, was amused at the excitement over the "cold weather" and chance of snow.

When things were somewhat quieter, Diane said to Mercer, "We've both spent hours with Lovely, yet I haven't picked up a single clue as to her notes. Not long ago she said she used them to write her memoir. Now, though, she can't find them. Has she mentioned them to you?"

"No. I've asked twice and got nothing. How important are they?"

"Don't know until we see them. She got spooked when she realized that they might be turned over to the other side. I even said something to Miss Naomi once and she claims to know nothing about the notes."

"Are you sure you want to see them?" Thomas asked.

"I don't know. Steven and I go back and forth. If we see them, then we have to produce them for Tidal Breeze. What if they're filled with inconsistencies? What if they conflict with her memoir, or her deposition? There's a good chance the notes could really muddy the water."

When the bottle was empty they agreed they should leave before drinking more. They gathered again at Mercer's cottage where the pot of gumbo was waiting on the stove. Mercer turned on the burner and sliced and buttered a baguette as Diane tossed the salad and Thomas selected another wine.

Midnight was the goal but they didn't make it. At eleven, Thomas walked onto the patio to check the snowfall and saw none. He and Mercer retired to the bedroom while Diane disappeared under a quilt on the couch.

10.

By midmorning the skies were clear, the sun was out, Santa had come and gone, and things were back to normal in North Florida.

Judge Lydia Salazar lived alone in a gated community seven miles west of Camino Island, on the mainland by a small lake that not too many years earlier had been somewhat rural. Now, though, the roads were congested. Her neighbors were complaining, but seriously, weren't they all part of the problem?

She was fifty-seven and had been elected in a close race seven years earlier. Reelection was around the corner and she was dreading another campaign. Like most sitting judges, she now believed that electing judges was a bad idea. She preferred to be appointed, one four-year term after another. Elections, though, were not going away and she spent little time fretting over the next one. Her docket was busy. She enjoyed her work and was well regarded by the lawyers who came before her.

Her first husband was long gone and she didn't miss him at all. Her son, Lenny, was only thirty minutes away and she saw him and his family often, especially now that he and his wife, Alissa, had produced two children. Judge Salazar was still amazed at how swiftly she had been consumed by the two little people who now dominated her thoughts. When they arrived for Christmas lunch, their grandmother Sally, as she was affectionately nicknamed, was waiting with another round of gifts and toys. Within minutes her den was destroyed, with paper, wrappings, and boxes everywhere. Sally was on the floor in the middle of it all, having a ball and reliving the days when her own kids were lost in Christmas magic. When she could corral them, she read stories by the tree, fed them gingerbread cookies, and found more gifts to open.

Over hot cider, the adults watched the kids and talked about the weather. The snow had come closer than anyone expected. Scattered flurries had been reported in southern Georgia, close enough to give them hope for next year. Alissa was from Mary-

land and missed an occasional snowfall but had no desire to
return there. She taught school and was taking a couple years
off to raise the kids. Their finances had been tight, but there
was good news. Lenny had finally found traction in the building
boom and maybe, just maybe, he had his first big break.

Lydia had seen something in the newspaper or online about
Old Dunes, but thought nothing of it. Another development was
hardly headline-worthy in their world. For her, the big news was
that Lenny had signed contracts to build at least eight upscale
condos in the second phase of Old Dunes. The massive development just might keep him busy for years as he built his company.
They were so optimistic about their future, they were already
talking about moving closer to the job sites.

And closer to Sally!

After a long lunch of turkey, creamed potatoes, and stuff-
ing, they loaded the kids into their car seats, and with Sally
sitting on the rear bench between them drove a few miles east
toward the coast. The entrance to Old Dunes was blocked by
a gate, but Lenny had an electronic pass, which he waved at a
sensor. The streets had been paved for several months. The
curbs and gutters were finished. Dozens of buildings were in
various phases of being framed—apartments, condos, zero-lot-
line homes, vast mansions, a central square lined with stores
for the future, the harbor and marina. Lenny pointed here and
there and relished being so involved with such an impressive
project. He proudly stopped in front of the first condo he was
building, a sprawling townhome that would hit the market for
almost a million bucks. There would be plenty of them, he was
certain.

With both kids napping beside her, Sally couldn't help but
be impressed. Her son had struggled mightily to get his little

construction business off the ground. Now, he was building million-dollar homes. And she could spend more time with her grandkids.

11.

Having made so little progress with the painting, Mercer was reluctant to waste another day, even though it was Christmas. Thomas balked and threatened a strike. His cell phone said forty-eight degrees, two shy of the threshold. Instead of bickering, they agreed to go for a long walk and enjoy the afternoon.

Warmer days were coming. They'd get it painted sooner or later. Why hurry? They were on beach time, right?

CHAPTER EIGHT
EARWIGGING

1.

On the first Monday of March, Judge Salazar held her quarterly docket call to review pending cases, schedule hearings and trials, and check the status of the many guardianships and conservatorships under her jurisdiction. With everything now fully digitized and available online, the docket call was more a ritual, a throwback to a simpler era when the lawyers enjoyed gathering in their grand courtroom early on a Monday morning to have coffee and pastries, pass along the gossip, and act important. Judge Salazar still expected them to show up, though attendance was no longer mandatory. After each docket call, the lawyers and judges moved down the street to a private dining room in the rear of an upscale restaurant and held their quarterly bar meetings. Some of them would later move on to a saloon across the street for another version of a bar meeting.

When Judge Salazar called the case, *"In Re Petition of Lovely Jackson,"* Steven Mahon and Mayes Barrow stood. A handful of spectators watched with little interest.

Sid Larramore from *The Register* watched from the front row.

At that moment, it was the most interesting case on the island, but he had gathered no new material for the story in a couple months. The letters to the editor had petered out and lost some of their bite. A few people were quietly in favor of Panther Cay because of the economic boost, but Camino Island was still a conservative place where most folks belonged to a church and claimed to attend regularly. Gambling was frowned upon. Could prostitution be far behind? And drugs? The majority, at least in Sid's opinion, were opposed to more development in the area.

The lawyers agreed that discovery was on track and they could not foresee anything that would interfere or delay the trial, set for May 18.

Judge Salazar thanked them and moved to the next case. The morning dragged on. Steven hung around and planned to attend the bar lunch, something he did only once a year. At 11:30, the judge adjourned court and encouraged the lawyers to regather at the restaurant down the street.

In the buffet line, Steven shadowed the judge and luckily found a seat next to her. With thirty lawyers in a dining room the conversation was guaranteed to be lively. Most of them talked as they were eating, either about their latest exciting cases or college basketball. The guest speaker was a lawyer from Jacksonville who was swamped with immigration cases, and he managed to hold their attention for about ten minutes. Unfortunately, he went on for thirty more. As soon as he finished, his audience virtually stampeded out of the room.

Judge Salazar turned to Steven and said, "Are you in a hurry?"

"No, it's a pretty slow Monday."

"Got time for coffee?"

"Sure. I'll get us some."

"Black, please."

"I may have a small slice of the caramel cake. You?"

"Great idea, but very small."

When the dining room was empty, they turned their chairs to face one another and had dessert. After two bites she said, "I've reviewed everything in the Dark Isle case and I find Lovely's story troubling. I've read her book and I've studied her deposition. I'm sure you know there are plenty of discrepancies."

Steven was hoping for a quiet word with Her Honor about the need to visit the island. His idea was to hire experts to search for the cemetery, and, if found, try to secure samples from the human remains that could be used for DNA testing. If the DNA from the old bones matched Lovely's, there would be no doubt that the important parts of her story were true. Steven still believed her, but Tidal Breeze and its lawyers were casting plenty of doubt. Such an expedition into the jungle would require Her Honor's cooperation.

This, though, was a curveball he did not see coming. It was virtually unheard of for a judge to want a private chat about a pending case. He'd spent his career in federal courts and had handled only a few cases in the local courthouses. He'd never met a federal judge who would remotely consider talking about a case. Maybe the rules were different on Main Street, but he didn't think so.

Flabbergasted, and cautious, he wasn't sure how to respond. He said, "Well, she's eighty years old and maybe her memory is not so sharp."

"Do you really believe she lived out there? And all that stuff about her family? What troubles me is that she didn't claim the island until the developers showed up. She waited over sixty years, if you can believe her story. And how could she possibly have known to hire an environmental lawyer?"

There was little doubt that Her Honor was not buying Lovely's story. Steven was stunned and scrambled for something harmless to say. He didn't want to argue but he was curious as to how far the judge might go. He said, "Oh, I believe her. Why else would a woman her age bother with the fight?"

"Money, perhaps."

"I'm not sure we should be discussing this," Steven said.

"You're right. I should not have brought it up. I'm just troubled, that's all."

Steven took a large bite of the cake and worked on it slowly as the seconds passed. He couldn't think of anything fitting to say at the moment, but since she was in such a talkative mood, he wanted to give her some more rope.

"Let's pretend we never had this conversation," she said.

"Okay."

Fat chance of that. Judge Salazar had already decided the case. To make bad matters worse, Steven got the clear and troubling impression that she suspected he and the other tree-huggers were just using Lovely as their first line of defense against Panther Cay.

Rattled and reeling, he excused himself and made a clumsy exit. Hers was just as awkward. He ducked around a corner and disappeared in an alley. When she'd had enough time to walk back to the courthouse, he returned to his office. Diane was at her card-table desk in the kitchen. "You're not going to believe this," he said. She missed nothing.

"You look pale," she replied.

"Let's go for a long drive."

2.

For the past fifteen years or so, Noelle had sold French Provincial antique furniture and furnishings to Aurelia Snow, a delightful lady and friend who lived four blocks away in one of the many handsome Victorians in central Santa Rosa. Her home was the only one Noelle coveted, and though it would soon go on the market, Bruce had made it clear that he was not moving. Virtually every rug, lamp, chandelier, and piece of furniture had come from Provence by way of Noelle's Antiques on Main Street, next door to Bay Books. The house was packed with armoires, wine-tasting tables, daybeds, poster beds, cabinets, buffets, vanities, and much more, all selected by Noelle for every room and corner of the house. The project had been challenging and rewarding, and Noelle and Aurelia had made several trips to France over the years searching for the right pieces.

Aurelia, sadly, was now slowing down. She'd lost a step or two because three years earlier, at the age of seventy-seven, she purchased a new hip. A year later, a new knee. Now, an ankle was stiff. Arthritis was getting worse. She avoided the stairs and, frankly, was tired of taking care of so much stuff. She had been living alone for over a year, since she socked her wealthy husband into assisted living. When she decided to sell her Victorian, Noelle was the first person she called. Most of the French stuff she'd bought, well, now she wanted to sell it back, and Noelle was willing to trade.

Aurelia was buying a new condo, one without stairs, and she wanted Noelle to oversee its interior design and decoration. She would use as much of her furniture as possible, but most of her collection simply wouldn't fit.

When the roof was up and the walls were roughed in, Aurelia decided it was time to start decorating. Noelle drove her across the river to a new development called Old Dunes to have the first look. As they entered the main gates and crept along the busy streets, they were startled at the beehive of construction.

"Are you sure you want to live here?" Noelle asked, obviously turned off by the sprawl.

"Yes, I've made up my mind. It'll be okay once everything is finished, don't you think?"

"I don't know. It'll be a drastic change."

They found the streets with new homes going up. A gaudy sign advertised: LUXURY CONDOS STARTING AT ONLY $950,000.

Bruce was of the opinion that the Snows' Victorian would hit the market for at least $4 million. Aurelia was looking at a windfall and she knew it. She had said to Noelle more than once, "All this money and nothing to spend it on. Barry's lost his marbles and can't go anywhere."

"Find a younger man," Noelle had said, only half serious.

A paint crew was busy with the exterior of Unit 416, Aurelia's. They got out and walked carefully around the ladders and drop cloths. They stepped through the front door and were met by a pleasant young man who introduced himself as Lenny Salazar, the contractor. For an hour, they looked at plans, measured walls, stared at windows. Lenny was a busy man, taking several phone calls, barking at his subs, even disappearing once for fifteen minutes. But he was thoroughly accommodating and willing to move walls and doors and tweak the floor plans. He even took a half-bath and said he could remove a corner and install a small sauna next to the laundry room.

The challenge was obvious. Aurelia was downsizing from a three-story home with 12,000 square feet to a one-level condo with 2,500. Nevertheless, she was excited about it. The more she walked across the bare floors, the more antiques she jettisoned. Noelle was only too happy to purchase and resell what she didn't want.

When they were finished, Lenny walked them outside, handed each a business card, and said the closing would take place whenever Aurelia was ready. The condo would be finished in sixty days and she could move in at her convenience. As she looked around and took in the noise—cement trucks roaring by, hammers pounding away, saws screaming, workers yelling—she decided she was not in such a hurry.

She asked, "I might wait a few months before I move in. It's awfully busy out here."

Lenny laughed and said, "Yes ma'am, it is. There are sixteen condos on this street, then we move to the next."

"How many of these are sold?"

"About half."

Aurelia laughed and asked, "Do I have the right to approve of my new neighbors?"

Lenny laughed too and said, "I assure you they're all nice people."

"Whatever. I'm in no hurry. It'll take a year to sell my house anyway."

3.

Steven's favorite escape from the office was a long walk along Main Street to a coffee shop. He usually dropped in to Bay Books and said hello to the staff. If Bruce was in, which he usually was, they might gossip for a few minutes.

He found him in his office, poring over an old book with a magnifying glass.

Steven said, "I got some dirt." Code for *We need to have a quiet lunch.*

Bruce smiled and said, "What a coincidence. So do I."

They met at noon the following day in a pizza joint around the corner. It was early March and the wind was blowing. No one was eating outdoors. The wine list left much to be desired, so they ordered sparkling water.

Once confidentiality was established, and Bruce could be

discreet when necessary, Steven replayed the troubling conversation he'd had the previous week with Judge Salazar.

He said, "She was completely out of line. No judge, regardless of how big or small the job is, should ever discuss a case with one of the lawyers without the opposing lawyers present. Most states have laws on the books prohibiting attorneys from trying to hustle or influence or curry favor with a judge. In the common law, which we inherited from England, there was even a term for it. 'Earwigging.' It was illegal and certainly unethical to earwig a judge."

"But you weren't the one doing the earwigging," Bruce said.

"Exactly. I can't understand why she felt the need to inform me that she thinks my case is weak. What did she gain? I'm really baffled. I've been here only six years and I rarely appear in her court. I've talked to a couple of local guys who do a lot of chancery work and it seems as though she has a reputation for loose lips. She's well regarded and there are few complaints, but she drops comments from time to time when she doesn't like a lawsuit or the testimony of a witness. I guess that doesn't matter. What matters is that she tipped her hand in favor of Panther Cay."

"And if you called her out?"

"It would only make things worse. As you know, there's no jury. She is the sole decision-maker. The verdict belongs to her. We can always appeal, but the Florida appellate courts rarely overturn a Chancellor in matters like these. She has enormous power and her verdict will be given great deference on appeal."

"Hard to believe she would bring this up at a bar lunch."

"Well, the lunch was over and we were alone. Still, it was strange. And I got the clear impression that she sort of wished she hadn't said anything."

"Lucky she did. At least you know where you stand. Can't you ask her to step aside?"

"That rarely works. In fact, it usually backfires. When you ask a judge to recuse herself, guess who makes the decision. The judge. And if she says no, then you're stuck with a judge who's really pissed off at you."

The pizza arrived and they had a bite.

Steven said, "And your dirt?"

"Nothing compared to this. Just a bit of gossip, which, oddly enough, is related to Her Honor. Do you know Aurelia Snow, lives in that big blue Victorian on Elm Street?"

"I don't think so."

"Nice lady. Husband's in memory care or one of those places and she's downsizing, selling the big house and moving into a new condo. She wanted Noelle to buy back a boatload of French antiques she's collected over the years. Anyway, Noelle drove her over to see the new place yesterday. It's in Old Dunes, the latest planned development on the back bay."

"I know all about it. We thought about stepping in, filing suit, trying to fight it, but found nothing to hang our hat on. Just another development, one of too many, and we decided to keep our powder dry."

"For Panther Cay."

"For Panther Cay, and after Panther Cay there will be another one. This is Florida."

"I love it. More books are sold per capita in Florida than any other state. Don't forget that. The population is a bit older and folks like to read."

"I bought a hundred books from you last year. Hardbacks, no discount."

"God bless you. And I'll bet your bookshelves are beautiful."

"Indeed they are. And the dirt?"

"Well, small world. The guy building Ms. Snow's fancy new condo is none other than Lenny Salazar, son of the judge."

"Didn't know she had a son. She's divorced, right?"

"Yes, a long time ago. She doesn't live on the island so I don't know much about her."

"What's your angle?"

"I don't have one. That's your world. I'm just a small-town bookseller." He took a bite and chewed. "But I wonder who owns Old Dunes."

"I thought it was some Texas swinger."

"Maybe, maybe not. The first newspaper story said it was a Houston company with an office in Tallahassee. I called Sid at *The Register* and he knew little. Might be worth digging into."

"Wait a minute. You're not thinking it might be Tidal Breeze?"

Bruce was nodding.

4.

At four that afternoon, Steven returned to the bookstore and brought Diane with him. They found Bruce in the rear stockroom, boxing up unsold books to return to the warehouse, an unpleasant task that he refused to delegate. He still opened every box of new books and placed them on display with great confidence that they would be sold, read, and enjoyed. Six months later, he sadly sent some back in defeat.

Steven and Diane collected espressos at the upstairs coffee bar and waited for Bruce at a quiet corner table. When he climbed the stairs, he ordered a latte and sat down. "This must be serious," he said with a smile.

"Diane's on the trail," Steven replied.

"It's not much of a trail, yet," Diane said. "The land for Old
Dunes was purchased five years ago by a Houston company
that set up a new corporation in Florida. It has done business
here before, primarily in the Naples area. It leased an office in
Orlando and went to work, got all the permits and approvals,
promised to be good boys and productive citizens. So far, no
complaints. The Texas guys have a nice reputation for building
quality resorts, hotels, golf courses, the works. It's a private corporation so not much in the way of public records, though I did
track down some of their other developments and learned that
they prefer to build, then hold and manage themselves. Not in
the habit of flipping. However, in September of last year, they
sold Old Dunes to a company registered in the Bahamas. Proper
paperwork was filed here by the new owner, Hibiscus Partners.
Couldn't find a thing about them. Like a lot of offshore havens,
the Bahamians keep things private, for a nice fee, of course.
Then, in early October Hibiscus sold Old Dunes to Rio Glendale, and the weeds get thicker. Rio Glendale is registered on the
tiny Caribbean island of Montserrat, a rather notorious haven
for shady corporations and tax evaders."

"I've never heard of Montserrat," Bruce said.

"They advertise in travel magazines and that's about it."

"Where is it?"

"It's a British territory, down the road from Nevis and St.
Kitts."

"Sorry I asked."

"Most of it was destroyed by a volcano a few years back."

"And they call it a haven?"

"Anyway, it's impossible to penetrate the record-keeping on
the island, same as the other Caribbean fronts."

"So, another dead end?"

"Maybe, maybe not." Diane was in her element, slowly peeling the onion. "You might not be surprised to learn that Tidal Breeze has a history of tax troubles. I've found two newspaper articles about dust-ups with the IRS, and both led to investigations in the Bahamas and Cayman Islands."

Steven said, "It's possible that Tidal Breeze bought Old Dunes through Rio Glendale and is keeping it offshore."

"And does this little conspiracy have a motive?" Bruce asked as he tried to keep up.

"Ever heard the word 'earwigging'?"

"Not since lunch."

"We're dreaming here, Bruce, speculating. Playing a game of what-ifs. Panther Cay will be far more profitable to Tidal Breeze than Old Dunes, so what if Tidal Breeze figures it can have both? It uses Old Dunes to snag Lenny Salazar, who just might be able to influence his mother."

"You're really throwing darts here, Steven."

"True. But as I said, we're just playing a game, for now anyway." Steven nodded to Diane, who said, "I've spent the past two hours studying building permits, something I don't recommend, both in Camino and Duval counties. For the past three years Lenny Salazar has built fourteen duplexes in Duval, federal government housing, average value about two hundred thousand. He also built a small apartment complex and a strip mall. He's a hustler, stays busy, good reputation with the trades. Last September he appeared at Old Dunes and started building condos worth a lot more. I called his office, said I was looking for a builder, and was told Mr. Salazar was too busy to call me back."

Bruce sipped his latte, looked at Steven, shrugged at Diane, and said, "Okay. I've read a million mysteries and I love a good plot. This one wouldn't make it to chapter three, but it has just enough suspicion to turn a few more pages. What's next?"

Diane said, "Well the plot does thicken a little. Of course every foreign corporation, as well as every out-of-state one, must have a registered agent here in Florida. Virtually every other state reciprocates. There are dozens of companies who do nothing but serve as registered agents, shuffle the paperwork, and provide an address. It's especially big business in Miami with so many South American companies doing business in the state. Rio Glendale is using a registered agency in Coral Gables. So far I've found two other offshore companies owned by Tidal Breeze who register at the same address. So Tidal Breeze knows them well. Again, there are literally tens of thousands of entities and it could be purely coincidental, but I'm still digging. It does look a little suspicious."

"Okay. That turns a few more pages. What's next?"

Steven said, "Not sure. The only way to know who owns Old Dunes is to sue the company, get 'em in court, and make 'em divulge their ownership."

"I can think of several lawyers around here who specialize in bogus lawsuits," Bruce said.

All three laughed. Then Bruce stopped laughing and asked, "What kind of lawsuit would it be?"

Steven said, "I really don't know. Not my area of expertise. I've thought of snooping around out there and trying to find an EPA violation somewhere, run to federal court and harass them for a while. But I really don't have the stomach for it, nor the time. And it would be a long shot at best."

Diane said, "I've checked all the dockets and no lawsuits have been filed against Old Dunes so far."

Steven said, "It's a matter of time. Every large construction site is good for a few lawsuits. Unpaid bills. Liens by subs. Workers get hurt every day."

"Is it that simple? You sue 'em and find out the real owners?"

"Usually. It's not always easy, but the rules of discovery are flexible and allow the parties to ask all sorts of questions. Real ownership is on the table and courts want to know the true identities of the litigants. We just need a plaintiff."

5.

Gifford Knox was no stranger to litigation. For more than twenty years, ever since his books began selling in impressive numbers, he had been involved in many environmental fights up and down the East Coast. The more he sold, the more money he donated to his favorite conservationists. He had testified in two trials involving fights to stop developers in his beloved Low Country. His testimony had been neither crucial nor revealing, but it had been good for front-page stories.

Nor was he opposed to pulling a stunt to thwart a development or harass a polluter. The stunt was Bruce's idea. He waited two days until the temperature in Santa Rosa was twenty degrees warmer than dreary Charleston, and he called Gifford with the invitation to come visit for a week or so. The timing was perfect. Gifford and his current wife, Maddy, were bored on the sailboat in Charleston Harbor. The early March weather was windy and raw, and a few days in the sun sounded wonderful.

The stunt sounded even better. Bruce was careful to keep Steven away from it. If it blew up, he didn't want the lawyer to have his ethics questioned. There was nothing illegal about their little plot; nonetheless, Steven did not need the state bar poking around with some pesky ethical questions. Bruce would take full responsibility. As a bookseller, he really had no code of ethics. As a writer, Gifford certainly did not.

The salesman, Arnold, met them at the MODEL HOME! and showed them a slick video that revealed the breadth and beauty of Old Dunes. Everything a person could possibly want, and just thirty minutes from the Jacksonville International Airport. They looked at house plans, with a keen eye on the McMansions along the waterfront. Gifford, who was using the name Giff—not that it mattered, because he might have been one of the top-ten bestselling writers in the country but lived in near total obscurity, like the other nine—had questions about the final cost per square foot, and so on. He and Maddy had scoped the development and knew that three of the huge homes were under construction. Arnold said two had been sold. The third was a spec house that quickly became Maddy's favorite, the one they just had to see.

Diane had dug through the records and knew that all the lots in the development were still owned by Old Dunes; thus, the company would be a defendant in any lawsuit.

Giff and Maddy followed Arnold's car to the waterfront and parked at the curb. They entered the house, which was framed and roofed and even had brick going up one exterior wall. Giff and Maddy had plenty of questions about how much they might be able to change the design. Could they move walls at this point? And windows and doors? And the patio was just too narrow. At times they had to yell over the banging, hammering, and sawing. The stairway to the second level was temporary construction steps, barely firm and solid enough to handle the traffic up and down. They climbed the stairs carefully. Gifford shook the handrail and saw that it wobbled a bit. They inspected the three large bedrooms upstairs, found problems with the layout of the master bath, and didn't like a bay window. With each minor problem, Arnold assured them that everything could be adjusted. With a $3 million price tag, he could almost taste his commission.

When they were finished with the upstairs, they headed

down. Arnold first, then Maddy, then Giff. He took a deep breath, yanked hard on the handrail, broke it, and tumbled forward, screaming as he fell. Maddy yelled too and managed to stop his fall at the bottom of the stairway. In the fall, Giff managed to bang his head without really hurting himself. Sprawled across the bottom step, he was covered in sawdust and apparently unconscious. Arnold bounced around, yelling at the workers. Someone dialed 911. Maddy leaned over her husband, who was not responsive.

They hauled him away in an ambulance. His vital signs were normal. The two medics found no broken bones but there was a knot over his left ear. Obvious head injury. Obvious because he was unconscious.

When he finally woke up an hour later his skull was throbbing with a massive headache. His vision was blurred. The doctor said his scans were fine and give him pain pills. No, he did not want to go home. Maddy insisted he stay for further observation. The following day he was observed some more and seemed okay, except for the complaints about headaches, blurred vision, and a strange ringing in his ears. Arnold came by twice to check on him and to apologize. Maddy said she'd been worried about the unstable stairway. Odd, thought Arnold, none of the workmen had noticed or complained.

After two days he was finally evicted from the hospital and returned to Bruce's home where they had a fine lunch on the veranda with two bottles of wine. At times, Gifford had trouble eating because he was laughing so hard. Maddy thought he was a terrible actor. They howled when describing poor Arnold darting around with his cell phone trying to get an ambulance out there, downright frantic about losing his commission.

Late in the day, an insurance adjuster for the company that covered Old Dunes called to check on Gifford. He reported ongoing headaches, bouts of blindness, even a minor seizure or two, and so on. He promised to give the guy a call after he saw a specialist in Charleston.

A week later he filed suit in federal court in Tallahassee. His lawyer was a buddy from Charleston who had stood by his side through many of his exploits and been to court with him several times. The lawyer did not know of the stunt, but was suspicious of the mounting medical bills. His client seemed perfectly normal, or as normal as usual, the alleged migraines and seizures notwithstanding. Gifford did admit that the primary purpose of the lawsuit was to smoke out the true owners of Old Dunes. Attached to the lawsuit were standard interrogatories and requests for documents that would provide some interesting information.

6.

Two days after the lawsuit was filed, Bruce met Steven and Diane for a late afternoon drink at the Pirate's Saloon. He handed them both a copy of the lawsuit, which was a mere three pages long, and watched their amused faces as they read.

Steven was smiling when he finished. "And what was Gifford Knox doing looking at a new home in Old Dunes?"

"He was looking at a new home in Old Dunes. Same as other folks."

"Did he buy one?"

"Still pondering, but doubtful. Really not his scene."

Diane said, "I thought he lived on a sailboat."

"He does. But there will be a nice marina out there and a place for him to dock. He's very curious about these new developments."

"I smell a rat," Steven said, still smiling.

"You should."

"And how is he recuperating?"

"He's coming along. Maddy says there should be no additional brain damage."

Steven tossed his copy on an empty chair and laughed. "You did this, didn't you?"

"Did what?" Bruce protested with a grin. "It takes very little to get Gifford involved in a good fight. You said yourself that the only way to 'pierce the corporate veil' as they say, was to sue the company and get their documents. Well, here's the lawsuit, and Gifford's lawyer is hot on the trail."

"Beautiful."

"I thought you'd like it. If Tidal Breeze does indeed own Old Dunes, then what?"

"Then we have a chat with Judge Salazar and explain that she has a rather serious conflict of interest. Her son is in business with one of the litigants. We'll press her to recuse herself. If she refuses, then we'll consider going to the state bar association. That would be very embarrassing for her."

"Do you think she knows who owns Old Dunes?" Diane asked.

Steven shook his head. "Highly unlikely, at least at this point. How many corporate names have you traced back to Tidal Breeze?"

"Dozens."

"Right. These guys are slick, sly, and very secretive. They have plenty of lawyers and tax advisors and operate in many places here and offshore. No, she doesn't have a clue. But, there might come a time when Tidal Breeze feels the need to apply some pressure."

Bruce said, "It's still so speculative."

"It is. But we're getting there, thanks to Gifford Knox and his clumsiness."

"What? Didn't you read the lawsuit? He's not clumsy. The stairs were shoddy, defective, and part of an unsafe work environment."

"Beautiful," Steven said again.

7.

"Why are we attracting lawsuits up there?" Wilson Larney asked as he stared out the window and gazed at the ocean. "This was supposed to be easier. Roll in, throw some cash around, buy off everyone, and start building. I can't believe it's almost April and we're still bogged down in court."

One lawyer, Pete Riddle, said, "It's a simple slip-and-fall in one of our new homes. The guy had some injuries but nothing serious. I've told the insurance company to settle it, and quick. The plaintiff's lawyers are poking around offshore."

"And the injured guy's some kind of big writer or something?"

Dud Nash, the other lawyer, said, "Oh yes, name's Gifford Knox. Good crime writer. I've read him."

"Never heard of him," Wilson said.

That's because you haven't cracked a novel since high school, Dud thought.

Wilson was frustrated but never angry. His father, Rex, the founder, had been a hothead who cursed and threw things at subordinates. Wilson was far more professional, and far richer, and believed in keeping his cool. However, it was apparent that he was losing patience with the slow progress at Panther Cay. He wanted the largest casino in North Florida and was convinced it would mop up with Atlanta traffic.

"When's the trial?" he asked.

Riddle replied, "Same. Still May eighteenth. Nothing should delay it."

"And we offered the old lady half a mil, right?"

"Right," replied Dud. "And she said no."

"She's never had a dime, lives on Social Security, and she turned down half a million in cash?"

"She did."

"Okay. Offer her one million dollars to go away. Got it?"

Jeff smiled and said, "Yes, sir, boss. We'll get it done."

"The boys in Tallahassee have the funding for the bridge. A hundred and sixty million dollars. The banks have approved our first series of construction loans, two hundred million. What the hell are we waiting for?"

8.

After six months on the island, Diane had met far more people than Steven had met in six years, not that he was trying to compete. She had a knack for remembering names, so people remembered her. She stopped by the bookstore almost every day, said hello to Bruce and to every other person who worked there, and took the time to chat for a few minutes. She knew the baristas in the coffee shops, the waitresses in the restaurants, the clerks in the dress shops. She visited Sid Larramore at *The Register* at least once a week and traded gossip. She also spent time in the vaults reading past issues. She jotted down every name that she might one day come across. She flirted with the beat cops, the deputies, and the charter boat captains at the harbor. She watched the court dockets and kept up with cases. She got fresh with some of the lawyers but never went too far.

And she had spent so much time with Lovely that they had

become close friends. Diane coaxed her, and Miss Naomi, to a new café downtown, one that was not around back in the day. They had a long lunch and had so much fun they did it again. Lovely invited her to come sit on the front porch and have iced tea. Lovely had so many stories, and Diane would stop her and say, "That's a new one. Mind if I tell Mercer?"

Mercer was always a topic of discussion. Diane told her everything, regardless of whether she had cleared it with Lovely. Occasionally, the topic of money was mixed into the conversation, and Lovely had little to say. Over time, though, Diane began to suspect that she wasn't exactly dependent on a Social Security check. Her life was simple and there was little to spend money on. She had purchased the house fifteen years earlier and there was no mortgage. Her only extravagance was clothing, her colorful robes and turbans and scarves. Lovely, always reticent, finally admitted that she ordered her wardrobe from a store in Queens. She produced a catalog—Kazari's African Boutique—and allowed Diane to flip through it. Pages and pages of colorful dresses and robes, and the clothing wasn't cheap.

"You must have quite a wardrobe," Diane said, practically begging for a look.

"It's nice," Lovely said. Her front door remained closed.

Once, on the porch, Diane was taking notes as they worked through Lovely's employment history. She was quick with the dates, but, as Diane had already learned, the dates were proving to be flexible. After she left Dark Isle at the age of fifteen, she moved to Santa Rosa and went to school. She and her mother were practically starving and both worked wherever they could, primarily around the canneries. When Lovely was in her early twenties, she began working as a housekeeper in various hotels along the beach. This was not unusual; many black women worked in the resorts, hotels, apartments, and fine homes. When she was about fifty-five, she landed a nicer job working in a large home, one of the Victorians, in central Santa Rosa. The owner was Mrs. Rooney, the widow of an older man who had passed years earlier. Mrs. Rooney was from "up north" and had a different view of race relations. She and Lovely became close friends and relied on each other. Lovely was still required to wear her housekeeper's uniform each day, and Mrs. Rooney would never think of having dinner with her in a restaurant, but things were slowly changing.

When Mrs. Rooney died, she left Lovely some money. She had never told anyone how much and wasn't about to tell Diane, regardless of how cleverly she prodded. Miss Naomi said she had never heard the story.

It helped explain why Lovely was not impressed with money. When Steven and Diane met her in Bruce's office and told her that there was a million dollars on the table, she scoffed at it. Her only reaction was "I wish they'd stop offering money. I ain't for sale."

It was exactly what Steven wanted to hear.

9.

In anticipation of spring break, Mercer began dropping hints that she wanted to return to the island and paint the inside of the cottage. Now that the outside was pristine, they should work on the interior. The walls had not been painted in decades. They owned the necessary supplies—brushes, ladders, pans, rollers, drop cloths, everything but the paint—and they were somewhat experienced now that they had painted the outside. The interior would be much easier, she thought.

Thomas wanted to go skiing in Utah. He mentioned this a couple times but it apparently went unheard. A mysterious phone call from his editor at *The Atlantic* got his attention. He was needed in New York to review the final edits for his lost submarine article. Away he went, and Mercer drove ten hours to the beach with only the dog. The little family was happy. She needed some quiet time to write and work on her book. Thomas, who had shown little talent with the brushes, had avoided manual labor. The dog would get to sleep on his side of the bed.

Mercer and Diane talked by phone at least an hour a day. They emailed and texted constantly and couldn't wait to hang out on the island. Even as a paralegal, or office assistant, or whatever she was supposed to be at her card-table desk in the cramped kitchen at the Barrier Island Legal Defense Fund, she was supposed to keep the firm's work confidential. She did not. At least not when she wanted to talk to Mercer about the Dark Isle litigation. Steven Mahon sort of gave her the green light. They reasoned that Mercer was writing an in-depth book about the case and would find out everything sooner or later. She could be trusted. Lovely had given her approval for the two women to discuss her life and the lawsuit.

The first night on the island, Diane arrived at the cottage with a pizza and a bottle of inexpensive red wine. They talked nonstop for three hours and watched a movie. Diane slept on the sofa. The following morning, she was up early with a pot of coffee and reading Mercer's first draft.

10.

Noelle cooked dinner for Mercer the following night and they ate on the veranda with Steven and Diane. With surprisingly little embellishment, Bruce told Mercer the story of Noelle sniffing out Lenny Salazar as she examined the new condo for her client. If Lenny had a direct financial connection to Tidal

Breeze, and one had certainly not been proven, Steven said he planned to go after the judge.

Mercer listened as if enthralled, though Diane had already covered all the details. Bruce was a gifted raconteur, especially after some wine. He liked nothing better than a long dinner "on the porch" with writer friends and other admirers. As always, Noelle said little. She was content to listen to the others and speak only when she had something to add.

Mercer was delighted with the new twists and turns. She had written 51,000 words, which she judged to be about half the book. And, most important, she had stopped thinking of tossing it. She liked her narrative so far and knew the best was yet to come. Not only would it be long enough but the subplots were spinning. Diane had blitzed through the draft in three hours and said it read like a crime thriller.

"When can I take a look at it?" Bruce asked.

"How about when it's finished?" Mercer replied.

"Come on. I'm intrigued by your first effort at nonfiction, which is one of my strong suits."

"Along with everything else."

"No, not true. I don't read much poetry. I think I should read the first half and do so with a red pen."

"I'll think about it."

"Which is a nice way of saying no."

"I'll think about it. The first half is still pretty rough."

"I disagree," Diane said. "I devoured it this morning before breakfast. It's amazing. The stuff about the ex-slaves on Dark Isle is so compelling."

"Thank you."

Bruce poured some more wine and said, "Come on, Mercer. If you want me to sell this book I need to read it."

"And you will, as soon as I finish."

"Which will be?"

"Depends on the story. If the Barrier Island Legal Defense Fund wins Lovely's title dispute, then there will be a happy ending this summer. Right, Steven?"

"I suppose. However, there is always the possibility of an appeal. That'll eat up a year, maybe a year and a half."

Diane said, "The average appeal from chancery court takes fourteen months in Florida."

"My ace paralegal," Steven said with a nod across the table.

Bruce said, "Well, I can't wait that long."

"You'll have other books to read while you wait," Mercer said.

"Are you kidding?" Noelle said. "He's reading three a week now."

"Just part of my job," Bruce said with a smile. "Reading great books, drinking great wine."

11.

There was no shortage of London-based law firms that specialized in Caribbean tax schemes and offshore maneuvering. Gifford's lawyer in Charleston found one with a tiny branch office on Montserrat. For a fee, and it was never clear whether the fee was aboveboard or below, the lawyer accessed the government's register of foreign companies and individuals claiming to be domiciled on the island. Rio Glendale was one of 8,700. Its Articles of Incorporation, which were treated as highly confidential under the island's laws, were signed by Nate Gooch, a junior partner under Pete Riddle. Half of Rio Glendale's stock was owned by Delmonte Land; the other half by Sandman Ventures. Both companies were owned by a Boca Raton–based subsidiary of Tidal Breeze. All of the entities were privately held and under the thumb of Wilson Larney and his family.

It was a decent effort at hide-and-seek, but not terribly creative. However, Wilson and the boys never thought they'd be sued over Old Dunes. The real pros in the business went through Singapore and Panama and left no trail whatsoever.

12.

In mid-April, one month before the trial, Steven arranged a meeting with Judge Salazar in her office down the hall from the courtroom. The purpose was to discuss the trial and decide who would testify and in what order. Before they got around to it, though, Steven startled her with "Judge, I have some rather troubling news for you."

She responded with a confused look. "Okay."

"It has come to our attention that your son, Lenny, is building condos at Old Dunes."

"And doing quite well."

"Yes. The problem is that Old Dunes is secretly owned by the Tidal Breeze Corporation of Miami."

Her reaction was one of genuine shock. She sighed and exhaled and seemed poised to say something in response, but nothing came out. Her instinct told her to believe it, because Steven Mahon would never say such a thing without concrete proof. He placed a file on her desk and said, "Here's the paper trail. It sails around the Caribbean a few times, which is not unusual for Tidal Breeze. The corporation is privately owned and very secretive."

"My son is doing quite well and I'm proud of him."

"And you should be. There is nothing in that file that is in any way critical of your son. I assume he doesn't know the identity of the owner."

"I seriously doubt he does. We've never discussed it. I had no idea."

"Of course you didn't. Tidal Breeze went to great lengths to hide behind a few of its offshore shell companies, a game it has played before."

She removed her reading glasses and massaged her temples. Steven let her suffer. She said, "It was the bar lunch, wasn't it? Last month. I said too much after the bar lunch."

"Not at all, Your Honor." Of course it was the bar lunch. Of course she said too much and caused them to panic and conspire to find a way to get her off the case. It was a needless, careless moment for a respected judge to comment on an important pending matter. What had she gained by tipping her hand? Nothing. Unless she secretly wanted to help Tidal Breeze, which Steven did not believe for a moment. She had no idea the company had maneuvered itself into the ownership of Old Dunes.

"Well, I said too much and I've regretted it ever since. Not like me at all, you know?"

"I know."

She regained her composure and said, "I have an open mind, Steven, and am prepared to hear the case."

Your mind is definitely not open. "Well, Judge, we think that's a bad idea. You said what you said and left little doubt where you stand. It's best if you step aside."

"Are you suggesting I recuse myself?"

"Exactly. You do not believe the testimony of our client and star witness. Ma'am, you've already made up your mind."

"I have not."

"I won't argue with you, Your Honor. If you refuse to step aside by your own motion, then we'll file a proper one in court. The best way out for you is to quietly recuse yourself now. In doing so, you will not be required to give a reason. File a one-page order and ask the Supreme Court to appoint a special master for this case."

"And if I don't?"

"Then you'll run the risk of being embarrassed. We'll file the recusal motion claiming that you have a substantial conflict of interest, though we won't specify what it is, not initially. The news will make the front page. If you deny the motion, then we'll file an expedited appeal. And, Your Honor, with all due respect, we'll file a complaint with the Board on Judicial Conduct. Potentially also front-page news."

Her cheeks flashed red with anger and she almost fired back. Instead she took a deep breath, and she said, "This is pretty aggressive hardball, Steven. I'm surprised."

"And I was surprised too when I realized you had already decided the case."

"I was wrong. And you're wrong to try to force me off the case."

"I'm protecting my client, that's all. And I learned hardball suing Exxon and DuPont. Quit now, Your Honor, before this story becomes something much larger. You can handle the damage now, but maybe not tomorrow. You're up for reelection next year."

"Don't you dare bring politics into this, Steven. I don't count votes before I decide a case."

"Of course not. But the voters may take a dim view of a judge with a substantial conflict of interest. And an ethics complaint. Panther Cay is unpopular around here. You enjoy a sterling reputation. Why risk it?"

She removed her reading glasses and wiped her tired eyes with a tissue. She gave up, and asked, "Was Tidal Breeze the original developer of Old Dunes?"

"No. The company wormed its way in back in September. It was a trap, Your Honor. An elaborate scheme to use your son to put pressure on you. Panther Cay will be worth a lot more to Tidal Breeze than Old Dunes. Why not have both of them?"

"My son has done nothing wrong."

"I have not said nor have I implied that he has."

"I want him protected."

"Then recuse yourself."

"Let me think about this. It's all rather sudden."

"I'll wait twenty-four hours, Your Honor, then file a recusal motion."

"You're being quite heavy-handed, Steven."

"I learned in the trenches."

"I won't forget this."

"Neither will I."

13.

At noon the following day, Judge Salazar filed a notice with the clerk and sent copies to all of the attorneys. Without stating a reason, she was recusing herself from the case and asking the Supreme Court to appoint a special master to hear it. Since the filing was a public record, she did not bother to notify the press. By the time Sid Larramore at *The Register* got wind of it two days later, Judge Salazar was out of town on a short vacation.

CHAPTER NINE
THE DIG

1.

To get away from the voters who'd turned him out of office, Clifton Burch and his wife moved away from the sprawl of Orlando and retired to the much quieter town of St. Augustine, on the Atlantic. He'd had the honor of serving as a circuit court judge for fourteen years and was highly regarded by his peers and the lawyers who appeared before him. In his final campaign, he'd been blindsided by an unknown right-winger who flooded the internet and television with attack ads claiming Judge Burch was "soft on crime." He was not, and his record spoke for itself. But attack ads work brilliantly when they are dumbed down and frighten voters. His sudden and unplanned retirement was at first traumatic, but he soon realized he could stay just as busy pinch-hitting in cases all over the state. The Supreme Court was constantly searching for retired judges to referee hot cases where the locals were running for cover. Judge Burch, at seventy-six and fit as a fiddle, quickly became known in legal circles as the go-to guy who was organized, efficient, unbiased, and eager to resolve even the thorniest of disputes. He knew nothing about the case and had never heard of Dark Isle, Panther Cay, Tidal Breeze, or the Barrier Island Legal Defense Fund. He took a call from the clerk of the Florida Supreme Court at 9:30 a.m. on a Tuesday, April 21, and by noon had spoken to all of the lawyers and was plowing through the pleadings. He promised to read the depositions, review all discovery, and be up to speed by the weekend. In the past three years, he had handled two title disputes and knew the law well. It wasn't that complicated. The trial was set for May 18 and there would be no delays.

Steven was delighted with the appointment of Judge Burch. He liked Lydia Salazar but she had been compromised, and he had no regrets in scheming to remove her. He called Gifford Knox in Charleston and thanked him again for getting injured. Gifford howled with laughter and vowed to sail down immediately to celebrate.

They had another discussion about the money for the expedition. Gifford committed $5,000 more, bringing his total to $15,000. Steven had passed the hat among the "greenies" and their nonprofits, and he had collected $25,000. Bruce Cable pledged $10,000.

Mercer added another $5,000 and was brooding about the possibility that her little "Lovely Project" might be turning into a money pit.

2.

The idea had been Diane's. Initially, the goal was to visit Dark Isle with a group of experts, find the cemetery that Lovely described, find the graves, dig up some bones, and test for DNA.

Tidal Breeze had chosen the scorched-earth defense that

Lovely's story was fiction, that she had never lived on the island. And, so far, the good guys had produced no hard evidence to the contrary. A DNA link to the Jackson ancestors would destroy the corporation's claims and severely damage its credibility.

Diane had convinced Steven before Christmas, and, though he was concerned about the costs, he gave her the green light to proceed with caution. Being cautious was not in her DNA, but she gamely tried to show restraint. She found the African Burial Project in Baltimore and paid $100 for a membership. Its mission, as stated on its website, was to locate and preserve the burial grounds of enslaved Africans, and to memorialize their lives, struggles, and contributions. Most of its work was centered from the mid-Atlantic northward. In the former slave states, where, obviously, there were far more lost burial sites, there had so far been little interest in the work of the ABP. The nonprofit had no presence in the state of Florida.

That was about to change. Diane made three trips to Baltimore, a twelve-hour drive each way, and paid her own expenses. She charmed her way into a pleasant acquaintanceship with the executive director, a former law professor named Marlo Wagner. Marlo read Lovely's book overnight and was immediately drawn to the story. ABP was on a tight budget, but it had contacts in the archaeological world. Marlo knew researchers who did nothing but look for old bones and burial grounds that were never supposed to be found.

At the same time, through the winter, Diane had made numerous trips to Florida State University in Tallahassee. Dr. Gilfoy, the chairman of its Department of Anthropology, explained, more than once, that there was no money in the budget for a "big dig" in a place like Dark Isle. He, his colleagues, and especially his students preferred digging in more exotic places like Egypt and China. However, Dr. Gilfoy and some retired archaeologists from around the state ran a small company on the side that might be interested. Diane gave him all the maps, photos, and history she had, and he eventually explained over lunch one day that such a project would require five to seven days on-site with a team of archaeologists and students. The cost would be in the neighborhood of $30,000. A nice contingency was needed because the team had no idea what it would face, especially in the aftermath of Hurricane Leo. There was a decent chance the cemetery, if it had ever existed, had been swept away by the storm.

While Steven worked his contacts in the conservation community, Diane pecked away with a dogged determination, trimming estimates and begging for discounts, and finally put together enough money and talent to make the project happen. One team of three archaeologists from an affiliate of the ABP, and another team of three from Dr. Gilfoy's firm in Tallahassee, would spend several days on the island digging through the cemetery, if it could be found. Any skeletal remains would be DNA-tested at a genetic lab in Austin.

Steven contacted Judge Burch and laid out the plan. Since Dark Isle was not officially owned by anyone, court approval was not crucial. However, Steven felt it was in the best interests of their case to inform all the lawyers.

Tidal Breeze, of course, objected to the idea. In a teleconference, Judge Burch abruptly informed Mayes Barrow, Pete Riddle, and Monty Martin that he found their objections frivolous and time-consuming and he had no patience with such tactics. Sufficiently burned, they got off the phone as soon as possible and reported to Wilson Larney. Steven and Diane got off the phone and high-fived. They liked this judge. He gave the green light and wanted a report as soon as one was ready.

3.

The last obstacle was Lovely Jackson. Because she admired Bruce and felt comfortable in his store, Diane made the decision to arrange another meeting there. As always, Miss Naomi drove her. As always, she was adorned in a colorful robe and turban. Bruce served coffee and oatmeal cookies, her favorite. Bruce also stayed in the room, his office, because Diane and Steven thought they might need his help. They were proposing something that they had not yet discussed with their client.

Steven began with a summary of the lawsuit, or "court case" as he called it, for her benefit. The trial would begin in a few weeks, and after months of depositions and paperwork and such, it was now time for the big event. In his opinion, Tidal Breeze and the other "bad guys" had done a good job of casting doubt on Lovely's claims of being the last rightful owner of the island. The best way to prove them wrong was to go to the island, find the cemetery, and hopefully find the remains of her ancestors. She had assured Diane many times that she knew exactly where they were buried.

To introduce Lovely to the miracle of DNA testing, Diane had, weeks earlier, told her the stories of two men who were wrongfully convicted and languished in prison for many years. They had little hope of being freed until their lawyers convinced a court to allow DNA testing of some hidden evidence. The tests proved the men were innocent, and the guilty man was identified. Lovely had been captivated by the story, so Diane told her another one. And another. Then she told her the story of Thomas Jefferson and Sally Hemings, one of his slaves, and the six children they produced—before, during, and after his presidency. For decades, white historians denied that President Jefferson had kept Ms. Hemings as his concubine, in spite of ample anecdotal evidence. DNA testing resolved the issue in 1998 when one of his descendants was genetically linked to one of hers.

Diane had explained that it might become necessary to use DNA testing in their effort to win the title dispute.

Steven was saying, "Our plan is to take a team onto the island and find the cemetery."

Lovely seemed to know what was coming and was already shaking her head. She closed her eyes and said, "Can't do that."

No one said a word. No one knew what to say.

"Can't do that," she repeated and opened her eyes. "Nalla hexed the island when she got there. She painted the beach with the blood of Monk, the white man who raped her on the ship. The white man who made her pregnant and gave her a boy who was half-and-half. In Africa, in her home village, Nalla was a high priestess of African spirits and medicine, the village doctor. She was the same on Dark Isle, same as her daughter and granddaughter and all my grandmothers, all seven of them, all the way down to me. Nalla's curse is still in the sand on the beach of Dark Isle. No white man has ever set foot on the beach and lived to talk about it."

Bruce and Steven glanced at each other. They, of course, had heard the legend of the curse, but were too sophisticated to believe it. Now, though, hearing it described by Lovely, it seemed more plausible.

She said, "A lot of men have gone to the island, white men, and none have survived. The spirits are there and they tell me the stories. I hear Nalla's voice and the voices of my grandmothers. I know the curse is there, in the sand. It is not wise to tempt the spirits."

There was a long silence as the white folks in the room absorbed this. Miss Naomi sat next to Lovely, patting her arm and looking as bewildered as the others. Diane, never shy, finally broke the ice with "Does the curse apply to white women?"

A long pause as Lovely hummed and stared at the floor. "I don't know. I'll ask the spirits."

Bruce had never gone near Dark Isle and was not tempted now. He glanced at Steven again, and it was obvious he was having the same thoughts.

Diane asked, "As a priestess, do you have the power to lift the curse?"

"I don't know. It's never been done. I'll ask the spirits." She looked at Miss Naomi and said, "I'd like to go home now."

4.

Two days passed with no word from Lovely. Diane called Miss Naomi twice but no one answered. She had a long chat with Marlo Wagner and explained the situation. At first Marlo made light of the old African curse, but grew more serious when she realized that Diane and the others were frightened by it. The legend of Dark Isle included many stories of white trespassers who had died mysteriously. Marlo also recalled something from a book she'd read about African mysticism: the curse went away with the death of the witch doctor, or mystic, or priestess. Or whatever they were called.

Diane assured her that Lovely was believable. Hearing and watching her had convinced them all. "We could almost feel a spirit in the room," she explained.

There was a sudden search for black archaeologists. Marlo knew two who had helped the African Burial Project and she promised to call them immediately.

Diane called Dr. Gilfoy at FSU and described the current wrinkle in their plans. He, too, scoffed at the idea of a curse, especially one put in place 260 years ago. He was not intimidated in the least and was still looking forward to the dig on the island.

5.

Over coffee, Bruce told Steven that he had a new legal strategy.

"And since when did you start giving legal advice?" Steven asked.

"Oh, I advise on many subjects. Here's the idea: Withdraw your lawsuit, give Tidal Breeze the green light, and let them invade the island. That'll piss off Lovely and her spirits and they'll take out a few surveyors and architects. Once Tidal Breeze starts losing people, then they'll tuck tail and run. The island will be saved."

"I've actually thought about that. But what if it's all a crock? Do you really believe there's an old African curse on the island?"

"No. But I ain't going over there. You?"

"I'm a lawyer, not an archaeologist. I'll stay behind. Diane, though, can't wait to jump in the middle of it."

"What if Lovely says no?"

"We'll still go to trial. DNA is a long shot anyway. It's hard to believe they could find some old bones after all these years, and especially after Leo."

"What are your chances without DNA?"

"Fifty-fifty. Our biggest problem has not changed. Lovely admits she left the island sixty-five years ago."

6.

Miss Naomi called late at night. Diane was house-sitting Mercer's cottage, something she was doing more and more. "Well, hello Miss Naomi."

"Lovely wants to talk in the morning on her porch. Just the three of us."

"I'll be there. What time?"

"Ten. And if you bring some of those coconut cookies, that'd be nice."

"Will do."

The porch was so narrow their toes almost touched. They sipped coffee and nibbled on cookies and talked about the weather until Lovely said, "If I go, things will be okay."

Diane waited for more, and when nothing came she said, "You want to go to the island?"

"That's right. If I go I can release the curse. And they can't find the cemetery without me."

"So, let me get this straight. It's okay for the team to go onto the island, all of them, including us white people? But only if you go too?"

"Yes. I must go."

"And I can go too?"

"I want you to go. The spirits are with me and they know that good people are trying to help."

"Okay. How soon can we go?"

"Wednesday of next week is a full moon. We go at midnight."

"Midnight?"

"Yes."

7.

The large pontoon boat was used for sunset excursions, booze cruises, private parties, and sightseeing around Camino Island. Steven wrangled a one-week lease from its owner for $2,500, supposedly at a discount. The team arrived at the island's main harbor late in the afternoon of April 22 and began loading gear and supplies onto the boat.

The team consisted of two men and a woman affiliated with the African Burial Project. All three were black, thanks to Marlo Wagner's charm and salesmanship, and they were led by Dr. Sargent, chair of the Department of Anthropology at Howard University in Washington. The truth was that once word of the expedition spread through the network, Marlo was flooded with requests from volunteers. With good nature and a dose of humor, she explained that black gravediggers were preferred for reasons to be discussed later. The dig might be too dangerous for white folks. Most of the archaeologists, black and white, knew each other and many had worked together.

The white team was led by Dr. Gilfoy, who years earlier had studied with Dr. Sargent at Cornell. All six had doctoral degrees and worked in both the classroom and the field. Dr. Sargent had published two books on lost African burial grounds and was considered the leading expert.

After dark, Bruce Cable arrived with Claude the Cajun Caterer and a case of wine. Dinner was served under the pontoon's canopy and the team dined on gumbo, jambalaya, and crawfish étouffée. The wine and beer flowed along with the stories. There were plenty of them, told by seasoned raconteurs who'd had amazing experiences digging in jungles, mountains, and deserts the world over. As the evening wore on, it slowly became apparent that Dr. Sargent had the best stories and the most experience with African burial sites, and, without seeming pushy or ambitious, he gradually took charge. There were plenty of egos around the table, but they were accustomed to teamwork in difficult places.

At 10:00 p.m., on schedule, Diane and Mercer arrived with Lovely Jackson, who had ditched the colorful robes and turbans and wore instead old jeans, boots, and a khaki shirt that was three sizes too big. The party belonged to her and she took her time meeting the team, all of whom were delighted to meet her.

Mercer had taken a one-week leave of absence from the classroom, something her dean wasn't exactly thrilled about but he really had no choice. She had a big book contract, something the other professors could only dream of.

They gathered around a table and looked at large maps and aerials of Dark Isle, both before and after Hurricane Leo. Lovely had never seen the island from the air and it took her a while to get oriented. She pointed to a small cove where the boats were kept at a dock. It was on the eastern edge of the island, facing Santa Rosa, and had been obliterated by Leo. It was a short walk from the dock to the village. The cemetery was on the western edge of the island, on a ridge that was the highest point.

The archaeologists had platted every square foot of the island, or as much as could be seen from the air. The density of the forests and the damage from Leo made it impossible to see any remains from the settlement. They pointed here and there on various maps, quizzed Lovely, scratched their heads, and slowly put together a plan.

At eleven o'clock, Ronnie, the boat captain, started the engines. Bruce and Steven helped shove the pontoon away from the pier, then said their goodbyes. Bruce called out, "If we don't see you again we will not attempt a rescue." Everyone laughed.

Inching across the still water under a full moon, the mood quieted as Santa Rosa faded behind them and Dark Isle loomed ahead. Twenty minutes after leaving the harbor, Ronnie throttled down, then killed the engines. "We're in five feet of water here. This is okay?"

"Okay," replied Diane.

A small dinghy was starboard and Ronnie unhooked it from the pontoon. Diane stepped into it first and found her balance. Mercer went second. "Watch your step," she said to Lovely as Ronnie held her arm and guided her down. The dinghy rocked and Lovely tilted before Diane caught her and eased her onto the bench. Ronnie handed Diane three large canvas bags and said, "The surf will take you in but there is a paddle if you need it."

The dinghy drifted away from the pontoon. Diane clicked on a flashlight and scanned the beach, which was thirty yards away. The shoreline and the entire island were pitch-black. She turned around and swept the light behind her to see the pontoon, as if making sure it and the team were still there. They were all leaning on the railing, watching, mesmerized. The moon came from behind a cloud and lit up the shore. Mercer took the paddle, a tool with which she had zero experience, and managed to splash some water. It wasn't clear if her efforts were productive, but the dinghy seemed to be inching closer to land.

Lovely sat in the front, staring ahead, silent, unflinching as the boat rocked gently forward. As a child she had played in the water but never spent time on boats. That was work for the men: fishing, shrimping, trading with the merchants in The Docks and around the canneries. She had learned to swim and wasn't afraid of the water, but that was so long ago. She thought of Nalla and her violent, horrifying arrival on this beach. Shipwrecked, naked, hungry, traumatized by the passage and then the storm. Nalla was never far from her thoughts.

Diane's stomach was flipping, and she could not remember being so frightened, but at the same time the adrenaline was pumping. She was exactly where she wanted to be and she trusted Lovely to protect her. Mercer put the paddle away and tried to enjoy the moment.

The bottom of the dinghy scraped the sand. The waves quietly broke onto the beach. Lovely began undoing the laces on her boots, then removed them and rolled up her jeans to her knees. Her first words in a long time were "You stay here until I call. No lights." Carefully, she worked one leg over the side, then slid into the ocean. The water was barely above her ankles. She took a canvas bag and gazed up and down the beach. Slowly, she began walking forward and was soon on wet sand.

The clouds were moving. When the moon peeked through, Diane and Mercer could see her clearly. When it disappeared they could barely see her outline.

Lovely walked halfway to the dunes, stopped, and found her spot. From the bag she removed a small tiki torch and shoved its handle six inches into the sand. When it was sturdy enough, she got another one and placed it ten feet from the first. She removed a lighter. The cotton wicks had been soaked in torch fuel and lit easily. The two lights glowed bright in the darkness.

Standing between the torches, Lovely raised both hands in front of her, then spread her arms to her sides. She spoke, barely audible even to herself, and called forth Nalla's spirit. Once Nalla was in place, Lovely called forth Candace, Sabra, Marya, Adora, Charity, and Essie, all of her maternal grandmothers. Then she called her own mother, Ruth. When their spirits were joined she prayed for Nalla to lift the curse.

From the dinghy, Diane and Mercer watched in muted fascination. They had been skeptical, to say the least, but at that moment whatever they were looking at was undoubtedly real.

From the pontoon, the team gawked at the distant torches and Lovely standing between them. As seasoned archaeologists they had been around the world and seen many things, but they would never again witness a scene like this one.

The distant rumble of thunder jolted them back to reality.

8.

Finally, Lovely returned to the dinghy and told Diane to call the pontoon. The island was safe.

Ronnie revved the engine just enough to gain momentum, then shut it off and lifted it. The pontoon glided to a stop in the sand near the dinghy. No one seemed eager to get off.

Dr. Sargent quipped, "I think you white boys should go first."

Dr. Gilfoy replied, "We'll follow you."

Diane said, "We walk to Lovely one at a time, between the torches, and she will say a prayer. Then you are clear."

"Are you sure?" asked Gilfoy.

"No, but we're doing what Lovely says. Follow me."

A lightning storm erupted over Cumberland Island to the north. The thunder was louder but still far away.

They walked a few steps along the beach and stopped near Lovely. Diane stepped forward, between the torches, and faced Lovely, who placed her left hand on her shoulder, closed her eyes, and mumbled something. Diane had no idea what she said, and she felt no different when the prayer was over. Mercer followed and went through the same ritual.

Methodically, and with no concern about the thunderstorm, Lovely blessed the six archaeologists, one at a time. Then she explained that the island was now safe for them, and they could get on with their work.

The first order of business was the unloading of the pontoon. Ronnie was still on it when Gilfoy asked Lovely, "Can he come onto the island?"

"Keep him on the boat."

"Will do."

The campsite was near the torches, a hundred feet or so from the surf, and far enough away not to worry about high tide. Dr. Gilfoy and Dr. Sargent agreed that it was best to camp on the beach and away from the dangers of the bush. Gilfoy had barely survived a cobra bite in India when he was thirty, and he preferred to avoid another encounter with a poisonous snake. Sargent knew that some of the deserted islands in the Low Country were crawling with eastern diamondbacks. He had seen some impressive ones stuffed and mounted.

One team began setting up the tents while the other scampered on and off the pontoon hauling supplies. When it was unloaded, Ronnie offered a quick farewell and good luck and said to call him when they needed something. He watched the storm as he hurried away.

The team had debated using the pontoon to shuttle back and forth each day. Staying in a nice hotel on Camino Island and eating in restaurants would be the easier route, but archaeologists preferred traveling when they had to carry their own toilet paper. They lived for the thrill of surviving a storm. They liked to sleep on the ground when on a dig, and cook over a fire. Each of the six could tell long stories of the great digs of their careers, hardworking expeditions that kept them away from the modern world.

Diane and Mercer shared a large canopied tent, the girls' tent, with Lovely and Dr. Pennington, a researcher at Howard University and a veteran of several African burial digs. It had four cots with inflatable mattresses. At two-thirty they settled into bed and turned off the lights. There were soft whispers from the other two tents as everyone tried to get comfortable. Things were still and quiet until lightning cracked nearby and thunder followed. Then the rain began.

9.

At times it was heavy and unrelenting and it didn't stop until dawn, when they staggered out, red-eyed and sleep-deprived, to inspect the damage and see about coffee. Of course everything was soaked, but the campsite was intact. The storage tent was made of heavier canvas and a stronger frame, and it was unfazed. A pot of coffee was soon brewing on a Coleman burner. The morning was cloudy and brisk. The forecast was no rain and a high of near eighty, perfect weather for a dig, but the clouds were hanging around. They interrupted cell phone service, which was unstable at best in clear weather. Internet service was also unstable.

Three "scouts" left to look around while the others fixed breakfast and inventoried gear. Lovely managed to sleep through the noise until eight o'clock. When she emerged from the tent she thanked Diane for a cup of coffee and informed the rest that she'd had a thought during the night. They were searching for the cemetery, not the village, and, as she now recalled, the cemetery was closer to the harbor on the other side of the island. They pulled out maps again and studied them. The scouts returned with grim looks and a report that they were in for some heavy lifting. "Pack the chain saws," one said.

Over instant oatmeal and bananas, they decided to use the boat after all. They radioed Ronnie and called him back to the island. He arrived an hour later and said the latest forecast was for overcast skies but no more rain. They loaded food and gear onto the pontoon and Ronnie circled it to the bay side where the mainland was less than a mile away. Dr. Gilfoy pointed and said, "This is where the state wants to build the bridge if Panther Cay is approved."

At eleven-thirty, the team packed itself with plenty of gear— three folding shovels, trowels, chisels, two chain saws, two machetes, goggles, tarps, a first aid kit, a handgun, cameras, sandwiches, and water—and marched off into the woods in search of a trail Lovely was certain they could find. They could not.

Diane and Mercer stayed on the pontoon with Lovely, under a canopy, and began killing time. Ronnie strung up three hammocks and invited them to relax. There had been much discussion about Lovely's stamina and the amount of "trail work" she could handle. She was in decent shape for an eighty-year-old but certainly not fit enough to fight her way through a jungle. The initial goal was to find the cemetery without her, and, when found, see if she could get there and help in the search for graves.

Mercer stretched out in a hammock, opened a paperback, and promptly fell asleep. Diane put in her earbuds and took a nap. Lovely sat in a chair on the deck, in the shade, and stared at the water, lost in her history.

10.

The team returned intact five hours later. They had found no sign of anything that remotely resembled a trail, and had quickly realized that a trail was something they would have to create. That was the bad news. The good news was that the three white men were still alive. Lovely's banishment of the curse was holding.

They had seen three rattlesnakes and killed two of them. So far, no sign of panthers or bobcats. At times the insects were as thick as a fog. The mosquitoes were huge but no match for their repellent. The aftermath of Leo was worse than expected. Thousands of trees had been snapped off and blown into huge drifts, like stacked cordwood. The island was a mile wide and they had fought their way through maybe one-third of it. They had seen nothing that had been made by humans.

Ronnie cast off and they puttered around the bay and back to the ocean side. He unloaded them and said goodbye. Cold beers were passed around by everyone but Lovely. A fire was made in a pit and the team rested. Exhausted, they decided to dine on sandwiches and go to bed early.

11.

The panthers waited until their island was pitch-black again. As if choreographed, one eased into place fifty yards up the beach to the north, and his partner took a position to the south. The first one began with a low, rumbling growl that grew louder and sounded as if it was preparing for an attack.

Seconds passed before it was answered down the beach. Then a full-throated scream pierced the night and shocked the sleeping campers. When it was answered to the south, Diane jumped out of her skin and almost shrieked herself. Back and forth the panthers went, screeching at each other as flashlights came on inside the tents.

Even when an archaeologist is afraid, he or she will hide it. The six sat up on their cots and listened, obviously startled.

Diane pulled the sheets over her head. Mercer was barely breathing. Dr. Pennington waited for the next scream. Lovely, though, calmly put her feet on the canvas floor and smiled.

More panther catcalls at full volume. Back and forth they went.

"What is it?" Diane asked, peeking from under the sheets.

"Two panthers," Lovely said. "Male and female. You never heard a panther?"

"No, oddly enough, I haven't."

"Heard 'em all the time when I was a kid."

"What are they doing?"

Dr. Pennington said, "It's what they're about to do. It's mating season, right, Lovely?"

"I think so. It's springtime. We had 'em around back then. You don't mess with a panther, especially this time of the year."

"Are we messing with them now? They don't seem too happy."

Lovely said, "This is their island. No, they don't like us being here."

It was almost 2:00 a.m. All three tents were zipped tight and no one was venturing out. Minutes passed as they waited anxiously for more noise, or, worse still, an attack of some variety. But the panthers went away.

Sleep was difficult but they managed nonetheless. They had not slept the night before and their first foray into the bush had drained them. They soon drifted away and were dead to the world when a panther eased to within two feet of Dr. Gilfoy's cot and growled through the canvas. Another was just outside the door of the girls' tent and howled on cue. Another was scratching the door of the supply tent.

And so it went. The panthers checked on their visitors several times throughout the night, curious about their tents and attracted to the smells of food.

12.

When the sun appeared on the horizon, Dr. Sargent and Dr. Gilfoy were sitting on the sand at the edge of the surf, sipping coffee from the first pot and talking softly. They were concerned that the project was a waste of time. They had not found anything that gave them hope. Nothing in the piles of debris or in the depths of the forest that indicated humans had ever been there. There were the usual beer cans and plastic bottles washed up on the beach, but nothing else. No pieces of glass or paper, plank, cut board, shred of fabric, smoothed stone—none of the clues they usually found in search of a lost civilization.

After half a day in the woods, they were not encouraged. However, that was nothing new for them. Their project was planned for seven days, and budgeted for that long, and they never backed away from a challenge. All of them had read Lovely's book and believed her story. The proof that had not been swept away by the storm was buried somewhere on the island, and they were determined to find it.

They needed bones.

Over breakfast they looked at more maps and aerials, all prepared before Leo and thus terribly outdated. The decision was made to wave off the pontoon for the day and hack through the woods from the ocean side. They loaded their gear in backpacks and left the campsite just after nine o'clock. Diane and Mercer tidied up the place and relaxed under a canopy with Lovely. Cell service and internet connections were still unstable.

Diane put down her paperback and asked, "How often do you think of Nalla?"

Lovely smiled and said, "All the time. We always believed that she and the others came ashore right along here. Two hundred and sixty years ago." She gazed at the ocean as if looking for a ship. "A slave girl, pregnant with a white man's child. Captured and taken in chains, shipped across the ocean like an animal. I guess she got lucky with the storm, don't you think?"

"I would never call it luck."

"Oh, I think they were all lucky to find this place. They were not slaves here. They fought and killed the white men who came after them, and they protected each other."

"Now the white men are back," Mercer said.

"Indeed they are. This time they're using money and lawyers and courts to take this island, not guns. But we'll win, won't we, Diane?"

"I believe so."

Lovely reached for her cane. "Let's walk on the beach while the sun is behind those clouds."

The sand was firmer at the edge of the water and they took off their boots. Lovely used the cane with her right hand and held on to Mercer's arm with her left.

But the walking was too strenuous and they turned around. Back at the campsite, they heard the distant whine of a chain saw.

13.

The scariest thing about a diamondback was not the venomous fangs, but the rattle itself. The rattle meant only one thing—the diamondback saw or heard you before you saw it. The rattle meant the snake was upset, frightened, ready to protect itself. If you were lucky and saw the snake soon after hearing the rattle, you could move away, give it plenty of room. But when you heard the rattle but couldn't find the snake, well, that was the scariest part.

After hearing two rattles but no sightings, the team was

on edge. They took a water break and rested on the trunk of a fallen oak, listening for snakes. Dr. Gilfoy took a drink, wiped his mouth with a sleeve, and saw something in a pile of rotted timbers thirty feet away. It had the glint of metal. Holding a shovel, he walked to the pile and moved some debris. Carefully, he picked up a two-foot section of cut board partially rotted and covered with mud.

"It's a hinge!" he announced with excitement. The other five quickly gathered around to inspect it. They had found the first sign of civilization.

"A three-inch butt hinge for a door," one said.

"Antique cast iron," said another.

"Could it be a cabinet hinge?"

"No, not at three inches. It's too big."

"Steeple finial. Definitely a door hinge."

"How old?"

"A hundred years."

"Yeah, early nineteen hundreds."

They passed it around so everyone could touch and feel it. A rare diamond would not have been more precious.

Dr. Sargent said, "Well, we now know that a hundred years ago there was a dwelling close by and it was advanced enough to have butt hinges on its doors." He pointed and said, "If you look at the tree line there you'll see that the terrain rises. Lovely said the cemetery was on the highest part of the island. If the houses were around here, might the cemetery be up there?"

"I like it," Dr. Pennington said.

"Let's give it a try."

For an hour they hacked and cut a trail to the top of a slight elevation and stopped at a small clearing choked with weeds and thick scrub brush. Lovely had said there were no trees in the cemetery. The gap in the woods might possibly be the site. They cut and cleared for another hour, found nothing, and stopped for lunch.

Dr. Sargent walked behind a thick tree to relieve himself. In a grove of saplings he noticed a row of indentations, all covered with grass, each about two feet from the next. Lovely had said there were no headstones to mark the graves because there were no stones or rocks on the island. Each grave had a small wooden cross with no name on it.

Sargent said, "I think these might be graves."

The dig was on.

14.

With ample sunlight left, they decided to call it a day and return to camp. The last thing they needed to worry about was getting lost in the dark. They left their chain saws, shovels, and other tools under a tree with a bright blue tarp over it. They kept the machetes and handgun to deal with the diamondbacks. Dr. Gilfoy had a small can of orange paint and sprayed trees along their return route. Now that they knew the way, the walk took thirty minutes.

They were worried about Lovely making the trek, but she insisted on being at the gravesite if bones were found. They were under her strict instruction not to remove anything from the graves without her being present. Otherwise, the spirits would be upset.

After a round of beers, they dined on canned beef stew and cheese crackers, then moved their chairs closer to the campfire. It was not yet 8:00 p.m. and too early for bed, though they desperately needed sleep. They had joked all day about the panthers disrupting their night. Surely they would leave them alone tonight.

Dr. Gilfoy asked the African American archaeologists about other slave burial projects they had worked on, and this led to several stories. Dr. Sargent had been involved in perhaps the most famous discovery. In 1991, in Lower Manhattan, a contractor was doing site work in preparation for the construction of a new federal courthouse and discovered the graves of several dozen slaves, all in wooden caskets. Controversy erupted on all fronts and construction was delayed. Archaeologists descended upon the site and more graves were found. In all, historians estimated that between 15,000 and 20,000 African Americans were buried there, not in a mass grave but in individual coffins. Some were freed blacks but most were slaves. Half were children, evidence of the high mortality rate. A total of 419 caskets were relocated, with names, and a monument was erected in memory of their lives. The federal courthouse was built elsewhere.

Lovely told the story of her father's death and burial. It was in her book and all of those around the fire had read about it. Jeremiah died in 1948. His body was placed in a casket built by his brother, a carpenter. She would never forget watching it lowered into the grave.

Like all the others, it faced east, toward the ocean, toward home in Africa.

"We'll find it tomorrow," Sargent promised.

15.

The night was still and peaceful, uninterrupted by storms or wild animals. They were up at sunrise and eager for a long, productive day with their shovels. Breakfast, again, was oatmeal and fruit, with plenty of strong coffee. The plan was for Lovely to leave early with them and supervise the opening of the graves.

If she needed rest, half the team would accompany her, Diane, and Mercer back to camp.

In the woods, she was stunned and saddened by the destruction. She mumbled over and over, "I can't believe this."

They stopped at the pile of timber and debris. Dr. Gilfoy showed her the hinge and the piece of the door it came from. "Could the village have been around here?"

"I don't know," she said, bewildered. "Everything is so destroyed, so different." She thought a moment as she looked around. "Maybe. Yes, our homes could've been here. The cemetery should be that way." She pointed in the right direction.

When the trail began its slight ascent, Lovely struggled to keep her balance. She leaned on Mercer and her cane and made every step count. Three of the archaeologists walked ahead of her, guarding the trail and looking for snakes. The other three walked patiently behind.

Lovely had made a list of her ancestors who were buried on the island. There were seventy-three in all, though some were buried in different places. A great-uncle had split with the family over a romance and moved away from the village. He and his people had their own little cemetery. As a child, she had known of other small burial grounds around the island. Two hundred years earlier the dead were buried in shallow graves with no caskets.

They stopped where they had worked the day before, in the clearing where the weeds and vines and saplings had been cut away. "We found some graves here," Dr. Sargent said. "Does anything look familiar?"

She was shaking her head and wiping her cheeks.

"We have to start somewhere, Lovely."

"I don't know," she said. "Nothing is the same."

They removed the blue tarp and gathered their shovels and

tools. The tarp was strung up to provide shade from the sun and Lovely took her place under it. She was overwhelmed and emotional and they left her alone.

The row of low spots in the earth seemed like the best place to start digging. Within half an hour they found bones, too small for an adult, and not intact. The skull was crushed and the feet were missing. They were less than two feet from the surface and there was no sign of a casket. Lovely backed everyone away and knelt beside the grave. Without touching the bones she held her hands over them, closed her eyes, and mumbled a prayer. She looked at the other indentations and said, "I remember now. The graves of the children, buried long before my time. Back when they didn't use caskets." She stood, looked around, and pointed. "Not long after Nalla died, a fever came to the island, killing most of the children. They buried them here, in a row, in shallow graves because they were in a hurry." She pointed again and continued, "My people are over there, in that corner of the cemetery."

Over there was a thicket packed with thorns and vines and certainly hiding snakes. The team put down their shovels and used their machetes, swing blades, and chain saws. For two hours they hacked at saplings and small oaks and dense brush and hauled it away to another corner, where, hopefully, they wouldn't have to touch it again. When the ground was cleared and scraped they studied the dirt and discussed the lay of the land. In one place there was a slight unevenness that, upon closer examination and expert study, looked somewhat out of place. The shovels went to work. The sandy soil was soft and easy to dig, not necessarily a good thing. If they found human remains, they would most likely be a mess. Moisture led to a more rapid deterioration of a human body and decimated traces of DNA.

Three feet down a shovel hit something solid. It was wood. Four of them dug earnestly, but carefully, and soon found a corner to what they knew was a coffin. It was an old box for sure, and its top was rotted and its sides had caved in. When they had scraped away as much dirt as possible, they began to find bones resting haphazardly.

Leo's storm surge on Camino Island was measured by experts at twenty-seven feet. Since Dark Isle had no inhabitants, the surge and winds were not measured there. The slight ridge where they were working was about twenty feet above sea level, and they had assumed that the entire island was under water during the storm. Judging from the mounds of rotting trees, it was not difficult to believe that a massive surge had swept through.

Poking through the skeletal remains, the archaeologists agreed that the floodwaters had inundated the casket.

Lovely hovered over the bones, chanted a prayer that was thoroughly indecipherable to the rest, and returned to the shade under the tarp. By noon, they were exhausted and hungry and decided to return to the camp. Lovely needed a nap.

16.

The second and third graves were excavated. The caskets were rotted, the bones scattered about inside, and nothing of value or interest had been buried with the bodies. Lovely blessed them, then backed away as the team picked through the bones, scraping gently, examining fragments, searching for clues, filming and photographing everything. When the sun began to fade, they covered their work with more blue tarps and trekked back to camp.

17.

The cemetery was an archaeologist's dream. There was no shortage of graves with old caskets filled with skeletal remains, and it was tempting to lose sight of their mission—to link a bone or two to Lovely's DNA. After three days of nonstop digging they realized it could go on for weeks.

Lovely was ready to leave. Everyone wanted a shower and a hot meal. When they finally agreed that they had enough clues, Dr. Sargent called for Ronnie and his pontoon.

18.

Six days later, Steven took the call from the DNA testing lab in Austin. Of the eight samples—five bones and three teeth—taken from four different caskets, six contained insufficient tissues to compare to Lovely's blood sample. The bones and teeth had been kept in conditions that were less than desirable and subjected to too much moisture and heat. Even though they had been resting approximately forty inches under the surface for decades, perhaps centuries, they had degraded. For the remaining two bones, both taken from jaws, there was sufficient tissue for a comparison.

The disheartening truth was that they did not match Lovely. If her ancestors were indeed buried on Dark Isle, there was no biological proof to offer in court.

CHAPTER TEN
THE TRIAL

1.

Gifford Knox, still allegedly suffering from headaches and seizures and still in the throes of protracted physical therapy, arrived on Camino Island, by sailboat, three days before the trial with every intention of stirring up trouble. His plan was to meet with black leaders both on the island and in Jacksonville and whip up some racial conflict. In his opinion, the trial was a clear example of a rich white corporation trying to steal hallowed land from a poor black woman. He'd seen it before in the Low Country of South Carolina and had even written a long magazine article about it.

But Steven Mahon was not sure it would help. Public opinion would not affect the outcome of the trial. Chancellor Clifton Burch had not been elected by the people and so far had played no favorites. Protests and press conferences would only irritate him.

Bruce managed to talk Gifford off the ledge and convinced him another blistering op-ed piece in a big newspaper would be more effective. Giff said he was working on one for *The New York Times*, and it was almost finished.

Gifford, using a cane as a prop when in public, arrived at the courthouse early on Monday, May 18, and took a seat in the front row, next to Mercer and Thomas. Bruce sat behind them. By 9:00 a.m. the courtroom was full.

2.

In chambers, Chancellor Burch and the lawyers sat around a table sipping coffee and discussing last-minute matters. He said, "I suppose you want to make opening statements."

Steven shrugged as if he could go either way. There was no jury to sway and the judge knew as much about the case as anyone. Monty Martin, the lead trial lawyer for Tidal Breeze, said, "I'd like to say a few words, Judge, for the record."

"Okay. Mr. Killebrew?"

"The same, Your Honor, just for the record."

Evan Killebrew was an assistant Attorney General representing the state of Florida.

"Very well, but keep it brief."

The lawyers entered the courtroom from a door behind the bench and took their seats. Three tables had been arranged, each facing His Honor. On the far left was the petitioner's table, where Ms. Lovely Jackson sat in glorious splendor, adorned in a bright red robe that touched the floor and a red-and-yellow-striped turban that seemed to reach for the ceiling. So far, no one had objected to her headwear in the courtroom. The three bailiffs, the opposing lawyers, the clerks—no one had said a word. Nor would they. Steven had whispered something to Chancellor Burch and he, too, was on board with her attire. Diane Krug sat to her left, like a real attorney, though she had yet to bother with law school.

The center table was manned by the state. Evan Killebrew had two associates and a paralegal as his entourage. To the far right Pete Riddle sat in the middle of the table as the proud agent of Tidal Breeze, Monty Martin on one side, a junior partner on the other, with paralegals and assistants protecting their flanks. Mayes Barrow had his nose buried in a file. The jury box had fourteen chairs, all empty.

A bailiff barked, "All rise for the Court!" The crowd snapped to attention and rose obediently. Judge Burch swept in, his black robe as long as Lovely's. As he sat down he said, "Please be seated. And good morning." He paused for a second as everyone sat down almost as fast as they had stood. "Good morning," he said again, loudly, into his microphone. "This is a title dispute involving land commonly known as Dark Isle. I've tried these cases before and never had more than five spectators, so I thank you for your interest. I hope you won't be bored to death. As you can see, there is no jury. In Florida we don't use juries for title disputes, same as forty-five other states. I've gone over the lineup of witnesses with the lawyers and we're confident we can wrap things up by late tomorrow afternoon or early Wednesday morning. We have plenty of time and we're not in a hurry. I will allow each party to take a few minutes for opening remarks. Mr. Mahon."

Steven walked to the podium beside the middle table and began with "Thank you, Your Honor. I am the executive director of the Barrier Island Legal Defense Fund and I'm here in that capacity. More important, I have the privilege of representing the petitioner, Lovely Jackson, and I must say it has been one of the highlights of my long career. She is the rightful owner of Dark Isle because it was owned by her ancestors, dating back to the mid-1700s. They were former slaves who knew nothing about land grants from the British crown, or rights of title handed down by other European intruders. Indeed, as former slaves, her people wanted no part of the laws passed by white men. They lived, worked, reproduced, had families, enjoyed life as free people, and died on Dark Isle, where they are now buried. Ms. Jackson is the last known descendant of the freed slaves and free people of Dark Isle. It belongs to her, Your Honor, not some ambitious developer from Miami."

He sat down and winked at Mercer.

Evan Killebrew stood next to his chair and without notes said, "Your Honor, under Florida law, all deserted and abandoned islands with no owner of record belong to the state. There are over eight hundred of these islands from here to Pensacola down to the Keys, and they have repeatedly been declared the property of Florida. It's that simple. Over sixty years ago the legislature passed a law making all uninhabited islands property of the state. We do not dispute the fact that people lived on Dark Isle for many years, but the proof will show that no one ever made a legal claim to the property. That is, until now. Now it seems to be in big demand. We expect the proof will also show that the last inhabitant, Ms. Jackson, left the island in 1955, some sixty-five years ago. No one has lived there since. It's a simple case, Your Honor. The title belongs to the taxpayers of the state of Florida."

"Thank you, Mr. Killebrew. And for the Tidal Breeze corporation."

Monty Martin walked to the podium and frowned at Steven Mahon, as if he had been offended by something. "Thank you, Your Honor. My client has a sterling reputation for developing resorts, hotels, luxury apartments, and shopping centers throughout Florida. It is family-owned and has been in business for almost fifty years. It employs six thousand Floridians and last year paid over thirty-one million dollars in corporate income taxes to the state treasury. Tidal Breeze is a solid corporate citizen and it's been my honor to represent the company for many years."

Diane scribbled on her legal pad and slid it to Steven: *$2000 an hour I'd be honored too!*

"Your Honor, there is simply no proof that Ms. Jackson ever lived on the island. In her memoir, her own words, she writes that she was born there but left the island with her mother sixty-five years ago. I assume her memoir will be admitted as evidence. We've all read it by now. It's a nice story, sort of reads like a novel. Has a rather fictional ring to it. But let's say it's all true. Even then, she abandoned the property decades ago. The law is clear in Florida. Possession has to be continuous, open, notorious, and exclusive, for at least seven years. She made no claim to the island until my client entered the picture with its plans to develop it into a major resort. Yes, my client has advertised that it will spend at least six hundred million dollars on the island. The state of Florida has tentatively agreed to build a new bridge. It is our position, Your Honor, as an interested third party, that title to this island was vested in the state of Florida when it became a state in 1845."

Monty took his seat.

"Thanks, Counselors. The petitioner may call her first witness."

Steven stood and said, "Lovely Jackson."

3.

There had been no requests for cameras in the courtroom. Judge Burch would have said no anyway. The lone sketch artist in the front row was from the Jacksonville daily, and she was having a grand time trying to capture the colorful image of the witness.

To match her red and yellow turban and her robe, Lovely wore a pair of round, red-framed bifocals, which she peered through at the clerk when she swore to tell the truth. She sat down in the witness chair, pulled the mike a bit closer, as Steven had instructed, looked out at the crowd, and smiled at Diane and Mercer. She saw Miss Naomi in the second row and gave her a little nod. She appeared to be anything but nervous. Proud, regal, onstage, and looking forward to telling her story.

Steven slowly walked her through the preliminaries with easy questions. She answered slowly and clearly. She was born on Dark Isle in 1940, left fifteen years later. They went through a series of questions and answers, just as they had rehearsed, that covered those fifteen years. Life on Dark Isle: her family, home, neighbors, village, school, chapel, their religion and daily routines, the fear that white people would take away their island, the fear of death and disease. From the age of seven Lovely went to school every day until noon, then went home and did chores. The women tended the gardens, cooked the meals, cleaned the houses. The men, even the young boys, fished and brought home the seafood, some of which they traded in Santa Rosa and on the mainland. No one had a real job; everyone pitched in. Death was always hanging like a cloud. Most of the men died in their fifties. Many children died. The cemetery was a busy place. Her uncle was a carpenter and built many coffins. The "priest," as they called him, had a black robe he'd bought somewhere on the mainland, and she was always afraid of it because it meant death. She had vivid memories of watching coffins lowered into graves.

After an hour and a half of nonstop narrative, Judge Burch called for a recess. Diane led Lovely to the ladies' room while the spectators talked in low voices.

"You're doing great," Diane said as they walked down the hall.

"I'm just talking, that's all."

Back in session, Steven handed Lovely a copy of her memoir, which she identified. He asked that it be admitted into evidence.

Monty Martin stood and said, "Your Honor, we have no objection as long as it's understood that we're not agreeing that everything in that book is actually true. We reserve the right to cross-examine the witness from her own book."

"Of course," said Judge Burch.

Steven returned to the podium and asked, "Ms. Jackson, why did you write this book?"

She took a long pause and studied the floor. "Well, I did it so my people will never be forgotten. I wanted to preserve the story of Dark Isle from the time my ancestors arrived from Africa. So many of the slave stories have not been told and have been forgotten. I want people to know and remember how they suffered, and how they survived. Today, we don't know the real history because it has not been taught, and it's not been taught because so much has been forgotten. People don't want to talk about what happened to the slaves."

He asked her about her writing process. How long did it take to write the book? Off and on, ten years. Did she seek advice? Not really, just read some magazine pieces. She wrote it in longhand and paid a young lady, a schoolteacher, to type it up for her. When it was finished she didn't know what to do with it. The same lady, the typist, said she should look for a publisher, but she wasn't sure how to go about it. Some time passed, nothing happened, then someone told her about a company that would print the book for $2,000 and make five hundred copies. That's how the book got published.

Steven was not about to ask if the five hundred copies had sold. He knew they had not and he wasn't about to embarrass his client. Instead, he switched gears and asked about the decision to leave (never "abandon") Dark Isle. Lovely took a deep breath and looked down. She and her mother were the only two left. The village was sad and depressing, and all their family and friends were gone. They had little to eat and some days ate nothing at all. A friend came to get them and finally convinced them it was time to go. They moved in with another friend on Camino Island and went to work in the canneries. After her mother died in 1971, Lovely got married to a man with a good job. She moved up a notch and worked in the hotels. She longed for the island and wanted to see it, but her husband had no interest. She paid a man named Herschel Landry, a fisherman with a boat, to take her out several times a year so she could tend to her family's graves in the cemetery. She did this for many years, until Herschel sold his boat and moved away. By then her husband had left her.

Lovely was suddenly tired and removed her glasses. It was almost noon and everyone needed a break. Judge Burch recessed until 2:00 p.m.

4.

The nearest diner was across the street from the courthouse. Since the weather was nice, Bruce reserved a table on the patio and welcomed Mercer and Thomas, Steven and Diane, and Lovely and Miss Naomi to his little corner. He ordered iced tea and coffee. Gifford Knox arrived a few minutes later, on a cane, and ordered a whiskey sour.

Lovely had performed brilliantly on direct examination, and, so far, there was nothing to worry about. She was a bit fatigued but thought a good lunch would get her ready for the afternoon.

Steven and Diane had spent hours with her, crafting her testimony, deciding what was important and what could be left out, anticipating attacks from the other side. Steven had even tried some old courtroom tricks to trip her, but they had not worked. She had been unflappable, both in rehearsal and this morning onstage.

Their discussion was about how long to keep Lovely on the witness stand. Telling her entire story would consume hours and hours and, at some point, become monotonous. Steven knew from experience that good witnesses were often destroyed because they said too much. On the other hand, a great witness needed to be heard. The truth was that Lovely's memoir was in evidence and had already been studied by Judge Burch and all the lawyers. The challenge was deciding how much to go over again and how much to leave alone.

Everyone at the table had an opinion about Judge Burch. Since he was the sole juror, his demeanor, body language, and reactions were of the utmost interest. So far, he was proving to be remarkably poker-faced. He absorbed every word, took a few notes, ruled on objections quickly, and gave away nothing. He appeared to be involved in the case and eager to hear the testimony.

5.

At 2:00 p.m., Lovely settled back into the witness chair and smiled at His Honor. Steven asked her if she had been to the island lately. She said yes, about three weeks ago, with the archaeologists. He asked her to describe the island now, and she took a deep breath. When she spoke, her voice cracked for the first time. She took a sip of water, straightened her back, and began talking. Steven interrupted a few times to keep her on course. Monty Martin politely objected twice when her narrative rambled on, but Judge Burch waved him off. They were going to hear everything Lovely Jackson wanted to tell them.

"And did you find the graves of your father and grandparents?"

"Well, we're not sure. We found a lot of graves but they were never marked. There were no stones or anything like that. Most of the caskets were rotted. The scientists did the testing with DNA but they found nothing. So, no, I can't say for sure that we found the graves of my blood kin."

On a large screen set up in the jury box, Diane flashed a color photo taken by Dr. Pennington when the team was at work in the cemetery. Tight string on stakes marked the graves. Neat piles of dirt stretched along one end of the cemetery. Two of the archaeologists were on their knees working with trowels.

"Does this photo look familiar?" Steven asked.

"Yes, sir. It does. We were right there just a few days ago."

"And do you know who was buried in the graves that were being excavated?"

"No, not exactly. But I came to believe that it was my folks in that corner of the cemetery. My Daddy and all my grandparents. But, as I said, the tests don't prove that."

"What did the cemetery look like years ago, back when you went out there with Herschel?"

"Oh, it was much nicer. Wasn't all grown up. There were some weeds and all because nobody lived there, we'd been gone a long time. Me and Herschel and a boy named Carp would cut some of the weeds around my family's graves, but it was not as nice as when I was a little girl."

"Why did you keep going back to the island?"

"Because Dark Isle belongs to my people, to my family, to me. I was the only one left. If I didn't go take care of things, or at least try to, there was nobody else."

6.

In 1990, Lovely read a story in *The Register* about a new state park that had just opened between Jacksonville and Tallahassee. Officials from the Florida Park Service were on hand for a ceremony and one of them claimed that the state had the finest system in the country, with over 160 state parks and growing. Lovely wrote a letter to the person quoted in the article, and suggested that Dark Isle, with its truly unique history, would be ideal for a park, sort of a memorial to the former slaves who lived and died there. Her first letter was not answered, but her second drew a response from a Mr. Williford, who, in polite and official language, said they were not interested at that time. She waited six months and wrote him back. There was no response. She paid the same schoolteacher a few bucks to type her letters and make copies.

Steven handed her the first letter and asked her to read it. She adjusted her red glasses and said, "Dear Mr. Williford. My name is Lovely Jackson and I am the last descendant of former slaves who lived on Dark Isle, near Camino Island. Dark Isle was the home of my people for over two hundred years. No one has lived there since 1955, when my mother and I had to leave. As the last descendant, I guess I am the owner of Dark Isle, and I would like to talk to you about turning it into another state park, to honor my people. I visit it often to care for the cemetery. Most of the old houses and buildings are falling in. But the island is very historic and I think people would enjoy visiting it, if it was fixed up somewhat. Please contact me at your convenience. Thank you for your time. Sincerely, Lovely Jackson."

She said there was no response. Her second letter was virtually identical to the first. When Mr. Williford did write back, he said, "Dear Ms. Jackson, Thanks for your kind letter of March 30, 1990. Your request for consideration is certainly interesting. The state of Florida currently has six proposed new parks. Unfortunately there is funding for only four of them. I will place your request in the proper file, to be considered in the future. Sincerely, Robert Williford."

Her third letter, six months later, was similar to the first two. Steven presented all the letters and asked that they be admitted into evidence. There was no objection.

"Now, Ms. Jackson, is it true that you tried to pay the property taxes on Dark Isle?"

"It's true. I've tried for many years."

"And how did you go about doing this?"

"Well, once a year I sent a check for one hundred dollars to the tax office across the street. Been doing that for a long time."

"And what happened to the check?"

"Well, this nice lady, Miss Henry, the tax lady, she always writes me a little letter and sends it back."

Steven stepped over and handed her two sheets of paper. "The one marked 'Exhibit Seven,' can you describe that?"

"It's a copy of my check to the tax assessor, dated January fourth, 2005. Below it, right here, is a copy of my note, saying: 'Dear Miss Henry, Here is my check for one hundred dollars for the property taxes on Dark Isle.'"

"And Exhibit Eight, what is that?"

"It's a letter from Miss Henry, says: 'Dear Ms. Jackson, Thank you once again for your check for the taxes on Dark Isle, but, once again, I cannot accept your money. Dark Isle is not on the county's tax roll, so no taxes are due.'"

"And when did you send in the first check for the taxes?"

"Nineteen sixty-four."

"And why did you do that?"

"Because I thought the owner of the property had to pay the taxes. My husband told me so, said if I didn't pay taxes then the county would foreclose on the property and I'd lose it. I saved my money and sent what I could."

"And how long did you do this?"

"Did it last January."

"Every year from 1964?"

"Yes, sir. Never missed a single year. I'd send the check, Miss Henry, or the lady before her, would send it back."

Steven picked up a thick file and said, "Your Honor, I have copies of the checks and the correspondence between my client and the county's tax assessors."

"Since 1964?" Judge Burch asked, obviously not eager to review the contents of the file.

"Yes, sir. Every year."

"And they're all the same? One hundred dollars every year?"

"Yes, sir."

"Very well. And you want them entered into evidence?"

"Yes, sir."

"Any objections?"

Neither Evan Killebrew nor Monty Martin objected, because they knew it would do no good. Judge Burch was admitting everything to review later.

Steven said, "Your Honor, I have Blanche Henry under subpoena to testify if needed. She's just across the street. Do you or counsel opposite wish to hear her testimony?"

Judge Burch looked at the two lawyers. Monty Martin stood and said, "I believe the point has been made, Your Honor. The evidence is in the record." Killebrew nodded his agreement.

7.

In his glory days as the top litigator for the Sierra Club, Steven had been known for his meticulous pre-trial preparation. For him, as for all great trial lawyers, it was the key to winning. Every phase of every trial was planned, then rehearsed over and over. Witnesses were given scripts, then coached by the trial team. Psychologists, even drama coaches, were sometimes hired to help witnesses. Phantom juries were paid to hear and evaluate the evidence. Of course, Steven had bigger budgets in those days. The Barrier Island Legal Defense Fund operated on a shoestring and couldn't afford the experts. What it could do, though, was put in the hours.

The Friday before the trial, with the courthouse practically deserted, Steven and Diane ushered Lovely into the empty courtroom, put her on the witness stand, and walked her through her testimony. Steven then turned the tables, playing the role of an opposing lawyer, and tried to confuse her on cross-examination. The following day, Saturday, Lovely and Miss Naomi spent hours in Steven's office polishing her testimony, cutting unnecessary dialogue, working on the soft spots. She would be by far the most important witness and she had to be believable. At the end of the day, both Steven and Diane were convinced she could go toe-to-toe with the "bad lawyers," as she called them.

When Steven tendered the witness early Tuesday morning, Monty Martin stepped confidently to the podium and said hello. Lovely glared at him and did not return the greeting.

"Ms. Jackson, when did you decide to file this petition to clear the title to Dark Isle?"

Diane hid a smile. The question had been put to Lovely at least three different ways over the weekend.

"Last summer," she answered. *Keep your answers short! Volunteer nothing!*

"And what prompted you to file this petition?"

"A casino."

"A casino?"

"That's what I said."

"Would you care to explain?"

"I don't understand your question."

"Okay. Why did a casino force you to file this petition?"

"Nobody forced me to. I did it because I wanted to. It's the right thing to do."

"And why is that?"

"Because the island doesn't belong to a casino. It belongs to me and my people, the ones buried on it."

Monty picked up a copy of her memoir and said, "According to your book, and also your deposition, you left Dark Isle in 1955. Is that correct?"

"It is."

"But you filed nothing in court until last summer, 2020."

"What's your question?"

"Why did you wait sixty-five years before trying to clear the title?"

Word for word, the exact question Diane had written weeks ago. She could also recite Lovely's answer.

"Because the island belongs to me and my people and it always has. No one else had ever tried to claim it, not until last summer when your client showed up. I filed my petition because somebody, namely your client, was trying to take my property."

"Who suggested to you that you file your petition?"

"Some friends."

"And who are these friends?"

"Is that really any of your business?"

Steven stood and said, "Your Honor, please, any out-of-court statements made by the witness and her friends and solicited by Mr. Martin will clearly be hearsay."

Burch shook his head and said, "I hear your objection but let's see where it goes. Ms. Jackson, I caution you not to repeat statements made by others."

Steven sat down, but only for a moment.

Monty Martin asked, "Ms. Jackson, when did you first meet with Mr. Steven Mahon?"

"I don't know. I didn't write it down."

"Had you ever met him before last summer?"

Steven stood again and said, "Objection, Your Honor, the relationship between me and my client is highly privileged. Not sure where Mr. Martin is going with this, but he's out of bounds."

Steven knew exactly where Monty was going, as did Judge Burch and the other lawyers. Tidal Breeze was itching to prove that Steven and his band of environmental zealots had recruited Lovely to file her petition, as the quickest way to stop Panther Cay. But its lawyers had been unable to get around the privileged relationship between lawyer and client. Nor would they be able to now, but Monty wanted to at least raise the suspicion.

Judge Burch was all over it and said, "Objection sustained. Move along, Mr. Martin."

Monty flipped through Lovely's memoir as if looking for something. "You use a lot of names and dates in this book, Ms. Jackson. Are all of these accurate?"

"As far as I can remember."

"Did you use notes or old family records, things like that?"

"I had some notebooks, long time ago."

"Where are those notebooks now?"

"I don't know. I lost them and can't find them." It was a fib but she didn't care. Protecting her land was far more important than being completely honest with a bunch of rich white men.

"On page one-twenty, you write that your great-grandmother, Charity, died in 1910. But in your deposition, given right here in this very courtroom last November, you testified that she died in 1912. What's the truth?"

Lovely shook her head as if chatting with an idiot. "The truth is that she's dead, been dead a long time now. The truth is that many of my stories rely on ones handed down by my people, so I suppose it's possible that some dates got mixed up."

"So, are all of your dates mixed up?"

"I didn't say that. You just did. You see, sir, my people didn't have a lot of education. We didn't have a schoolhouse or teachers or books out there on the island. The state of Florida didn't care about us. We didn't exist as far as it was concerned. Now it claims to be the owner. How nice. Where was the state of Florida a hundred years ago when it was building schools and roads and hospitals and bridges everywhere else? Not one penny was ever spent on Dark Isle."

Monty suddenly wanted to sit down. He was getting nowhere with the witness. In fact, he was probably losing ground. His staff had pored over her book and her deposition and made a list of eleven discrepancies regarding dates and names. Now that list suddenly seemed worthless.

Diane's list had thirteen mistakes, all of which had been discussed with Lovely, who was poised to explain them away.

Monty whispered to one of his associates and killed a few seconds. He smiled at Lovely, who was not smiling at all, and said, "Now, Ms. Jackson, I'm intrigued by these lost notebooks. When did you start writing in them?"

"I don't know. I don't write things down like you do, sir. On the island we didn't always have pencils and pens and papers and notebooks, things like that to write with. I went to school in a little square building that we called a chapel because it was our only church. We were lucky to have two or three textbooks to pass around. I don't know where they came from. Half the kids didn't even go to school. My parents could barely read and write. I learned most of what I know after I left the island and went to school here, in the old black school down in The Docks. Even that school didn't have a lot of extra stuff, not like the white schools."

Monty felt like apologizing. He had planned to make hay out of the missing notebooks and portray them as important documents that should have been handed over during discovery. Now, the notebooks also seemed useless.

Again, he changed the subject. "Now, Ms. Jackson, on page seventy-eight of your book there is a rather graphic story in which Nalla, you ancestor, cuts the throat of a man who raped her. She then dripped his blood along the beach. Was this some type of a curse?"

Her eyes glowed as she nodded and said, "Yes, it was."

"Can you describe this curse?"

"Yes. Nalla had powers. She was a doctor who could heal people. She talked to spirits and could tell fortunes. After she sacrificed the man called Monk she spread his blood in the sand and said any white man who came onto the island would die a horrible death."

"And you believe this to be true?"

"I know it's true."

"How do you know it's true?"

Lovely glared at him for a long time as everyone strained to hear what she was about to say. She leaned an inch closer to the mike and said, "I know the spirits. I know when someone has gone onto the island."

Monty offered a proud smile, as if he had finally cracked the witness and discredited her. "But you were on the island three weeks ago, with the archaeologists, right?"

"That's right."

"Some were white, some were black. Correct?"

"That's right."

"And no one was killed or injured, no one died, correct?"

"That's right."

"What happened to the curse?"

"I was there and I lifted it."

"So you have that power?"

"I do."

"Is the curse still lifted, or is it back on the island?"

"I'm not sure. Why don't you go find out?"

The laughter was instant, loud, and contagious. Not a single person tried not to laugh. Judge Burch covered his mike with his hand and enjoyed the moment. All the lawyers were amused. Some of the spectators practically howled. Even Monty couldn't help but appreciate the humor.

Judge Burch finally tapped his gavel and said, "Okay, okay. Let's have some order. Continue, Mr. Martin."

Monty was still chuckling when he said, "I'll pass, but thank you." He stopped smiling and asked, "Now, before your visit, when was the last time the curse of Dark Isle claimed a victim?"

"Last spring, about a year ago." Her matter-of-factness slowed Monty for a second.

He sized her up, or tried to, and asked, "Okay, what happened?"

"Four men went to the island. All four were dead within a week."

"Four white men?"

"That's right."

"Do you know their names?"

"No."

"Okay. What were they doing there?"

"Don't know."

"All right. Were their deaths reported anywhere?"

She shrugged as if she had no way of knowing. "Can't say."

"What caused their deaths?"

"A bacteria got in their skin."

The cardinal rule of trial procedure is: Never ask a question if you don't know the answer. Monty had learned this in law school and had adhered to it strictly for almost thirty years. But, at that moment, he simply couldn't stop.

"And this bacteria was caused by the curse?"

"That's right."

8.

Gifford Knox sat in the back row and reveled in Lovely's performance. Next to him was Thalia Chan, a reporter for *The New York Times,* a woman he had known for a decade. Her favorite topic was environmental problems caused by big companies, and she had written several long pieces on Gifford and his exploits. She had seen him arrested twice, hauled into court, fined, and threatened. She had seen him testify in a coal ash case. Over the course of their friendship, Gifford had fed her many stories and plenty of inside dirt that was off the record. He was her favorite "unnamed source," and he had never leaked something that wasn't accurate.

Gifford had told her about Dark Isle months earlier. He had outlined the key players and repeated things he'd heard over dinner and drinks. He had not told her or anyone else about his fake accident and bogus lawsuit. Even for a bigmouth like Gifford, there were some things that should be kept quiet.

A big story in the *Times* was coming, and no one but Gifford knew about it. He couldn't wait.

9.

After a day and a half on the witness stand, Lovely was excused and allowed to sit at the table between Steven and Diane. Her performance could not have been better.

Steven's next witness was Dr. Sargent, the archaeologist from Howard University. They went through the usual back-and-forth establishing his expertise—education, training, writings, experience, and so on. Of particular interest was his work with various African burial projects, beginning in Manhattan decades earlier and continuing to the present. On a large screen mounted in front of the jury box, Dr. Sargent started with a less-than-detailed map of Dark Isle, with most of the details given by Lovely. They included the approximate area of the settlement, the rows of houses, and the cemetery. He showed color photos taken during their recent expedition. Photos of the damage and debris caused by Hurricane Leo; photos of their team clearing the brush and foliage from the burial sites; photos of the actual dig. He said they found remnants of about eighty graves, some with wooden caskets, some without. He had photos of the badly deteriorated caskets. The cemetery was about twenty feet above sea level at its highest point. Leo's storm surge on Dark Isle had never been determined, but the National Weather Service had decided that on the north end of Camino Island it had risen to twenty-seven feet. The eye then passed directly over Dark Isle, so it was reasonable to assume that the entire island had been under water. Even the most recent graves showed signs of severe water damage. Dr. Sargent said that, in his opinion, the graves and caskets were soaked with seawater for several hours, thus seriously degrading the samples needed for DNA testing.

None of the bones and teeth matched Lovely's sample.

Dr. Sargent estimated that there were probably about two hundred graves in the one site they found. According to Lovely's history, there were other burial sites scattered around the island.

After two hours on the stand, Dr. Sargent had said enough. Judge Burch needed some coffee.

10.

Diane had chatted several times by phone with Loyd Landry, Herschel's son. She had visited them months earlier in New Bern, North Carolina. She had left the visit certain that Herschel, at ninety-three, had lost too much of his memory to be involved in litigation. She had also emailed Loyd a number of times, just to keep him apprised of the case. He knew the trial date, and the previous Sunday he had called with the startling news that his father wanted to return to Camino Island.

According to Loyd, after meeting Diane at his nursing home, Herschel began quizzing his son about her and her visit. He remembered Lovely and Dark Isle, and the more they talked the more he recalled. On the good days. On the bad days, he didn't know where he was.

On Monday morning, an hour before the trial started, Loyd texted Diane that they were in the car, their road trip had begun, the old guy was thrilled to be out of the nursing home, and they would get there as soon as they could. They were about ten hours away but several pit stops were likely.

And pray for a good day.

At three-thirty Tuesday afternoon, Judge Burch tapped his gavel and said court was in session. Mr. Mahon, please call your next witness. The main door opened, and Herschel came rolling down the aisle with Loyd pushing his wheelchair. For some reason he held a cane across his lap. When they approached the witness stand, Steven explained to the court that Mr. Landry could not sit anywhere but in his wheelchair and that he would need a portable mike. Loyd would be allowed to hold it and sit next to him. Without much of a struggle, the court reporter administered the oath and the direct examination began.

Herschel looked around the courtroom and couldn't see much. However, when his eyes met Lovely's, he smiled and nodded and mumbled something. Steven asked him his name, age, address, and a few other basics, and he gave the right answers in a slow, soft, hoarse voice, but with the mike at his lips every word was clear enough.

"Many years ago, did you know Lovely Jackson, the lady sitting over there?"

Another smile. "Yes I did. I liked her. She liked me."

Lovely kept smiling at him. She didn't care what he said about their relationship sixty years ago. All she wanted was the truth.

"And you were a fisherman on Camino Island and had a boat?"

Monty Martin stood and said, "Your Honor, I realize these are unusual circumstances, but how much can Mr. Mahon be allowed to lead the witness?"

"I understand, Mr. Martin. You have a valid objection, but I'm going to allow this gentleman to tell his story. Please."

"You owned a boat near the canneries in Santa Rosa, right?"

"That's right. I was a fisherman."

"Did you ever take Lovely Jackson over to Dark Isle to visit the cemetery?"

It took a while for the question to register, but then he began nodding. "Yes, that's right. We went over there all the time."

"And what did you do over there?"

"Cut the grass, pulled weeds around the graves. Her people."

"Did you go alone?"

The question vexed him and he didn't answer.

"Did a boy named Carp go with you?"

"Oh yes, Carp. Good boy."

"Where is Carp now?"

"Don't know."

"Do you remember his last name?"

"No," he mumbled.

"How old were you when you took Lovely to her island?"

"Thirty, I guess."

"And how long did this go on?"

"Oh, a long time. Many years. I liked her. She liked me. We liked to go over there together, alone."

11.

The rebuttal began Wednesday morning when the Attorney General himself was sworn in as a witness. His presence was certainly not necessary but spoke volumes to the influence Tidal

Breeze had in the state, or at least over the AG. The company, the Larney family, and its many employees, investors, and affiliated businesses were heavy contributors to his campaigns.

The gist of his brief testimony was that in Florida the law was clear, and had been on the books for over sixty years now. Because of nature and occasionally because of man-made projects, shorelines, reefs, even streams and tributaries change with time. Small islands disappear. Others are created. Still others merge and split. There were currently about eight hundred deserted islands in the waters off the coasts of Florida, and all of them were deemed, by law, to be property of the state.

In his learned opinion, Dark Isle belonged to the state of Florida.

When offered the chance to cross-examine such an important person, Steven toyed with the idea of exploring his closeness to Tidal Breeze. They could discuss the company's behind-the-scenes efforts to secure the island before the Court ruled. While such questioning would be a lot of fun, it would be a sideshow, not productive, so Steven waved off the opportunity as if the AG didn't matter at all.

If the appearance of the AG was designed to impress Judge Burch, there was no indication that it did. For the first time, His Honor seemed slightly impatient.

The next five witnesses added some color to the proceedings. All were working men who earned their money from the sea in various ways. All were natives of the area or had lived there for many years. All were middle-aged and white, and none of them really wanted to be there.

Skip Purdy went first. He was forty-five, a shrimper whose father had been a shrimper. He'd been fishing, for money and for pleasure, the waters around Camino Island and the Camino River since he was a kid. He knew all the islands well, including Dark Isle. No, he had never set foot on it, had no reason to, and knew no one who had. He had never seen any sign of life there—no human, no animal, nothing.

On cross-examination, Steven asked, "Mr. Purdy, you still run a shrimp boat, is that correct?"

"Yes, sir."

"And you should be out there today, right?"

"Yes, sir."

"Instead, you're here in this courtroom, correct?"

"Pretty obvious."

"Are you being paid to testify?"

Monty had prepped his witnesses well and the question was expected. "Yes, sir, I'm being paid, same as you."

"How much?"

Monty stood with a smile and said, "Your Honor, please."

"Objection sustained. Do not answer."

"No further questions."

"You are excused, Mr. Purdy."

Donnie Bohannon owned a charter service and specialized in catching sailfish in the Atlantic. He was forty-one, with the lined, bronze face and bleached hair of a man who spent his life in the sun. He had never been to Dark Isle but passed by almost every day, to and from the central marina in Santa Rosa. In the past eighteen years, he had seen nothing on the beaches. Hurricane Leo hit it hard and destroyed many trees, but there was no sign of life.

Roger Sullivan was a fishing guide who worked the bay side in smaller craft. The one-mile gap between Dark Isle and the mainland was a prime breeding pool for grouper, wahoo, and flounder. He passed close to the island every day and had seen no signs of life in many years. There was once a herd of deer, but they disappeared after Leo.

Ozzie Winston was a retired harbormaster at the Santa Rosa marina and a native of Camino Island. Brad Shore ran a scuba operation. Their testimony was more of the same: a knowledge of Dark Isle based on years of passing by it, familiarity with its legends and stories, and certainty that there had been zero human activity on the island in their lifetimes.

Monty's point was simple and effective: Even if Lovely visited her island for years, as she claimed, those visits had stopped long ago.

As the lunch hour approached, he made the decision to rest his case. In preparation for the trial, his strategy had been to attack the credibility of Lovely's case by casting doubts about her story. However, she had done a marvelous job in holding her own, and Monty was convinced Judge Burch was sympathetic to her.

What else could Tidal Breeze and the state of Florida prove? Dark Isle had in fact been inhabited by former slaves, both before and after statehood. Lovely claimed to be the last of their descendants and her testimony was believable. How could they prove otherwise? The archaeologists had found a real cemetery.

Judge Burch was always ready for lunch, but when he realized the lawyers were winding down he said, "I'll allow each party to take a few minutes for a recap. But I don't need to hear much. Mr. Mahon."

The lawyers were caught off guard, but none had an advantage. Steven stood, without notes, and said, "Sure, Judge. We began this dispute with Tidal Breeze denying everything, the usual tactic. Tidal Breeze denied humans ever inhabited Dark Isle and denied my client ever lived there. We know now that those denials were hogwash. It's so refreshing to see the state of Florida suddenly have a keen interest in the island. For almost two hundred years the state had nothing to do with it. No schools, no roads, no bridges, no clinics, no electricity, no phone service. Nothing, absolutely nothing, Your Honor. Lovely Jackson and her people lived in poverty on their island. Health care didn't exist. Diseases were common. The life expectancy was at least twenty years lower than average. But they survived because they had to and because they were proud and treasured their freedom. Now, the state has crawled into bed with a big-time developer, Tidal Breeze, and the state is in this courtroom right now fighting for ownership of Dark Isle.

"And something else to think about, Judge. The state and Tidal Breeze make much of their allegation that Lovely abandoned the island when she was fifteen years old. But did she? Did she really relinquish control? Most of us educated white men scoff at the notion of a curse hexed upon the island over two hundred years ago by a young African witch doctor, or voodoo priestess. We might snicker and whisper that it's a fantasy no reasonable person could really believe. We're much too sophisticated for such silliness. Well, if that's so, then I challenge any of my colleagues on the other side of the courtroom to take a shot. Go down to the marina, rent a boat, take a ride across the bay, and have a stroll around Dark Isle."

Evan Killebrew had said little during the trial. He wasn't expected to, not with such high-powered talent in the room. He stepped to the podium and said, "Well, Your Honor, putting aside the rather colorful history that we have enjoyed so far this week, I urge the Court to turn its attention back to the law, the black-and-white language of the statute that clearly says all deserted and abandoned islands in our waters belong to the state of Florida. Beyond that, what the state does with its property is not relevant in this lawsuit. If the state wants to sell the island to Tidal Breeze, or to anyone else, then that is simply not relevant today."

Killebrew sat down as Monty stepped to the podium. "I'll be brief."

"I know you will."

"Thank you. For sixty-five years, Ms. Jackson did nothing to enforce her legal rights as the owner of the island."

Judge Burch startled them with "Excuse me, Mr. Martin, but she tried to pay the property taxes for about fifty years."

"Yes, but since she didn't own the property, then no taxes were due, Your Honor. No one owed taxes on the island because there was no owner."

Judge Burch looked away, unconvinced.

"A year ago, the local paper, *The Register,* ran a front-page story about a proposed development called Panther Cay. Suddenly, after sixty-five years of silence, Ms. Jackson hires a lawyer, Mr. Mahon, a noted environmental litigator, to represent her in a title action. Mr. Mahon, by his own admission, does not do property or title work. In the same newspaper, he was quoted and was, shall we say, rather disdainful of Panther Cay. He promised legal action by his nonprofit."

"What are you saying, Mr. Martin?" Judge Burch interrupted again.

"I'm saying it looks suspicious."

"You're saying Mr. Mahon tracked down Ms. Jackson, solicited her case, and filed it to stop the development?"

"That's close enough."

"Big deal. Half the bar now solicits cases. Haven't you seen the billboards? Please move along."

Monty kept smiling and said, "Sure, Judge. I agree with Mr. Killebrew that we need to get back to the law, and it's very simple. To prevail on the grounds of adverse possession, a person must possess the property openly, actually, notoriously, exclusively, and continually for seven uninterrupted years before filing suit to confirm title. Seven years ago was 2014. There's not one shred of evidence, not even from Ms. Jackson herself, that she has been to Dark Isle, for any reason, in at least ten years. Maybe twenty. Maybe thirty.

"The island has a fascinating history, Your Honor, but it's just that—history. With a lot of gaps in it. We urge you to stick to the law and award title to the state of Florida."

Judge Burch closed his notebook and said, "Anything else, gentlemen?"

Nothing.

"All right. Congratulations on a case well tried. As an old judge who's refereed many cases, I always appreciate good lawyers. Thank you for your professionalism. I'll have a decision within thirty days."

CHAPTER ELEVEN
A NEW FOUNDATION

1.

The first bombshell landed the following day when *The New York Times* ran a front-page story about the trial. It was below the fold, and the most startling aspect of it was a large color photograph of Lovely Jackson entering the courthouse the day before. She was wearing one of her standard robes, a bright yellow one that trailed to the ground and seemed to glow, and a baby blue striped turban. She offered a winsome smile at the camera.

The story by Thalia Chan made no pretense of being balanced. The headline was "African Burial Site Thwarts Land Grab by Florida Developer." For Tidal Breeze, it was all downhill after that. The company was portrayed as another slash-and-burn developer hell-bent on cashing in on the casino craze. An unnamed source said Tidal Breeze coveted the Atlanta gambling market and had found the perfect spot just south of the Georgia state line. Another source (no doubt Gifford Knox) said the company had a dreadful record of environmental problems and would destroy the island and the waters around it. Ms. Chan did a passable job of laying out the facts and describing the trial.

The bulk of her story, though, was about African burial grounds and the efforts to find and preserve them. She talked to Dr. Sargent of Howard University, who described the cemetery on Dark Isle as "a major find on one of the most unique places in the history of American slavery." Marlo Wagner of the African Burial Project was thrilled with the discovery and promised her full cooperation in stopping any development. Florida's three black congressmen promised a federal investigation into the "desecration of hallowed ground." The longer the story went, the more race became a factor. The executive director of Florida's NAACP promised swift action. The chairwoman of the Black Caucus in the Florida legislature vowed that if the Court awarded title to the state, the state would never sell Dark Isle to any developer. It must be preserved. The battle lines were clear, with no room for gray areas. A rich white corporation was attempting to take historically significant land once owned by former slaves.

2.

Mercer couldn't write fast enough. The trial had pushed her into overdrive and she worked through the nights. Now the story was suddenly national, and as she struggled to absorb the flood of new material, she feared getting lost in it. She was also worried that too much exposure might dampen interest in her book, whenever it was published. Thomas reassured her that the publicity would only heighten awareness of Lovely's story.

Mercer called Miss Naomi and urged her to ask Lovely to avoid talking to anyone. Though reporters could not get her on the phone, they might try and find her in The Docks. Just keep the door locked and avoid strangers.

Late in the afternoon, Mercer and Thomas met Steven, Diane, Bruce, and Gifford at the patio bar of the Ritz-Carlton, away from downtown and prying ears. The story by Thalia Chan had gone viral and they felt like celebrating. Gifford confessed that he had introduced Thalia to the story, and once she realized its potential, he fed her bits and pieces of inside info.

Bruce, ever the bookseller, had already contacted Lovely's vanity publisher and ordered five hundred more copies. His thin supply sold out before lunch and he was expecting a wave. And he wanted to talk to Lovely about another signing, as soon as possible.

How might the news affect Judge Burch's decision? Steven had mixed feelings. The case was not complicated and he expected a decision soon enough. The trial had gone their way because of Lovely's performance on the stand, but the law was not squarely on their side. There was no doubt that neither Lovely nor anyone else had claimed the island in the past seven years.

Steven took a drink and said with a smile, "Regardless, folks, this little brouhaha is over. My phone is still ringing. The African burial folks have gone ballistic. The environmentalists are cheering them on. The politicians and civil rights groups can't wait to get involved. There's no way Tidal Breeze can survive the attacks."

"So we've won?" Bruce asked.

"Yes and no. My best guess is that Lovely has a fifty-fifty chance of prevailing. But if she loses, she still wins because the state will either yield to pressure and back down, or sell to Tidal Breeze and then watch from the sidelines as the litigation roils for the next ten years. In the end, no federal court in the country will allow an historic burial ground, especially one filled with the bones of enslaved people, to be tampered with in any way."

Bruce asked, "Can they protect the cemetery while developing the rest of the island?"

"Doubtful. The cemetery is in the middle of the island, on the highest point. Plus, Lovely said there are other small burial grounds on the island. Friends, I hate to tell you this, but Tidal Breeze is screwed. Lovely has won."

Bruce quipped, "I guess I need to order even more books."

Mercer said, "And I guess I need to finish mine."

3.

The second bombshell arrived by email at exactly 9:00 a.m. the following Monday. Diane saw it first, in the office kitchen, at her cluttered card-table desk, sagging now under too much junk. It was an opinion from Judge Burch.

Both thoughtful and terse, the first five pages covered the facts, both contested and uncontested; then he spent two pages on the law of adverse possession.

His final paragraph read: "It is the opinion of the court that the Petitioner, Ms. Lovely Jackson, has met the burden of proving her claim of ownership of Dark Isle under the Florida statutes referenced above. It is therefore ordered and decreed that the title to Dark Isle shall be confirmed in her name, as the sole owner, and that the claims of the state of Florida are hereby dismissed. It is so ordered. Signed, Clifton R. Burch, Special Master."

Within minutes, the opinion was zipping around the island. Then it went viral and the little Barrier Island Legal Defense Fund was bombarded with phone calls and emails.

4.

By noon, Bruce had Bay Books ready for a party. A table near his office was covered with hors d'oeuvres, finger sandwiches, and wine bottles. And, of course, a stack of Lovely's book. Sniffing free wine, and after being hazed by Bruce, the writers showed up. Myra and Leigh, Amy Slater, Bob Cobb. Sid Larramore from the newspaper. Several of Diane's friends. Mercer and Thomas and two of their friends. A dozen or so loyal customers who never missed a gathering arrived in fine spirits. When Lovely entered behind Miss Naomi, she was greeted with a loud ovation. She preened and bowed and kept saying, "Oh thank you. Oh thank you."

She declined a glass of wine but took a soda. When it was time for words, Steven tapped his glass and offered a toast to the best client he'd ever had the privilege of representing.

Bruce announced there would be a book signing on Friday. He asked Lovely to pose with her book for a round of photos, and within minutes they were posted on Bay Books's social media.

5.

Tuesday morning, Monty Martin issued a statement saying he was obviously disappointed with the Court's ruling but had great respect for Judge Burch. He would appeal immediately on behalf of his client and was optimistic about their chances. Tidal Breeze had no intention of walking away from Panther Cay, a "futuristic project" that would provide jobs for thousands of Floridians.

Wilson Larney read the statement and shook his head. He was sitting on the sofa in his splendid office, looking at the Atlantic, having coffee with Dud Nash. No one else was present.

"How would you rate Monty's work in the trial?" Wilson asked.

"Good. We had a bad set of facts, Wilson. Plain and simple. We didn't know about the burial site."

"It was in her book."

"Yes, but we didn't really believe her book, did we? We paid Harmon a ton of money to check out the island. They found nothing."

"And those four guys died?"

"Yep, later. In four different places."

"And Harmon hid this from us?"

"Yep. The truth is that once the cemetery was discovered, we were flat out of luck."

"You know we're getting hammered. I just got a call from our PR people. The blacks in Dade County are threatening to boycott our casinos. That's about twenty percent of the traffic. We're getting calls from black activists everywhere."

"I know, I know."

"And the chances on appeal are slim?"

"Eighty percent of the time the Supremes stick with the local judges in these types of cases. It's a real long shot. And if we get lucky and win on appeal, then we have even bigger problems on the island. The litigation could take years."

"How much have we spent on legal fees so far?"

"About a million."

Wilson grimaced, as always, when discussing fees paid to Dud's firm. "Ballpark, how much would the federal litigation cost us?"

"Twenty-five million over eight to ten years, with a good chance of losing."

"Why are your fees so high?"

"Gee, you haven't asked that question in, what, a week now? We charge that much because we're worth it."

"I don't feel so great right now. It's a PR nightmare and you know how I hate publicity."

"My advice is to let things cool off. We have thirty days to file a notice of appeal."

"Things aren't going to cool off, Dud. We've kicked a hornet's nest and they'll eat us alive."

6.

The second article from the *Times* was prominently featured on page eight, under the headline "Florida Court Rules Against Resort Developer." Thalia Chan recapped the opinion from Judge Burch and included a statement from Lovely that read, "I am relieved that the Court has chosen to protect the sacred property of my ancestors. This is a great day for the descendants of enslaved Africans." In response to a question written and submitted by Thalia through Diane, Lovely said, "I hope the state of Florida will take some of the money it planned to spend on a bridge and create a memorial to my people." Steven Mahon was quoted: "The court did what was right and just and in doing so averted an environmental disaster." The story was accompanied by an aerial photo, taken by a drone, of Dark Isle.

Neither Tidal Breeze nor the Attorney General's office could be reached for comment.

7.

Two days before the deadline for filing a notice of appeal, Tidal Breeze issued a statement that read: "In honor and memory of the enslaved people who lived and died on Dark Isle, the Tidal Breeze Corporation of Miami is withdrawing its plans to develop Panther Cay. The company respects the Court's decision and will not appeal it to the Supreme Court of Florida."

Steven Mahon and Diane whooped it up in their cramped offices and danced a jig. Diane then called Miss Naomi with the news and drove to The Docks to share the moment with Lovely. They wept with her on her front porch and savored the victory. It was such a magical moment, one still difficult to believe.

"You did it, Lovely," Diane said more than once. "You held your ground, fought for your people, took a mighty developer to court, and kicked his ass. You did it."

"I had plenty of help, my dear. Plenty of help."

Mercer called her agent, Etta Shuttleworth, in New York with the news, then spoke to her editor, Lana Gallagher, at Viking. "How many words have you written?" she asked. Typical editor.

"I don't know, maybe a hundred thousand. I'm throwing away pages almost as fast I write them."

"Then stop throwing them out and finish the book. I'll give you a deadline if you want one."

"Have you ever had a writer ask for a deadline?"

"No, of course not. But if I see the first draft by the first of October we can publish next spring."

"Sounds like a deadline."

Not surprisingly, Bruce called within half an hour of the news and informed Mercer that a celebratory dinner had been planned for that night. He was rounding up guests, but it would be the usual suspects, minus Gifford, who had sailed back to Charleston.

"Do you think Lovely would come?" he asked.

"I doubt it but let's try. It can't be a long night, Bruce. Thomas is kicking me out of bed at six every morning to write."

"Mercer, dear, who in their right mind would ever kick you out of bed?"

"You're hopeless."

8.

Not long after she began her takeover of the BILDF, Diane realized that if she wanted to be paid at least a minimum wage, not to mention wrangling a desk or even a nicer card table, she would have to raise the money herself. Steven loathed fundraising and couldn't be bothered. The roughly $200,000 that trickled in each year was almost by accident. The Sierra Club was a legendary, A-list nonprofit with a big budget, and while there he had been free to sue and litigate at will, without worrying about the overhead. Old habits die hard and now he almost refused to worry about money. The secretary, Pauline, was part-time, rather lazy, and content with her meager paycheck. Diane wasn't driven by money but she had an eye on law school. She convinced Steven to let her overhaul their lame website and expand their social media profile. He approved her initial changes, and she gradually brought their little nonprofit into the 2020s.

The Dark Isle case gave Diane something to write about almost nonstop. Their following slowly increased, as did their donor base. When she arrived in town the nonprofit's donations had averaged $19,000 a month, barely enough to cover their modest salaries and fund its low-budget style of litigation. Seven months later, it grossed $31,000 for the month of May, with Diane cranking out trial updates late every night. Thalia Chan's stories in the *Times* had led to a serious uptick in BILDF's profile.

Inspired by this success, Diane became intrigued with online marketing and its seemingly endless possibilities. Immediately after the trial was over, she raised the idea of a separate nonprofit to raise money for a memorial on Dark Isle. The story was still big news and there was plenty of interest. She discussed it with

Steven, of course, then Mercer and Thomas, Gifford, and Bruce. The most challenging conversation was with Lovely herself, who still wasn't sure what a website actually was.

About the time Tidal Breeze threw in the towel, Diane created the Nalla Foundation. Its mission was "to preserve and honor the memories of the freed Africans who settled on Dark Isle and who could never go home." The goals were to: (1) locate and renovate the burial sites; (2) build a memorial to the dead; (3) rebuild some of the settlement for tourism; and (4) seek funding from individuals, foundations, corporations, and governments, all for the preservation of Dark Isle and its history. Bruce and Noelle donated the first $10,000 as seed money, and Diane harangued Steven into a "loan" of another $10,000 from BILDF. She took most of the money and hired an online marketing firm. She anointed herself as the executive director, primarily because the IRS required one and there were no other prospects. A salary was also required, so she signed on, initially, for a hundred dollars a month, slightly less than she was earning as a full-time intern at Barrier Island.

With Lovely's lawsuit out of the way, Steven got busy elsewhere. Its rather sudden completion freed up hundreds of hours and he fell into a more relaxed schedule. Diane hazed him into renting nicer office space, and she was finally able to give away the damned card table. They hired a full-time secretary who had no legal training but could handle the front desk. She was also about to spend half her time with the Nalla Foundation, though she had not been informed of that.

Diane worked tirelessly establishing her new foundation. She wrote grant proposals by the dozen, solicited donors, gave interviews, and played the social media game. After a slow start, the money began coming in, small checks at first from individuals, then bigger ones from other foundations. In July, the African Burial Project sent a check for $50,000. More importantly, it agreed to share its donor list on a confidential basis. Diane went after the donors with a slick direct-mail attack and raised $120,000. She gave herself a reasonable pay raise and informed Steven that she was taking a ninety-day leave of absence from Barrier Island. She did not request one. She just took it.

She had tea on the porch with Lovely and Miss Naomi each afternoon and lunch every Wednesday at a barbecue place in The Docks. In the weeks after the trial there were dozens of requests to interview Lovely, all of which were directed to Diane, who distrusted journalists almost as much as Lovely. However, she had learned that her client and friend was a powerful fund-raiser. Her story was irresistible and she was fun to talk to. Each interview, in print or on camera, generated more interest in the Nalla Foundation, and more income.

Bay Books had sold over six thousand copies of her book.

It was during tea one hot afternoon when Diane first noticed the hesitation. Lovely was talking about her latest visit with Mercer the day before when she got stuck on the "water." The "w" sound would not come through. Her lips quivered and she closed her eyes. Diane shot a look at Miss Naomi, who looked away. It happened again moments later. Then she complained of a sudden headache and wanted to take a nap. Walking back to Miss Naomi's, Diane asked, "Has that happened before?"

"Yes, I'm afraid so. It started last week, at least that's the first I noticed it."

"Has she seen a doctor?"

"She doesn't like doctors, says she trusts the spirits."

"Please call me if it happens again. There's definitely something going on."

"I know, I know. I'm so worried about her."

9.

Mercer passed 110,000 words in mid-August. The trial, and the ending, was in sight. She wrote for four hours each morning, took a long hot walk on the beach with Thomas, then lunch and a nap. By two she was back at her desk. She was worried about writing too much, always a concern for her because she believed, and taught her students, that most books were too long. No one can tell a writer when to quit or what to cut. A strong editor can make changes or even reject a book for its length, but generally speaking, a writer is on her own with few limits.

Thomas had become quite the consultant. With his submarine story finished and due to appear in the October issue, he devoted his time to Mercer and her work. He read and edited every page, offered no shortage of editorial comments, and listened to her worries and complaints. Because he had lived so much of the story during the past year, he knew the material and still found the history of Dark Isle remarkably compelling.

Two days before they packed for their return to Ole Miss, Mercer invited Diane to lunch and an afternoon of reading. They dined on salads and avoided the wine, and when they finished Mercer handed over the manuscript.

"Are you finally finished?" Diane asked.

"Almost. I'll polish it up next month and turn it in October first. You've read the first half. Here's the rest."

"I can't wait."

"We're going into town. Do you need anything?"

"No."

"Make yourself at home. Here's a red pen, the one Thomas loves, so don't be shy about your comments."

They left and Diane made a nest on the patio, under a ceiling fan, with the ocean in the distance, and was once again soon lost in Lovely's world.

10.

In September, Gifford Knox settled his bogus personal injury suit against Old Dunes for $35,000. He gave one-third to his lawyer, spent $4,000 on uninsured medical bills for nonexistent injuries, and walked away with about $20,000. He sent half of it to the Nalla Foundation and kept the rest as compensation for his troubles.

Also on the legal front, at Diane's urging Lovely finally agreed to sign a simple will. She had trusted Steven for a long time and was happy for him to prepare one. With no blood heirs, she left her home and personal property to her dearest friend, Naomi Reed. As for her "money," the cash in her two bank accounts, she gave half to Naomi and the other half to the Nalla Foundation.

She also signed a warranty deed giving her beloved Dark Isle to the Nalla Foundation, to be held in trust forever and preserved in sacred memory of her ancestors.

With the deed in hand, Diane flew to Washington to meet with some important people. Now that she had the benefit of an expense account, she stayed at the famous Willard Hotel, down the street from the White House. Her first appointment was with a black-owned architectural firm that specialized in restoring historical sites deemed important to African American history. The architects were excited about the Dark Isle project and signed on. Almost as important, they had innumerable contacts in the preservation field. They promised to start making calls, and planned to visit the island in October. They were confident money could be raised.

Diane met with the National Trust, National Park Service,

African-American Historical Trust, African-American Preservation Society, Lilly Foundation, DeWist Foundation, and two of Florida's black congressmen. She had been unable to arrange meetings with its two senators.

Late on Diane's fourth night in D.C., Miss Naomi called with the urgent news that Lovely was in the hospital with what appeared to be a stroke. Diane canceled her meetings the following day and flew home. She hurried from Jacksonville to Camino Island and met Miss Naomi at the hospital, where Lovely was resting comfortably.

The doctor said there were several mini-strokes, all of which were worrisome but none of which caused permanent damage. However, there was a greater likelihood of a serious stroke around the corner. Lovely was able to walk just fine and insisted on going home. The doctor finally discharged her. Back on her porch and sipping lemonade, she seemed as spunky as ever.

11.

The Passage, by Mercer Mann, was well received in New York. After a few tweaks by Lana Gallagher, her editor, and the usual misunderstandings with the folks in copyediting, the manuscript was put on the fast track for publication in late spring. Viking felt an urgency in getting it into the stores because of the timeliness of the story. The trial was now five months in the past, a lifetime in the twenty-four-hour news cycle, and interest in the story seemed to be waning. For Mercer, and every other writer, sooner was better.

Bruce insisted on reading the manuscript before Mercer submitted it to Viking. He saw no structural problems but had a few editorial comments, all of which she ignored. They could quarrel later. He loved the book, but admittedly was probably not a fair critic. He felt like he had lived the story, plus he was, and always would be, smitten with Mercer.

During her Christmas break, Mercer and Thomas flew to New York for a brief victory lap. The trip was primarily about food and drink. They had a long lunch with Lana Gallagher and the president of Viking. They had an even longer dinner with Etta Shuttleworth and her husband. They shopped a little, went to a concert, and enjoyed a light snowfall as they walked in Central Park.

From New York they flew to Jacksonville, then drove to Camino Island, where they would celebrate Christmas. Bay Books was decorated to the max and teeming with customers. When Bruce saw them he dropped whatever he was doing and waved them into his office where he hugged Mercer a bit too long and smacked a kiss on her cheek. He bear-hugged Thomas as if he hadn't seen him in years. "I talked to Lana Gallagher this morning," he said, as if he routinely chatted with senior editors at the major publishing houses. On second thought, he probably did. "She adores the book, as you know, and thinks the first printing will be a hundred thousand."

That was news to Mercer.

"I said no way, Lana, this thing is going well north of two hundred thousand. Get the printing presses all greased up. You bought it too cheap."

Mercer and Thomas exchanged amused grins.

"Now, we need to start planning your book tour, beginning with a killer launch party here on the pub date."

Mercer couldn't stifle a laugh.

So Bruce. He just couldn't help himself.

CHAPTER TWELVE
WITH NALLA CLOSE BY

1.

On her fifth trip to Washington, D.C., Diane hit pay dirt. With Marlo Wagner at her side, she met with three foundations she had been cultivating virtually nonstop for months. The African-American Historical Trust stepped forward with a grant of $500,000, and it was matched dollar-for-dollar with grants from the DeWist Foundation and the Potomac Preservation Fund.

The Nalla Foundation had raised $320,000 since its inception, and Diane was already spending most of that on the architects and other preliminary matters, one of which was the clearing of a roadway from the beach to the cemetery on Dark Isle.

Lovely said the curse was lifted, and so far there had been no casualties among the white guys laboring on the island. It was the source of endless ribbing by the black guys. Workers of all colors kept a keen watch for the rattlesnakes.

With $1.5 million in hand, Diane contracted with Drs. Sargent and Gilfoy to begin the first of several cemetery digs. In early April, she finally received an artist's rendering of the memorial that she liked, after spending almost $60,000 on several that she did not. A marketing firm took the art and produced a slick direct-mail solicitation that went to 300,000 potential donors. In addition to the art, there was a color photo of Lovely and three paragraphs about her story. It was enormously successful, generating over $400,000 in the first two months.

Also in April, Diane decided to forgo law school for another year. She had been accepted at Emory, her first choice, and the school agreed to another one-year deferment, but her dreams of a career in environmental law were fading. She was too busy with the foundation. She said goodbye to Steven and his little nonprofit and rented more space. She hired the second employee. When notified by the IRS that she had failed to list her board of directors, she quickly sent in the names of Steven Mahon, Bruce Cable, Gifford Knox, Mercer Mann, and Naomi Reed. Then she got busy and forgot to tell them that they had been elected to the board of the Nalla Foundation.

At the beginning of the legislative session in Tallahassee, the Black Caucus held a press conference to announce the filing of a bill that would create a memorial to the enslaved people who had lived on Dark Isle. The bill sought $2 million in initial funding, a modest amount for a wealthy state with an impressive budget surplus. The bill died in a subcommittee, then was resurrected only to be killed again upon final adjournment.

Diane and Mercer were at the state capitol, lobbying in a vain effort, when time expired. It was a tough loss, but most caucus members were optimistic about next year. Among the many lessons Diane was learning was that private money was preferable over local, state, and federal dollars.

The Nalla Foundation was raising money and had enough to keep it busy for quite some time. It was about to get a big boost with the publication of *The Passage*.

2.

The early reviews were nothing short of remarkable. *Publishers Weekly, Kirkus, Booklist,* and *Goodreads* raved on and on, so much so that Viking increased its first printing to 125,000 copies. Momentum was building, and the buzz in the publishing world was that *The Passage* could be the summer hit on the nonfiction side.

Viking wanted to throw a launch party in New York, but Bruce Cable would have none of it. He wouldn't even discuss it with Mercer. The book was born in the waters around Camino Island, and that was where it would be celebrated first. He ordered two thousand copies, a record for Bay Books, and harangued Mercer into pre-signing all of them the day before the launch. He rented the town's brand-spanking-new amphitheater on the beach, a gift from the legislature to honor those who died in Hurricane Leo. He sold tickets for fifty dollars apiece, which included an autographed book, pregame rum punch on the beach, and a donation to the Nalla Foundation. The weather cooperated, the night was perfect, and a huge crowd showed up. Bruce was, of course, the master of ceremonies, and he introduced some important people to say a few words: Diane Krug, executive director of the Nalla Foundation; the mayor of Santa Rosa; the chairman of the Black Caucus in Tallahassee; and Marlo Wagner, director of the African Burial Project in Baltimore.

The star of the evening was Mercer Mann, and she spoke for

a few minutes before surprising the crowd with another intro-
duction. When Lovely Jackson walked across the stage and took
a bow, the crowd stood and cheered. When it settled down, she
stepped behind the podium, pulled the mike a little closer, and
thanked everyone for coming. She thanked Mercer for her book,
and Diane for the foundation and its wonderful work, and Bruce
at the bookstore. From a pocket somewhere in the midst of her
teal-tinted robe, she pulled out a paperback, her own story. She
set the scene, then read:

*The women held the children close to stay warm. The wind was
blowing in from the ocean and they were cold. Where were they?
They had no idea. They had survived a terrible storm. A storm
so long and awful and violent it had broken the ship into pieces
and sent hundreds of screaming people to their deaths. Nalla and
the other women and children had somehow survived by clinging
to a wooden post, a mast from the ship. The ship. A slave ship that
had taken them from their homes and families and children in
Africa. A ship that was now destroyed, sunk and at the bottom
of the ocean, where it belonged, where it could create no more
misery. A child cried and Nalla drew him close. She kissed his
head and thought of her own son, over there, across the water.
She cried too but only to herself.*

    *The waves broke onto the beach not far away. Dawn was
breaking and there was light in the east. The women were still
naked. The cheap burlap skirts they had been given on board had
been washed away in the storm. They had not eaten in days. The
children wanted food but the women just sat there in the sand,
beside a dune, and stared at the ocean, waiting for another day
in which they had no idea what might happen. Could another
ship come to take them home, take them back to Africa? Death
was everywhere. Nalla had seen so much of it she wondered if*

she might now be dead too. Finally dead and finished with this nightmare, now going home with the spirits to see her husband and little boy.

Lovely read slowly and pronounced her words clearly, as if she had done it before. The crowd was silent, and mesmerized. Mercer watched from the side of the stage and knew she had a tough act to follow.

The women heard voices and drew even closer together. The voices of men, but calm. In the early morning light, the women could see men walking along the beach and coming their way. Dark men, with pleasant voices. Nalla called out and the men walked over. Four African men, one with a rifle. Behind them were three women, all from the ship. When they saw Nalla and the others they ran toward them and the women hugged and cried, so happy to see others who had survived the storm.

The men watched and smiled. They were shirtless and barefoot but wore the same odd britches as the white men on the ship. They spoke in a tongue the women did not understand. But the message was clear: You are safe here. You are with your people.

Lovely closed her book, said a polite "Thank you," and walked away as the crowd stood again. Mercer gave her a hug, then walked, somewhat nervously, to the podium.

3.

From Camino Island, the team—Mercer, Thomas, Lovely, and Diane—flew to Washington, D.C. It was Lovely's first flight and the preparation for it had taken weeks. She sat between Diane and Mercer, kept her eyes closed most of the way, and seemed to be in a trance. She declined food and drink and said little.

The event was hosted by Politics & Prose, a long-standing independent bookstore in the area, and it was held at the historic Howard Theatre. Marlo Wagner had cracked the whip, ginned up interest in the event and the book, and a long list of African American groups bought tickets. The theater was sold out. Marlo and Diane presented a short video as an overview of the project on Dark Isle. Lovely spoke and read and once again stole the show. Mercer had a good night in front of a rowdy crowd.

The following day, she and Lovely were interviewed by *The Washington Post*, whose Book World had raved about *The Passage*. Its legendary editor, Jonathan Yardley, stepped out of retirement to do the interview and the three had a delightful time.

From Washington, Mercer and Thomas took the train to Philadelphia. Diane managed to get Lovely home to Santa Rosa, where, once back on her porch with a glass of sugary iced tea, she declared that she would never again set foot on an airplane. It was obvious to Diane and Miss Naomi, though, that Lovely rather liked being onstage.

4.

Dr. Sargent could not attend the book event at the Howard Theatre, though he had been invited and asked to introduce Diane and Marlo. He had his hands full of bones on Dark Isle. By late June, their second dig was well underway.

During the first one a month earlier, the team had recovered thirty-eight graves. With each find, they carefully lifted out whatever they found, usually bones and sections of the decomposed wooden caskets. The remains of each were cleaned, photographed, indexed, and placed into a small metal coffin that was then sealed tight. The grave was dug deeper, wider, and longer until it was four feet by two and exactly fifty inches deep. The metal coffin was then lowered and buried.

As always, it was hard, tedious work, and by late June the Florida heat was pushing ninety-five degrees. The team had set up camp near the cemetery, on a patch of land that had been cleared by bulldozers, and some of them preferred to cook and sleep in the wild. The panthers often made the nights interesting, but no one was injured. Indeed, halfway through the second dig, no one had yet to actually see one. The pontoon boat arrived each morning with water and supplies, and it returned late in the day to collect those who needed a hot shower and some air-conditioning. Each team member had the option of sleeping in a hotel in Santa Rosa, and as the days wore on, more and more left the island at night.

On two occasions, Diane escorted Lovely to the island to check on things. The temporary pier made their arrival much easier. The gravel drive through the woods seemed like a luxury. They rode in a John Deere Gator driven by a student at Howard, who was thrilled to finally meet Lovely.

The cemetery was changing dramatically. The overgrown vegetation and brush were gone, the entire area had been cleared. Rows of string and yellow tape marked the graves that had been found but not yet unburied. Small, neat mounds of dirt were piled beside other graves. Most of the working area was covered by large canopies to shield against the sun. Lovely sat in the shade, sipped cold water, and chatted with the archaeologists and students, who were in awe of her. The bleached bones they were touching and handling so carefully belonged to her ancestors.

Everyone wanted a photo with Lovely.

During the second visit, as they were on the pontoon boat

and headed back to Santa Rosa, Lovely asked Diane, "Can I be buried with my people, here on Dark Isle?"

"Well, the state of Florida doesn't really care. It allows a person to be buried on private property. However, Camino County passed an ordinance years ago requiring all burials to be in registered cemeteries."

"How do you know so much?"

"I've read too many old newspapers."

5.

The Passage debuted at #4 on the nonfiction bestseller list, prompting Viking to push the print button for another 25,000 copies. Mercer's book tour took her to New York, Boston, New Haven, Syracuse, Buffalo, then back down to Baltimore, and Philadelphia again. At each stop she did as many print interviews as her PR team could schedule, went to as many bookstores as humanly possible, and even managed some radio and local television. The third week after publication, the book moved up to #2.

She and Thomas went to the beach for the July Fourth holiday and caught up with Lovely, Diane, and Bruce. After three days of rest, she took off again, without Thomas, for a swing through the Midwest, stopping in Louisville, Pittsburgh, Cleveland, Indianapolis, and Chicago. For the most part book tours were relics from the past, but Viking was willing to fund as much as Mercer could stand. With Bruce's constant encouragement, she had agreed to forty cities in fifty days.

On July 18, some five weeks after publication, *The Passage* hit #1 on the list. Mercer was leaving a hotel room in Wichita when she got the call from Etta Shuttleworth in New York. "You made it, girl! Number one!"

Mercer sat on the edge of her bed, tried not to cry, and called Thomas. He promised to meet her in Denver. After that, she called Bruce, who, of course, already knew. Etta called back with the news that Viking was printing another 50,000 copies.

6.

In an author's note at the end of *The Passage*, Mercer thanked the many people who had helped with her research. She wrote a wonderful tribute to Lovely Jackson, a friend who had lived the life she had just described and who had unselfishly allowed Mercer to "borrow" her story. Mercer also made a pitch for money. She described the Nalla Foundation and its plans for a memorial on Dark Isle, finishing with: "It's a small nonprofit, just barely getting started, so if you have a spare buck, send them a check."

The checks were arriving, and not all of them were from spare funds. Almost all were individuals who read and were inspired by the book. By the time *The Passage* hit #1, its admirers had sent checks totaling almost $90,000.

7.

When the phone buzzed at 2:34 in the morning, Mercer found it, knocked it to the floor, picked it up, saw that it was from Diane, and knew immediately something had happened to Lovely.

"Mercer, where are you?"

A helluva question. She looked around the dark room as if the furniture or curtains might hold a clue to the city. "Portland, I think. What's wrong."

"Miss Naomi found Lovely on the floor tonight. She couldn't get up. We're at the hospital now and she's doing okay, resting, probably another stroke. I hate to bother you in the middle of the night but you told me to call."

"That's okay, Diane. No worries. Can she say anything?"

"Don't know. She's sedated but it doesn't appear to be that severe."

"I can't get home right now."

"Don't even think about it. There's nothing to do. The doctors will watch her for a day or two. We should know more tomorrow. How's the book tour?"

"Up and down. The crowds are nice but it's beginning to get old."

"Hey girl, you're number one. Savor the moment."

"Thanks."

"We're all very proud of you, Mercer. The entire island is enjoying your big moment. Including Lovely. It's all she talks about."

"Give her a hug and tell her I'm sending prayers."

"Will do."

8.

The damage was not slight, the stroke was neither a "mini" nor a "mild." After two days in the hospital, Lovely realized that her left leg and arm were not working too well. Physical therapists gently pulled and stretched, with little success. They put her in a wheelchair for the first time in her life and rolled her down the hall to lunch. Diane and Miss Naomi checked on her every day. They were told that she would no longer be able to live alone. She had to have care.

When told this, Lovely objected strenuously but there was no one to argue with. After ten days in the hospital, she was moved to a rehab facility in Jacksonville where she stayed for two weeks before being moved to an assisted living home ten miles west of Camino Island.

When Mercer completed her tour and returned to the beach, she and Thomas drove over to see Lovely. It was not an uplifting visit. Diane warned them that she was not improving.

Lovely looked much older and the left side of her face sagged. Her speech was slurred and she said little. She was happy to see Mercer but immediately began crying. Mercer sat on the edge of her bed for an hour, rubbing her arm and telling her about the bookstores she had visited and all the people across the country who now knew about Lovely Jackson and Dark Isle.

Mercer returned the next day, and the next, and alternated times with Diane. The nurses said their visits buoyed Lovely's spirits, but she was clearly declining.

In late August, Mercer and Thomas said goodbye and began their drive back to Ole Miss. Classes started in three days. Mercer promised Lovely she would see her soon, but she suspected that was their final visit.

Barely audible, Lovely thanked her for such a wonderful book, for caring so much about her and her people. "You made us famous," she said.

Mercer left in tears and cried for an hour in the car.

Diane called every day with the same update. Nothing much had changed, things had certainly not improved.

On September 28, Lovely Jackson died at the age of eighty-two, the very last descendant of the proud people who lived on Dark Isle.

9.

Pursuant to the instructions written by Lovely and given to Miss Naomi, her body was cremated and her ashes were put in the black and gold ceramic African vase she had owned for decades. It was on the middle shelf of her bookcase in the den.

Two months later, when Mercer and Thomas were on the island during the Thanksgiving break, they gathered at the harbor one afternoon with Diane and Miss Naomi. Ronnie, in a thirty-eight-foot fishing boat, took them across the chilly waters to the pontoon pier at Dark Isle. Their mission was a secret. They had told no one. Ronnie was curious but never asked.

They walked the gravel drive to the center of the island, to the cemetery where they admired the work that had been done by the archaeological teams. The remains of over 120 people had been dug up, cleaned, photographed, indexed, and reburied in metal coffins.

In one corner, where Lovely believed her family to have been buried, Thomas unfolded a small shovel and dug a hole. They placed the vase into it, secured it with packed dirt, and covered it up.

Lovely's last wish was to rest in eternal peace with Nalla close by.